UP SHE FALLS

Nonfiction books by Bob Trask

Living Free
God's Phone Number
Romancing the Soul

UP SHE FALLS

A Novel

Bob Trask

Cover Design: Ghislain Viau
Interior Design: Julie Klein
ISBN: 978-09612164-5-0

For Chauncey Anne

Freedom! That was the thought that sung in her heart so that even though the future was so dim, it was iridescent like the mist over the river where the morning sun fell upon it. Freedom! Not only freedom from a bond that irked, and a companionship which depressed her; freedom, not only from the death which had threatened, but freedom from the love that had degraded her; freedom from all spiritual ties, the freedom of a disembodied spirit, and with freedom, courage, and a valiant unconcern for whatever was to come.

—W. Somerset Maugham, *The Painted Veil*

1

Now, can you tell me this: why are people killing one another? I don't get it. What the hell must be going on in one's mind to deliberately snuff out a fellow human being? As a San Francisco prosecutor, I should know the answer to that, right? Yet after working dozens of murder cases, I'm as puzzled as ever. I've seen lots of homicide scenes and autopsy pictures and, well, they're not pretty. I realize there must be an underlying rage in some people that overcomes their rational minds. Maybe their parents never taught them how to handle anger so it doesn't destroy them and others. Is that it?

And then, of course there are the sociopaths. Oh boy, those folks are cold and cunning, and they have no moral compass. But that's a whole different ball of yarn, isn't it? Strange and vicious beings who kill just for the thrill of killing. It's like an addiction.

I've been thinking about something else too, about how some killers get off because they're deemed to be not sane at the time of the crime. But if that's a genuine excuse, shouldn't most killers get off? Because how in hell could anyone sane do something as insane as killing a fellow human being?

Now I'm ranting, aren't I? It's just that, on the Friday afternoon I'm going to tell you about, I'd had my fill of death and darkness and was wondering if, as sensitive as I am, I'd picked the right profession. I've always been conservative in my thinking and my voting. I believe people should be held accountable for what they do. Yet more and more I'm beginning to feel like a bottom-feeder. Most of the people I prosecute can't even afford a lawyer; one has to be provided for them, and those are too often not really defending their clients as much as getting them to accept a plea agreement. At the same time, people who have the money to hire the best attorneys are getting away with all kinds of crimes, including murder. They either walk free or get a slap on the wrist.

I was in rush hour traffic on that Friday afternoon, driving my little red Mustang from Oakland to San Francisco over the Bay Bridge, having just finished the deposition of a sweet old guy who'd watched a bartender kill a man by shoving him down a flight of stairs. I needed a credible witness and I'd hoped this old gentleman would step up, but now it wasn't going to happen. Initially, he told the police he saw the bartender arguing with the guy and then suddenly shoved him down the stairs. Now he can no longer remember what happened; maybe someone told him about a staircase with his name on it.

2

Anyway, I was done with it all for two glorious days; my weekend and I were headed for my cozy home out in the Avenues—my digs, my sanctuary. No wife beaters, no killers, no robbers. Just my books, a cup of tea, and only two blocks from my home, a beach with white surf to comb the crazies out of my head.

About me? I'm a scrappy thirty-six-year old woman. Some call me aggressive; others call me not-so-nice names. It's true, I do push a few buttons, but maybe people shouldn't have so many buttons. My health is good and I'm reasonably attractive, unless you are put off by the fact that I have one brown eye and one blue eye. It's called heterochromia, and fewer than one in two hundred thousand people have it. It embarrassed the hell out of me when I was a teenager, but now I feel kind of special. Physically, I was a late bloomer. I was twenty-two in my last year of law school, and I looked like I was seventeen. I'm sure some women would like that, but attorneys who look like teenagers are seldom the pick of the litter. Yet luck, good grades, and dogged persistence opened a few doors, and now I have this job, and despite my complaining, I'm successful and reasonably content.

Still, recently I wonder if I've missed my life train or maybe got off at the wrong stop. Something inside me feels unfinished. It's like driving away from your house, wondering if you've left the stove on or the door open. So yes, my life is good, and yet I keep hearing Peggy Lee singing "Is That All There Is?"

I wove through the bridge traffic, thinking that over the

weekend, I'd hook up with my old college roommate and best friend Jill. Long-legged, red-haired, crazy Jill. She's a psychologist with files of troubled patients while, as a prosecutor, I have files of injured and dead people. I needed a break, and maybe she did too. It had been a while since we'd laughed together. We were both single and enjoying our freedom, and yet the loneliness sometimes ached. And that's puzzling because neither one of us is that hard to look at, and we're both fun to be around. Our problem has been finding guys who want to do more than get stoned and get laid. I've pretty much given up on that crop of artichokes.

I moved my little red Mustang over to the curb lane as I approached the midspan of the bridge. And unbeknownst to me, I was fast approaching the end of my life as I knew it.

3

At midspan of the bridge, the traffic ground to a halt, and pretty quick I saw that it wasn't going to be moving anytime soon. I turned off the engine and got out of the car to look, figuring there must be a wreck somewhere ahead. I walked over to the bridge railing and looked forward past the stopped traffic. When I saw the flashing lights, a sudden chill went through me, and all at once, I could barely breathe. My legs turned to rubber, and I'd have surely fallen to the sidewalk if I hadn't been holding onto the railing. I took some deep breaths and tried to get myself balanced, but I was getting disoriented and feeling spaced out. It made no sense; I was fine and then, wham! I looked toward the lights again, and then was flying out of myself. It was truly weird. I'd never felt anything like it and it scared the hell out of me. I figured I needed to be anchored, so I made my way back to my car and got in.

Within a few seconds, my mind had cleared a bit and I was able to breathe again. Then my phone rang and I dug it out of my purse. "Hello, this is Keegan Tate."

"Oh, Keegan. Thank you for answering. It is so good to hear your sweet voice at last."

It was a woman's voice, soft as butter and like a warm embrace. I didn't recognize it. It belonged to someone dear to me; that I knew instantly. I just couldn't place her.

"Thanks," I said, "but who is this?"

"Keegan, right now I am feeling your presence, your warm presence. Thank you. You are so dear to me."

"Okay, but see, I'm feeling a little embarrassed here because I can't place your voice. Please tell me who you are."

"Keegan dear, soon enough you will know all about me and all about us. But right now you and I have very little time, so please listen. Are you hearing me?"

"Yes." I was nodding, though she couldn't see me over the phone. "I'm listening, and yes, I'm hearing you."

"Okay, then: Keegan, you must find the Three. Tell me you got that."

"What three?" I was puzzled. "What three? I'm sorry, but I don't understand what you're talking about. I think this is going to go a lot easier if you'll just tell me who you are."

"Thank you, dear Keegan," the voice on the phone replied. "Thank you for being you. Now we're connected, and we will be forever. Just don't forget that everything depends upon you following your heart until you find the Three. That's the way it will work."

Then the line went dead.

I stared at the phone in my hand; my mind had gone numb. I knew this woman; I knew her well, just couldn't place her. Her number was still there on my phone, so I called the number back. The phone rang and rang until, just as I was about to hang up, a man's voice came on. "Hello?" he said. "Who is this?"

I frowned. Dammit, I didn't want this man; I wanted that Three lady.

"Listen: I just got a call from a woman at this number. I need to talk to her."

There was a pause, then the man said, "Ma'am, I'm an officer with the San Francisco Police. Please tell me who you are."

A police officer? I shook my head. What the hell was going on? "All right," I said. "My name's Keegan Tate. I'm a San Francisco assistant district attorney. And like I said, I just this minute got a call from the woman at this number, and I need to talk to her. Will you please put her on?"

There was another long pause. "Now, you're saying you just got a call from a woman at this number, is that right?"

"Yes, and I redialed it from my phone. It's this number."

"And how long ago was that?"

What nonsense! I glanced ahead at the flashing red and blue lights on the bridge ahead of me. "It was one minute ago or maybe less. Why? What's going on?"

"Ms. Tate, there's gotta be a mistake here. I'm right now working a traffic accident on the Oakland Bay Bridge. This phone was ringing on the seat of the car, so I answered it."

"Well, I'm on the bridge too, and I can see your lights flashing about a hundred yards ahead of me. Now, will you please just hand the phone to the woman who called me?"

"Ms. Tate, I'm not sure how to tell you this, but the woman who was driving this car is here in front of me, and she's deceased. She most certainly did not call you in the last fifteen minutes because I've been here at least that long and, well, she couldn't have called anyone."

My mind went flat. I couldn't even think of what to say. I asked, "If she's been dead for at least fifteen minutes, then is there another woman nearby who could have used that phone?"

"No, ma'am. She is the only person in this car, and everyone else is in their own car. Now, I'd be happy to talk to you more about this some other time, but right now I'm pretty busy."

The line went dead.

A fire engine followed by an ambulance wove its way through the cars and I sat—manikin-dumb—frowning at them.

Eventually I got out of my car again and walked back to the side of the bridge, leaned against the rail, and looked north toward Angel Island. There, to my amazement, a shimmering cloud of bright birds was wheeling above the island in a beautiful sinuous formation. As I watched, they began moving out over the bay, hypnotizing me with their flowing undulations. Then they headed toward me.

4

As the flock flew closer, I realized that they weren't birds at all but some kind of tiny glowing spots of light. They were whirling like a murmuration of starlings, and I was being pulled up into the midst of them. Crazily, I felt my heart soaring with them. I had come undone from myself and was out of my mind, drifting into a bliss I've never known.

It gradually occurred to me that these bits of light might be photons, subatomic particles of light. Silly as it sounds, I felt like I was being cleansed and blessed by their flowing presence, not only around me but inside me as well. Never had I felt anything so beautiful. If I had looked down, I would not have been surprised to see that I was ascending high over the bridge and traffic. I reached out my hand, and my entire arm immediately became streaming light. I could hardly breathe.

I felt myself pulled from my body through every pore—like when you're standing at the shoreline and the receding water pulls sand from beneath your feet. And because I was no longer in my body, I realized that I must be dying, but it was okay because I was no longer the person known as Keegan Tate; I was one with the universe. Yet I hadn't lost myself; instead, I found a self I'd once known but had forgotten.

"Miss! Can you hear me? Come on now. Please! You're holding up traffic. Let's get you back in your car!"

I looked back over my shoulder. A policeman was stretching his hand out to me. Couldn't he see the lights?

I heard myself say, "The dead lady: she called me on the phone."

The officer had an angelic face, but his expression was grim and determined. The lights glittered on his brow. I shook my head in amazement.

He must have thought I was telling him no. "Now, miss! Right now. You need to get back in your car. You're holding up traffic."

I found my voice and smiled at him. "I'm okay, really. I'm going back to my car now."

I was starkly aware of a new reality around me—the bridge, the colors of cars, the radiance of light on steel, all dappled in divine light, all brand-new. I looked at the officer and saw gentleness in his broad face, sky blue eyes, and wide mouth. I saw him as a little boy, watching me in wonder.

"You're going to be okay driving now?" he asked.

"Oh yeah, sure." I nodded. "Sure. I'm good."

I felt like I'd awakened from a life-long sleep and into this sparkling new reality. I wanted to say more to the officer—like how angelic he looked and how touched I was by his kindness and concern—but I couldn't find the words, so I went to my car. And I stared at it, barely recognizing it as my own. In fact, nothing looked, smelled, or felt as it had a mere hour ago.

I drove across the bridge into the city, still surrounded by the satiny ribbons of rippling light. I shook my head, wondering how much Johanna's death had unbuttoned me.

Johanna? I knew no one named Johanna. I shuddered. What the hell was happening to me? I knew I was driving my car, but I was also floating as if on some river of light. I felt stoned, yet my mind, my cognition, were sharper than I ever remembered. What happened to me back there? And what did Joanna mean by *Find the Three*? And how did she even call me if she was already dead?

I took a deep breath; I needed to get out of that trance or otherworldly zone or whatever it was. I was a practical, conservative-minded woman who didn't believe in tarot cards, Ouija boards, or any of the New Thought crapola. And yet here I was, being bathed in this altered reality. My hands were glowing on the steering wheel, and I was being washed in luminescence. Washed? What, was I being cleansed? Is that what was happening? It sure felt like it.

I became so giddy that I started laughing out loud. I was Alice in Wonderland! I opened my windows and listened to the orchestra of cable cars clanging, cables sizzling, cars honking, voices calling. Life's beautiful ballet was in full voice, and I was hearing its harmony for the first time. And all because of Johanna dying?

Why do I keep calling her Johanna? I wondered, then thought, Well, I can't just keep calling her the lady who died on the bridge, can I? She'd become too close to me for that. Too close? Hang on, Keegan. You never met this lady, never even saw her, and now you're close?

Yes, I thought, somehow we are.

5

I got home and went straight to my bedroom, shed my work clothes, donned an old pair of jeans, a purple sweatshirt, worn tennies, and hiked two blocks to the beach. The late afternoon sun was splashing gold across the western sea as I walked along the water's edge. Bright, busy shorebirds skittered across the wet sand ahead as my heart beat in rhythm with the welcoming waves and the breeze that whispered freedom. Everything was fresh, the world was delicious, and I found myself laughing again. Here I was, a prosecuting attorney, walking by myself amidst the waves and laughing while tears rolled down my cheeks. Crazy!

The swirling lights had by then dimmed, but their energy was still flowing through me. I was seeing through new eyes and hearing through new ears. I had no frame of reference, no conscious foundation from which to understand what was happening, and yet my mind was as clear as the afternoon sky, as clear as a child's. I wondered if maybe this truly was the final dance of my life and that I was now slipping away into eternity. But if this was dying, so what? It didn't scare me anymore. A peace was expanding within me; again and again I had this lingering, repeating thought: all is well. And as difficult as it would have been to explain it, I saw this: every thing was everything. I told you it would be hard to explain. And yet it was true. All things were one thing: the sea, clouds, birds, wind, me—all one thing.

That afternoon, when I looked at the life I'd lived, it seemed like someone else's. For years I had focused on my daily accomplishments. But now, stepping—or should I say dancing—in harmony with waves and whispering sand, I knew I'd missed something important. I had been repeating the same routines daily, weekly, and monthly. I had done so because they were familiar and comfortable, and I felt capable there.

Was my life no more than a habit, then? Was I like a thoroughbred racehorse, running faster and faster but always in circles around the same track? I realized I had spent most of my life training to be an attorney and had been content with my career and with my life. So why did that suddenly feel so empty? Because Johanna had died? Well, hey, death wasn't that new to me.

I first encountered death when I was six. I was playing jacks on the front porch when Nan, my dog, came running over to greet me, all wiggly butt and tail, all warmth and sloppy kisses. She was a floppy-eared mutt with one blue eye and one brown, just like me. Daddy had brought her home when she was a puppy, and we grew up together.

Nan wandered into the road later that afternoon and got whacked by a pickup truck that never even stopped. I held her in my arms while she whimpered, then shuddered and fell away. I held her limp body against my chest and sobbed. We buried her out behind the barn, and I cried every day for weeks. I was never the same girl after that. Then a year later, my brother James died, and I fell into despair that had no bottom. For many months I lived in a dark and hopeless fog. Then nearly a year later, I slowly, ever so slowly crawled back to the surface. Healing that depression was the hardest thing I've ever had to do.

6

My job as a prosecutor was steady, reliable, and satisfying, and I tried to ignore my lack of romance. I'd been pretty much alone since coming to the city. *The city*—wherever you go in the world, when you hear someone say "the city," you know they're talking about San Francisco. And yes, it's a place with plenty of enchanting single men. I dated a few of them when I first came, but they were make-believe relationships: say the right thing, wear the right clothes, go to the appropriate parties, and try to matter. Eventually, I simply lost interest. Oh sure, there were nights when my heart ached for someone I could snuggle with, and sometimes I felt the ache more than I could stand. And I still dreamed that the right guy would ride up on his white charger and say, "Been waitin' long?" I always laughed when I allowed myself this foolishness. I was more content to wait for Mr. Right to appear than to hang my panties on the clothesline in singles bars. Meanwhile, I could hang out in my sweats with a glass of wine and a good book, and I was doing just fine.

I bent down to pick up a striped shell from the sand and tucked it in my pocket for my porch collection. On my right was the sound of the rolling surf. A white seagull caught the breeze, sang its cry, and sailed across a darkening sky. Its song blended with sand scrunching around my shoes as I walked, all sacred music in holy time.

As the sun slid slowly into the sea, I sat on the cool sand to watch, and when a soft blanket of twilight fell over me, I lay back on the sand into a sensation of lightness and light.

The sky darkened from pink to deep purple. I lay there in tranquility, knowing I had never really experienced a day folding into night. As I was free-falling into that strange new reality, my old reference points were dissolving. I didn't know this sunset nor this twilight; I didn't know these awakening stars. I also knew I couldn't go on like that. I had a job to do, a career, cases on my desk that needed handling. I breathed gently and told myself it would be all right tomorrow.

I got home, whipped up a salad of spinach, avocado, mushrooms, and tomatoes with pine nuts and sat out on the porch to eat and watch stars and listen to silence. The streaming light show had gradually disappeared, but I still drifted on a river of wonder. Sometimes when I closed my eyes, a red "3" appeared. My dad once told me to pay attention when something comes in threes. And I had read somewhere that three was a sacred number. I also remembered that a Greek philosopher considered three the number of wisdom—the beginning, middle, and end, the number of the Divine, signifying harmony. Harmony. Yes, that evening, harmony was exactly the right word.

I went to bed early, not dreading it like I thought I would. Instead, I felt like I was snuggled in someone's arms. I fell into a deep and peaceful sleep.

In the early morning hours, I dreamed I saw Johanna lying face down on a car seat while I hovered over her, weeping. Then she rolled over and looked up at me, smiling, her brown eyes deep and intelligent. There was no blood or other sign of trauma. She said something to me, something I couldn't understand, and I jerked awake. My sheets were drenched in sweat, and now I clearly heard what she had said: *Keegan, find the Three.*

It was still dark, but with sleep no longer an option, I slipped into my blue robe, padded into the kitchen, and turned on the light over the stove. I made a cup of tea and then sat watching the steam curl up from the cup. I was entranced; it was very like the light show I'd seen the afternoon before, and it gave me the same feeling.

Johanna's face was still vivid, and I wondered if maybe my mind was slipping away. Because by now this strangeness should have been receding, but no, it was not; it was beginning to take over my mind.

And yet as my old thinking told me to be worried, to find a way out, a larger part of me was floating in a calm embrace, and I felt comforted. Hey, how could that not be good?

"Keegan, come on," I said aloud. "Are you now one of those airy-fairy persons on some mind trip? Come on! You are a sensible, logical-minded professional, a prosecuting assistant district attorney, for God's sake! You believe in facts, right? Solid, objective facts. You've got a fact-based career, and you are damn good at it. You face complex situations daily and think your way through them. Logic is your platform, your foundation. It's who you are. Now, are you going to let this little scene derail all that?"

I drank three cups of oolong tea, trying to get back to home base. I tried, failed, and finally gave up, and as dawn blushed the living room curtains, I went to shower.

7

I pulled on an old green sweatshirt and jeans, toasted an English muffin, and headed to Golden Gate Park. I parked near the beautiful San Francisco Botanical Garden, turned off my engine, leaned back in my seat to think, and fell fast asleep. Sometime later, I awakened to nearby voices, got out of my car, and walked into the fresh kaleidoscope of colors and sounds: leaves rustling in the morning breeze and people dressed in bright clothes, singing words to one another. It was a living Monet painting. The world was alive and laughing. I've never been big on religion, but I remembered that Jesus said the kingdom of heaven was within us. Well, then, heaven is where I was. Or maybe I was dreaming? It sure felt like a dream. Either that or I was headed for the looney bin.

Then I seriously pondered that maybe Johanna's death had unbuttoned something in my mind. I was constantly seeing "3" in my mind. I wandered around in a stoned bliss. Eventually I stopped and leaned against a tree, wondering if I might be slipping into crazy. I needed to know, didn't I? I needed to talk to Jill. She was a psychologist and my best buddy. Surely she'd be able to make sense of this.

She was in the middle of painting a bedroom when I got her on the phone but said to come over. I was at her door within the hour, bearing fish and chips and cold lemonade.

That blue-eyed, red-haired, long-legged former dancer is a genius. We'd kept each other sane through college and had since become closer than sisters. We took our food and drinks to her back porch and began eating as I described my situation and Johanna's death. I told her about *Find the Three* and how I kept seeing that number.

Halfway through her last piece of fish, Jill stopped eating and studied me with raised eyebrows. "Okay, then, Keegs, want to get down to this? This prism you're looking through sounds pretty great to me. Damn, lady! How come you have all the luck? I'd love to see what you see—including your mysterious Three."

I shrugged. "But, Jill, is something wrong with me? Am I losing my marbles? You know I'm not a crier, but dammit, I'm in tears almost all the time now. This thing's taking over my life, and I don't know how to shut it down. I've never even heard of a thing like this, have you?"

Jill swallowed her last bite of fish, washed it down with the last of her lemonade, and wiped her hands. She studied me, a faint smile on her face and an unasked question hanging in the air.

I broke the silence. "Jill, are you hearing me? Everything's in motion, swirling around me, and I can't tell if it's coming from me or somewhere else. Like right now, shadows and colored lights are floating across your face that are so beautiful it scares me. And if I'm not losing my mind, then what the hell's going on? And how will I ever go back to prosecuting people when all I see is their beauty? I'm not sure if I'll ever be able to see anyone as bad again. And that, my dear, would be a huge problem for a prosecutor. Don't you think?"

Jill reached for my hand, "Keegs, cool down. Right now, you're going through the aftermath of talking to a woman who was supposedly dead. That would knock anyone off their track for a while, don't you think? And you're not just anyone; you've always been a super sensitive kid. You know that."

"You always say I'm ornery."

She grinned. "Well, and I'm not taking that back. But this is a new you, Keegs. You're being touched by something that you're never going to forget. You may never see life as you did before, but from where I'm sitting, that doesn't look so bad."

I wiped the crumbs from my mouth. "So what is this, then? PTSD?"

"Nope." She shook her head, and her red hair shimmered. "Not yet anyway, and we're not going let it get there, are we? We'll talk every day until you get your balance back."

"And the Three? What about the Three?"

She shrugged. "What about it? What's the harm in thinking about a number?"

I felt my anxiety melting away. I was okay; I wasn't going nuts. I'd still be able to do my job. And though my life might be a little different, it could continue intact.

Jill reached for my lemonade. "You're not going to finish this?" When I shook my head, she drained the glass, then set it on the table between us. "Look, Keegs, I wasn't kidding when I said I'd love to see what you see. It must be beautiful. Why not just go with it? Half the loonies in this town are dropping acid or something, just trying to get where you are. Trust your mind, girl. Relax and enjoy the ride."

I felt like crying. Of course Jill would understand. I launched myself into her arms and let her hold me.

"All better?" she asked after some time had passed.

"Yes. Yes, thanks. I'll be okay."

"Well, then, will you please get out of here so I can finish my painting?"

8

She walked me to the door, and we hugged again. "Thanks for lunch," she said. "I usually charge more, but your story's enough."

I stepped down off the porch and started toward my car, then pivoted around just as Jill was closing the door. "And hey, Jill, don't worry about your mom, okay? She's going to be fine."

She opened the door again and stared at me, her head cocked. "What did you just say?"

The words were bubbling up on their own. "Your mom. She's going to be fine now."

She tilted her head even more. "Keegs, what the hell are you talking about?"

"I'm talking about your mom, Jill. The stroke—didn't you mention it?" I shrugged. "Anyway, it's just a tiny clot, and it's nearly dissolved already."

The blood drained from her face. "Keegan, come back in here."

I couldn't remember the last time she had called me Keegan. I went back inside and waited while Jill went into another room. I could hear her talking on the phone.

When she returned, she was crying. "My mom did have a stroke. The ambulance took her to the hospital. It's too soon to know how serious it is."

"You mean you didn't know?"

"No, I didn't. And how did you?"

"Whoa! I've got no idea, Jill." I stepped toward her. "Now, will you just listen to me? She is going to be okay."

She stared at me. "So you said you saw lights, and now

you're talking about my mom's brain two thousand miles from here? What the hell, Keegs?"

What could I tell her? She was the psychologist. "Hey," I said with forced lightness, "let's not make this a bigger deal than it is, okay?"

I moved to put my arms around her, but she stepped back and folded her arms over her chest, looking at me like she didn't know me. Then she unfolded her arms and gave me a stiff sideways hug. "Okay, let's talk later. I've got to get back to my dad."

I wanted to say again that her mother would be fine. But instead, I turned and stepped outside. I heard the door click shut behind me.

9

Back I went to Golden Gate Park, hurting in my heart, feeling like I'd just been shot. All the glory I had felt had become a ball of darkness. From bliss to sorrow. And yet beneath that hurt was a foundation of me that was new and that I didn't recognize. I walked amidst flowers and trees, trying to regain the ecstasy, but darkness had dimmed the brilliance. I sat on a bench under a branching tree to consider what had happened with Jill and her mother, telling myself all would be well, but Jill's cold goodbye was still crushing my heart. I moved over on the bench so I was in the sunshine and tried to smile, thinking it might lift my mood. It didn't work. I gave up and walked back to my car, intending to go home.

An hour later, I was still sitting, eyes closed, trying to heal my hurt when I was jolted to the present moment by tapping on the window.

A tall policeman leaned down and looked at me with a curious expression. When I unrolled the window, he straightened up. He had broad shoulders and a gentle face. "Sorry to bother you, ma'am. I'm just making sure you're okay."

"Yes, sure, I'm okay. Why do you ask?"

I studied his face, thinking he looked familiar. Then it occurred to me that he reminded me of James, my brother who had died. I blushed when I realized I was staring at him. But he was watching me with the same intensity.

He stepped back. "Okay, then, you take care." He turned and walked a few steps away, then stopped and looked back as if he wanted to say something. Then he shook his head and walked on.

I started my car and pulled up alongside him. "Officer, may I ask you something?"

He stopped and looked down at me, and there it was again. I knew this man!

"Sure, ma'am. What can I do for you?"

I hesitated, wondering if he would think me loony. "When you stopped back there and turned around, was there something you wanted to say? Maybe something you wanted to ask?"

He looked away into the trees for a long moment, biting his lower lip. Then he took a deep breath and moved closer. "When I came up to your car over there"—he gestured with his chin—"I thought I saw something. Now I figure it had to be my imagination."

"And what is it you thought you saw?"

He bit his bottom lip again and studied me. Then he said slowly, "Well, I thought I saw a bright light around you. It almost looked like you were on fire."

And then I was sobbing. I tried to choke it back, but I couldn't stop. I turned off the engine and put my face in my hands. I heard the passenger door open, felt the car shift with his weight, and felt his hand on my shoulder. Twenty-four hours of bottled-up emotion poured out, and I couldn't stop it. I didn't want to stop it. I had to let it out. He sat quietly the whole time, his hand never leaving my shoulder.

When I finally stopped and was gulping for air, he removed his hand, leaving my shoulder empty and small.

"What's your name?"

"Keegan. Keegan Tate."

"I'm Noah Parker. So now, Keegan Tate, maybe you want to tell me what's going on here?"

I pulled a tissue from my purse and blew my nose. My eyes must have been swollen and red; I'd had a complete meltdown in front of this kind stranger. *Way to go, Keegan!*

I told him the whole story: Johanna's death and her

message on the bridge. The strange lights. Jill's mother. I must have sounded like one of the crime victims I questioned for my job, and I wasn't too pleased about that. But I was in this strange new dimension with no map and no way to figure out a path. I just told him my feelings.

When I finished, he sat silently, looking out through the windshield. Then he got out of the car and came around to my side. He crouched down so his eyes were even with mine, "Keegan Tate, here's my card. My personal number's on the back. You can call me if you need to. Anytime."

Then he straightened up and smiled. "And this isn't me trying to pick you up. I think that, well, maybe we should stay in touch until this thing straightens itself out."

I looked at his card: Lieutenant Noah Parker. I looked up at him. "Until what thing straightens itself out, Lieutenant?"

He raised his hands as if in surrender. "Hey, look, when I saw that light around you . . ." He paused, studied my face, and continued. "Something shifted inside me. Something changed, and I feel like I'm floating. I've been trying to ignore it, but now that I've heard your story, I think I maybe caught the bug, whatever that means. I've got no idea what's going on here, and right now my mind's floating about a hundred feet high, watching all this."

He shook his head. "I know I'm not making good sense and, well, I'm a police officer, and things are supposed to make sense. But it's probably nothing; it'll fade away. But until it does, if you ever want to talk about it." He nodded his chin at the card in my hand.

"Thank you, Lieutenant Parker. And I might call you. You've been so kind."

I drove home thinking about him. His scent was still in the car, his smile warming me. I didn't understand how, but I knew him, just like I'd known Johanna when I heard her voice on my phone.

10

I sat on my porch in my favorite red sweater, drinking tea and practicing my new favorite pastime: watching clouds. They were hypnotic. White billowed sailing ships blowing across the deep blue sky, pulling me up to float with them. I stayed on the porch until the sky turned a deep purple and the first star winked at me. I was surprised to feel hot tears on my cheeks. They weren't sad tears but rather an accompaniment to that sweet presence that now lived in me.

I wasn't hungry but knew I should eat, so I drifted inside and made a salad. As I tore fresh basil leaves, a rich woodland flavor filled my nostrils, and my mouth watered. The first bite was an avalanche of flavors that I'd never tasted before, and I realized I was having a first-time experience, that it was what I'd been experiencing over the past few days. Everything—clouds, colors, the taste of tea—it was all new. I was a child again, seeing, smelling, touching, and tasting things anew with no previous idea of how they should be. I felt like I was growing younger and my life was becoming new. I gradually saw that in growing up, my senses had become dulled by repetition and I had lost my sense of delight. Now life was a kaleidoscope: I saw music curling in the air, I saw messages in clouds, I tasted the sea in my pores, and the beauty of life swam in me. I wondered: was this what being born again felt like?

Thinking I needed a dose of everyday reality, I plopped on the couch with my tea and flipped on the TV. An attractive blonde with a drill sergeant personality said, "Now we turn to the story of a woman whose life ended on the Oakland Bay

Bridge late Friday afternoon. Some of you may have been caught in that hour-and-a-half-long traffic jam on the Oakland Bay Bridge that day. We now know that it was a fatal accident that ended the life of fifty-eight-year-old Johanna Gooding, a resident of Oakland and mother of three grown children."

I barely heard anything after "Johanna." I stared at the ceiling. My mind was whirling. Her name was Johanna? Dammit. Dammit! Just when I thought I was regaining my balance, my world was off tilt again. What the hell? I *knew* the woman's name was Johanna, and I *knew* about Jill's mom from six states away. Who or what was I becoming?

I called the cop.

He answered on the second ring. "Lieutenant Parker, this is Keegan Tate. From the park?"

"Oh. Hi, Keegan."

"Her name was Johanna?"

"Yes, but—well, you knew that, didn't you? You told me her name at the park. And since then, I've been trying to figure out how you knew her name if you'd never met her."

"Is that a question, Lieutenant? What exactly are you suggesting?"

"Whoa! Hang on a minute. So you're now mad at me?"

"I'm not mad. It's just that I've spilled my guts to you, and you acted like it was all new information. Want to tell me what that was about? Were you trying to find holes in my story?"

I knew my voice had gone up an octave and I was chattering like a monkey, but I couldn't stop. "See, I've pretty much reached my peak for mysteries—and now you've become one of them. So unless you suspect me of something, why in hell wouldn't you have just told me I had her name right?"

"Okay, okay." He sighed. "Yes, I should have told you that.

I guess I was being a cop, and I apologize for that. I don't suspect you of anything, Keegan. I've just been trying to figure out how you could know her name. And now I get that you're trying to figure that out too. And that makes sense."

I took a breath. "All right, Lieutenant. I see. Sorry for jumping on you, but this whole damn thing's just getting crazier and crazier."

"Would you please stop calling me 'lieutenant'? My name is Noah."

"Okay, then, Noah."

"And, Keegs, I need to tell you something, but I'd rather do it in person."

I paused. "Did you just call me Keegs? Where'd that come from?"

"I don't know where it came from. I won't do it again."

"No, no, I don't mind you calling me Keegs. It's just that only two other people in my life ever called me that; my brother who died, and my friend Jill. For some reason, I don't mind it from you."

"Then Keegs it is. It does fit you."

I grinned. "Now, you wanted to talk to me in person about something?"

"I do. When can I do that?"

"Well, what are you doing right now?"

11

I gave Noah directions to my house and put the kettle on for more tea. Fifteen minutes later, Noah Parker stepped into my home, filling it with his presence. It somehow felt like Christmas. It was enchanting. It was also scary.

I invited him to sit at the dining table and handed him a mug of tea. He asked for cream and sugar, which surprised me.

"You're a sissy."

"You're right," he said, and smiled. "I am a sissy. I like cream and sugar in my tea." He took a sip. "Whoa, this is good!"

"Psychedelic mushrooms and ginseng. You like?"

"No, really. What the heck is this?"

"A specially imported oolong."

"Oolong," he said. "My new favorite."

I joined him at the table. "You know," I said, "it's strange. Ever since Johanna happened, anytime I drink or eat something, it feels like the first time."

He stared at me, his eyes opening wide. "For real? Because that's me too, Keegs! I've been doing stuff for years that suddenly feels like it's the first time." He frowned. "What do you think that means?"

"No idea," I said. "But why you? You only heard my story. That's your only connection."

"And that's what I wanted to talk to you about, Keegs. Please don't get mad again."

"I won't."

"I was the cop on the other end of the phone when you called Johanna."

I stared at him, stunned. "You? That was you?"

"Yep." He nodded. "It was me. I'm sorry I didn't tell you before, but when we met in the park, you were pretty upset, and I thought you had enough going on without me piling my stuff on too."

I studied his face. There was strength and kindness in his eyes. I felt I could trust him. "Noah," I said with a deep sigh, "it's a relief to know I'm not alone in this."

"Oh," he said, "you're not alone, because the things you're going through, I'm going through too. I haven't been the same since that day on the bridge. I think Johanna's touched us both somehow."

We moved into the living room and sat together on the couch. By then, his presence was fitting into my little home, and it felt just fine, so I stopped resisting and began enjoying his company. He put down his tea when I talked and listened, studying me with deep brown eyes. He was easy to talk to and easy to like. We talked late into the evening, starting with our experiences with Johanna, then about how we were each dealing with our strange new thoughts.

At one point, I found his eyes shifting between each of mine. "See something interesting?" I asked.

"Your eyes. How'd you get so lucky?"

"Wow. First time anyone ever called it lucky."

He set his cup down. "You're kidding me, right? You're an amazing woman, and you must know that by now. But your eyes? It's just that I feel you looking into me like no one else ever has."

"And it doesn't make you uncomfortable?"

He leaned back, smiling. "Far from uncomfortable; that I can assure you."

We then fell into a comfortable silence, and his eyes closed. For the first time since Johanna died, I felt myself relaxing.

After a while, his eyes opened abruptly, and he got to his feet. "I've got an early shift tomorrow, so I'm going to shove off. You want to meet for lunch?"

"How about if I fix something here?"

"No, let's go out. I've got a place in mind."

"Where?"

He smiled. "You'll see."

12

When Noah picked me up precisely at eleven thirty, he still wouldn't tell me where we were going. We drove across Market Street into the Mission District and parked next to a weedy lot. Across the street, I saw an old storefront with CASSIE'S PLACE painted on the window. It was a place I'd passed for years without noticing it. It looked like it could use a fresh coat of paint.

"You're sure about this?" I asked.

Noah grinned. "Trust me."

We crossed the street and entered a cluttered alley that smelled of garbage, and then Noah opened a side door and we went in, but instead of shabby or rundown, the room we walked into was a small café, warm, well-kept, and softly lit. I stopped and looked around. The room where we stood and an adjacent room were bathed in soft light. I counted six tables each with four chairs. In that atmosphere was palpable gentleness. I felt safe.

Noah guided me to a wooden table scarred with old knicks and cigarette burns.

As we sat, a petite woman in a loose cream-colored blouse and dark violet skirt came out from what must have been the kitchen. She was smiling, her dark eyes sparkling as she looked at Noah.

She embraced him. "You damn kid! How come you never come to see your auntie?"

Noah seemed accustomed to her teasing. "You kidding? I was here last week."

"A week? What? So now you think that's enough?"

He laughed. "Tia Ana, this is Keegan."

She looked at me, and her face softened, "Oh, a nice name for such a pretty lady." She came around the table, took my hand, and held it. "My, you are beautiful, aren't you?"

I blushed. "Well, thanks. You're kind."

"Well, it's true. You've been blessed. And I can already tell that we're going to be good friends. Will you please call me Tia? It means auntie." She let go of my hand, then stepped back and regarded me. "I'm going to be your guardian angel."

I smiled at her. "Well, now, that's good to hear. Noah brought me to the right place because I need a guardian angel."

Despite her diminutive size and gentle demeanor, I saw strength in her deep brown eyes, almost a sleeping fierceness. And just as with Noah and Johanna, I knew immediately that she had been in my life—maybe forever. It seemed like I was returning to a family I'd once known but had forgotten.

Tia sat across from me. "Now, my niece, let me ask you this: why are you hanging around with this scoundrel?" She reached out and gave Noah's shoulder a push. "This sweet guy is a son to me—the best son ever. You found a winner here, my niece." Then she frowned. "You mind me calling you 'niece'?"

"No, I don't mind. It feels good."

"Well, forgive me, but I'm also going to call you 'Little Bird' sometimes because that's how I see you."

"I'm a little bird?"

She laughed. "Not the way you say it, no. The little bird I'm seeing is confident and she's free to do what she likes. She sees a place she wants to be, she spreads her wings and goes there. She is also gentle, and that's her power."

I was blushing and smiling. No one had ever said such a thing to me. This lady was seeing life on a level I'd never known. I was fascinated.

Then without missing a beat, she looked back and forth

between the two of us with innocent eyes. "So when's the wedding?"

Noah pretended to be shocked. "You evil woman."

But she laughed. "Now, you two want to order your lunch? Or do you want me to figure it out on my own?"

"You figure it out," Noah said. "You always know best."

She left the table and came back with two mugs of coffee, cream, and sugar, then disappeared into the kitchen.

"She's a delight," I said, taking a sip of coffee. It was full and rich and was a first-time experience. I sat for a moment, relishing it. "Delicious," I said. "She must be a really good cook."

"Cook?" Noah smiled. "Oh yeah, Tia's a great cook, but you'll see she's way more than just a cook."

"What do you mean?"

He raised his chin to the kitchen. "You'll soon see."

Tia reappeared with a tray holding three deep crockery bowls of chicken gumbo and a plate heaped with hot cornbread, butter, and honey. "I'll get you more coffee in a minute," she said. "I've got a fresh pot brewing."

The gumbo was thick and delicious, and the cornbread was just the right amount of sweet. I looked around; we were in a cozy restaurant with good food, yet we were the only two diners.

Tia was back in the kitchen.

"Noah," I said, setting down my spoon, "no one's here, and it's noon. How does she keep this place open with no customers?"

13

Noah looked at me in silence, raised his eyebrows, then went on eating. I gave up and went back to my gumbo. Gumbo: there was something in it that eluded me; more than the flavor, it seemed filled with tranquility. The more I ate, the more peaceful and centered I felt. I was on a sunny beach with no worries in the world.

Then I got it. I put my spoon down; we weren't here for lunch. "Okay, buddy, out with it. What's happening here? Is this Tia really your aunt?"

Noah placed his spoon beside his bowl, looked over at the kitchen, then back at me. "No, not by blood, but I've known her my whole life. She was my mom's best friend."

I waited.

"Mom died when I was thirteen. Tia took me in and raised me. I called her this morning and told her what was going on with us, and she said we should come for lunch. Hey, we agreed we needed help, right? Well, then, Tia's the one we need."

I was skeptical. "You really think she gets how weird this is?"

"Keegs, she says it was no accident, us sharing that event on the bridge. She says it was all part of an arrangement."

"A what?"

"An arrangement. You know, like a plan."

I frowned and leaned back, watching him. "What are you saying, Noah? Are you saying this was someone's plan? And all of this"—I nodded toward the kitchen and around the room—"this is a part of it? A part of Johanna's death?"

He held up his hands. "Whoa, now, wait a minute. I'm not

saying I or anyone else planned it. I'm saying that we could be part of something . . . something deeper." He shrugged. "I don't know what it is. Maybe some mystical arrangement that we can't wrap our heads around right now."

I tilted my head. I know he saw the smirk on my face. "What in the hell are you even talking about, Noah?"

He sighed, exasperated. "I'm talking about something happening here that's bigger than you and me. And no, I don't understand it, but damn, can't you see that there's some kind of underlying something, a pattern or a force or something at work here? Can you explain all the mysterious connections any other way?"

I was so intent on Noah's words that I never felt Tia approach the table with pieces of berry pie on flowered plates and a fresh pot of coffee.

"You two be careful now," she said, setting down the plates. "It's real easy to start pushing against each other when we get scared or confused. This isn't the time."

She poured us each a cup of coffee, then poured herself a cup and sat down. "I'm not concerned about what's happening, and I wish you two would just relax about it. Oh yes, I know—it's all strange, and nothing makes sense, and you want answers. You want answers that will make you feel better, answers that fit with the lives you've always known." She looked from one to the other of us. "But that movie is over, and that ship has sailed. Nothing from now on is going to fit together in the same way. You two need to accept that truth before we can move on from here." She took a sip of coffee, looking away for a minute, then back to us. "You'll both see that this couldn't happen if you weren't ready. It just doesn't work that way."

I was getting annoyed by this nonsense. "What?" I asked. I knew my voice had become the prosecutor, but I didn't really care. "Just what is it that doesn't work what way?"

"This awakening," she replied. "This awakening you're going through. Look, you two, you're not the only ones who've ever been here. This is as old as time."

"What?" I demanded. "What's older than time?"

She leaned back and raised her hands as if asking me to settle down. "Now listen! Just listen, both of you. She leaned on the table and let her hands weave her words. "If you try to figure this out, it's going to become more frustrating because it's not something you can make sense of with your thinking mind, your intellect. It's just going to get more difficult. You're just going to go through a lot of unnecessary confusion and waste a lot of valuable time."

"Well," I said, tilting my head and looking at both of them, "I've got this solid belief that things have to make sense."

She looked at me. "And making sense; that's how you stay safe. It's making sense based on everything you know, right? Based on your memories."

I had no immediate answer.

Your entire evaluation of life is based on your past experiences, isn't it? But then what about experiences you've never had before? Like this one?"

She stood up, pushed her chair in, and leaned on it, studying me. I felt her eyes questioning me.

"Your mind," she said, "only knows what it has experienced. This is very different. This is beyond your brain and mind, beyond what you know and are comfortable with."

She pushed away from the chair and came closer to me. "Doesn't make sense? Would there ever have been electric lights or airplanes if things first had to make sense?" She walked to the wall, straightened a slightly askew picture, then turned back to us. "You two are receiving a priceless gift right now. Priceless! Very few people are chosen, and you two have been. And you don't need to understand. Understanding is not the goal—knowing is. And if you can just be patient while you get your sea legs, you'll be in acceptance. Then as you unfold into this new reality, you will eventually come to understand. Then with acceptance, we can all get on with the next step."

"Acceptance?" Noah asked. "Acceptance of what, Tia? We don't even know what we're accepting."

She looked at him with a frown. "It's not acceptance of *anything* but of *everything*. My son, you'll do good to memorize this: *it is the way it is—it is the way.*"

"Well, Tia," he said, "that doesn't work real well for me. I want to change things and make things different and better. I don't want to just say it is the way it is."

She smiled at him. "You missed the most important part: *It is the way!*"

14

I threw my hands up. "Wait a minute. Wait just a minute! I don't care one whit about this acceptance business. And what the hell is this next step you're talking about? What am I not getting here?" I knew my voice was too loud, but I didn't care. "It all sounds to me like we're getting ready to make a movie . . . maybe about some aliens or something else weird." I leaned toward Tia Ana and asked as gently as possible, "And what, may I ask, is your part in all this?"

She leaned back against the wall and stared at me, shaking her head in surprise. "Well, now," she said, "I apologize. I assumed you knew who I am and why you came to see me."

She looked at Noah, who shrugged sheepishly. "Hey, don't look at me. I only came for lunch."

Then he looked at me. "Okay, I guess that's on me. If I had told you who Tia is, I thought you'd intellectualize it and refuse. I now see that was wrong."

He turned to Tia. "I just told Keegs I knew someone who could help. I didn't go into any detail."

"Well, then," she said, sitting back down, folding her hands on the table, and looking at him, "that leaves quite a gap in her understanding, don't you think?"

Noah reached for my hand. "I'm really sorry, Keegs. I apologize." He stood up, walked over to Tia, leaned down, and put his arms around her, looking back at me. "You see, Tia is a shaman; she's what might be called a holy woman." He kissed the top of her head, then stood back and looked at her with affection. "Tia's already traveled this road we're on, and I hope you'll come to trust her as much as I do."

It was awkward for me; I did like Tia, but this whole cosmic *being chosen* thing felt like a bad dream, and it was going too far. It was a make-believe fairy tale, and I was here with a fairy godmother. I'd been trying to hide my misgivings and be a good sport, but this was now a stage play I didn't want to be in.

I asked Tia, "When does this stop feeling insane?"

Tia studied me. "Let me ask: did you talk to Johanna at all before she died?"

"No. Noah said she was dead when she called me."

"Yes," said Noah. He had returned to his chair and leaned on its back, his face level with mine. "She was very much dead, Tia. Her phone was lying on the car seat."

Tia held up one hand as if to ask for silence and looked beyond us into the space of the empty restaurant, frowning slightly. She held that silence for a moment, then looked back at each of us. "Okay, then," she said, and nodded. "Then that's when it happened."

"When what happened?" I frowned.

"The transference, dear. The assignment."

I stared at her, dumbfounded.

Tia glanced between Noah and me. "Now, you will both need to get ready because this is going to change your reality, change your lives completely. You're waking up in a new consciousness that may sometimes scare you. But believe me, it's not to be feared at all."

"Oh, easy for you to say," Noah remarked.

"Yes, it is, because I know this reality well. It's more beautiful than anything you can imagine. And scary? Well, not once you've surrendered to it, it isn't."

Well," Noah said, "I'm not too big on surrender. I think I'd rather stand my ground."

Tia laughed. "You warrior, do you think it might be possible to put down your sword long enough to let the Light come in?"

He straightened up and folded his arms across his chest. "Tia, what light?" Then he looked at me, his eyes bright. "Hold on a minute. Could that be the light I saw around you at the park?"

He turned back to Tia. "The light I saw around Keegs when I first met her? It was beautiful but also scary; I'd never seen anything like that."

Tia looked at him from under raised eyebrows. "Do you think you can now accept this: that the light you saw was not *around* Keegan, it *was* Keegan?"

Noah stared at me as if stunned.

I blew out a breath and shook my head. "Can we all just stop a minute? Now I'm a light? Really? Don't either one of you think that this is getting a little weird?"

"Yeah," said Noah. "I want to be on the team here, Tia. I do. I want to understand this, but I'm looking at Keegan right now, and she sure is not Light."

"Oh, but she is!" Tia exclaimed. "She is beautiful!"

He looked at her skeptically. "And you can see that?"

"Yes, and I also see the Light that you are too, my son."

As I listened and watched, I fell further and further away from them and from this spacey conversation. Next they'd be levitating tables. This was not reality. I knew there could be no coming back if I went any farther down this road. I'd be leaping out of the nest I held dear, abandoning my truth for some weird, structureless make-believe.

Yet I was somehow reluctant to dismiss it. After all, I had talked to a dead woman, hadn't I? At least I thought I had. I closed my eyes and tried to imagine fitting this scenario into my life as a prosecuting attorney, a life I loved. And sure, my job had its challenges, but overall I did love it. I loved the foundation that law was built on: facts, evidence, and concrete written statutes. It gave me a secure foundation, no lights as people, no unquantifiable ideas.

15

Tia and Noah were still talking, talking about how everything is made of consciousness or something like that. I wasn't really listening anymore because I realized that I might eventually become hypnotized by this bizarre reality, one not based on anything but fantasies and wishes. Fun, yes, but still pure fantasy.

This was for someone else. If it was a gift, it had come to the wrong person. Maybe a nice hippy lady could feel right at home here. Me? I'd spent years of my life sacrificing to get the education and experience I needed, steadfastly determined to make it to where I was today, and I was not about to give it up for nonsense. I looked at the two of them and decided it was time for me to get back on solid ground.

"Listen," I said, looking at each of them in turn, "I am deeply grateful for the kindness and the support you've both given me. I truly am." I took a deep breath. "But this, all this"—I gestured around the café with my hand—"this is not me. It's not the life I signed up for. And it is not the life I want."

Seeing the hurt in Noah's eyes made my heart hurt, yet I knew this was my critical moment because if I went farther down this yellow brick road, I might not get back. I had to put the brakes on now. And I did.

"I have no intention of surrendering or whatever it is I'm supposed to surrender to," I told them. "I'm not the right candidate for this job."

They both watched me in silence. Noah had closed up like a clam.

"Please try to understand; I just want my life back. I must have it back. But I thank you both; you are kind and wonderful, and I'm happy I met you."

Tia raised her eyebrows and tilted her head to the side. "My niece, you're sure about this? Really sure?"

I nodded. "I'm absolutely sure, Tia. This just isn't my thing. I'm not into it. I've got a really good life, and I'm not about to mess with it. I hope you'll understand."

She studied me for a moment, then nodded. "Well, then, my niece, you must follow your heart, and if that means living your life exactly as it has been, well, then, you do that. After all, it has been a very good life, hasn't it?"

"Yes, it has, and I love it."

I looked at Noah, who was looking down at the table. "Can we still be friends?

"Oh, we'll still be friends," Tia said, answering for him. "We all will. This won't change that."

I sighed in relief. "Okay, then, will you please tell me how I can get rid of . . . this craziness that's been blowing through my life since Johanna? Seeing and hearing things and knowing things that are none of my business? Can I just get rid of this and go back to being me?"

Tia looked at me as if she could see into my soul. I was to eventually earn that this was her look when she spotted an opening in my ego wall. "So you want to put this new self in a box," she said, "and tuck it down into the closet of your mind and not have to deal with it anymore. Is that it?"

"Yes," I nodded. "Yes, that's exactly it. That's what I want to do. Can you help me do that?"

Noah spoke up, shaking his head. "Dammit, Keegs! Dammit! Can you just wait a minute?" His face was tight. "I'm trying to get my head around what you're saying, and it's making no sense! Do you want to just toss all this away now? Isn't this the most amazing and wonderful thing you've ever felt? Do you think this is some kind of . . . some kind of fantasy trip? Like we've all been dropping acid or something?"

I nodded to him. "Well, yeah, something like that."

He got up and began pacing around the room, his hands stuffed in his pockets. Then he returned to our table, stopped, and looked at me. "Keegs," he said, looking at the ceiling, "this is more real than anything either of us has ever experienced. I can't believe you don't see that. And you know what? I think you do see it. Please, please stop before you make maybe the biggest mistake of your life. This is a gift, Keegs, yours and mine."

I looked down at the table, trying to avoid the pain in his eyes. "Yeah, Noah, I get that it's a gift for you. But for me, it's becoming more of a curse. It's taking from me everything I hold dear. I didn't ask for this, and I don't want it. I don't want to see and know things that are not my business. I just want my old life back."

Noah pulled out his chair and sank into it, stunned. His eyes burned into me.

Tia Ana broke the silence. "I hear you, my niece, and I'm with you. But in answer to your question about stopping what's happening with you"—she shook her head—"I don't think it's possible to get the genie back in the bottle. I can help you with an expanding consciousness, but I have no idea how to squeeze you back into a smaller one." She looked into the distance for a moment. "But then again, maybe I do have something that will at least help when you start feeling overwhelmed."

"Please tell me!"

She looked at me with such tenderness that I knew she understood. "When you feel yourself losing your balance, stop and take four slow, deep breaths, making sure to completely exhale each time. Will you try that right now?"

I did as she asked, and the tightness inside me immediately released.

"Did that work for you, dear?"

I nodded. "Yes. Yes, it did. I'm more relaxed now."

"Good. Now, here's the next step: find a thought that
balances you and repeat it as many times a day as you need to
feel safe."

"A thought?"

"Yes. Some kind of grounding thought, like 'I am loved' or
'I am safe.'"

"I am loved, *and* I am safe." I said it three times.

"Oh yeah," I told her. "That does feel good; kind of re-
assuring."

"Then make that your affirmation," she said. "Use it every
day, as many times as you need to. Let 'I am loved and I am
safe' be your mental foundation, your identity."

"I simply hold the thought that I am loved and I am safe?"

"Yes. Let it settle deep into your thinking and keep you in
peace. Will you do that?"

I smiled. She was more wonderful than I'd expected. She
wanted me to be happy just as I was. "Thank you, Tia. I'm
doing it now. I am loved, and I am safe."

"Good. And remember to breathe slow breaths." She
reached for my hand. "You're going to be just fine."

Noah abruptly pushed back his chair and stood up. His
voice was icy. "Why, Keegs? Just tell me that. Why in the hell
would you do this? Why would you throw away this golden
opportunity? Can't you see what it is? Can't you see how
wonderful it is?"

Tia went to him and put her hand on his chest. "Noah, it's
okay. It's okay. Let it go. It's her right."

"But, Tia," he said, turning to her, his eyes opening wide,
"this beautiful, powerful opportunity ... how can she just
throw it away?"

"Son, please hear me. This is *her* journey. Didn't Buddha say, 'The best way to God is all ways'? So then let's support our Keegan doing what her heart calls her to do."

Noah walked out of the room.

16

My life went on for three weeks after that fateful lunch, but honestly, it was not the same. I was deeply sad for a reason I couldn't place. Surely my leaving Noah and Tia—who I barely knew—couldn't be causing such distress, yet there it was, nearly a depression. And what was even stranger was that elevated feeling, that feeling of spaciousness, kept expanding every day, and I needed to be an on-the-ground woman who works for the district attorney's office in San Francisco, California. But more and more, it felt like my mind was no longer contained on one path; it was floating in a giant coliseum of possibilities. And I was still haunted by that bothersome Three, which was bugging me in my dreams and more often in my days, a kitten meowing to be fed, making sure I wouldn't forget it.

And Noah, dear Noah, was almost never out of my mind. I knew I'd get over him in time and had done the right thing by pulling out of that crazy situation. That whole New Thought thing might work for some people, but it wasn't my world. My mental and physical security and way of life were based on logical, provable thinking, on things I could understand. Maybe Tia and Noah were okay chasing rainbows, but I couldn't; I wouldn't. I would not go there with them.

Then why did I feel bereft of their company? Well, it was because their nearness had been sweet as honey, and as strange as it sounds, my heart felt a bit naked without them. Every day I saw again the look on Noah's face just before he walked out of the café. It will fade, I told myself. Just give it some time. All this will go away. "See, Keegan?" I said out loud. "You see how close you came to getting sucked into some kind of cult? You thought you were above that. This is San Francisco; pay attention now, girl!"

And I'd like to say that the effects of Johanna's death had faded, but I was still conscious of a silky river of light presence around me. Was such a thing really there, or had something come loose in my brain? Then again, the feeling of being surrounded by a soft presence did not seem to exactly emanate from Johanna's death; it just awakened me to it. Because I knew as well as I knew the taste of chocolate that it had been there my whole life, holding and protecting me, and that Johanna had just made me notice it.

But there was no way I was going to let it change my career or the course of my good life, thank you! Not one more step would I take down that yellow brick road. I would follow the path I had set for my life's work. Period!

It was puzzling: when I walked away from Tia and Noah, I expected my life to go right back to its old rhythm, but it had not. Maybe it was because I had not entirely let Johanna go. Or maybe it was because she hadn't let go of me. How could I ignore that I was still enchanted by something beyond what I imagined? Clouds still pulled me up into them and into the space between them—that indescribably precious space that touched me almost to tears. "Okay, Keegan, stop it! Stop gnawing at this; you've made up your logical, well-educated mind. You can fantasize once in a while—no danger in that—but do not let lights and clouds take you down a rabbit hole!"

Tia would smile to see that I knew when my mom was calling even before she dialed and that I was reaching for the phone before it rang. I had no idea how that worked, but it was fun.

I also could not shake the feeling that Johanna was looking over my shoulder, waiting for me. To do what? Make sure I'd find her mysterious Three? It made me uneasy, even a little frightened, when I thought about her and her Three. That's when I followed Tia Ana's advice: I took four breaths and repeated, "I am loved, and I am safe." I was probably saying those words five hundred times a day. And in contradiction to my logical mind, they worked; they grounded me.

Then this morning, as I was standing under a hot shower, refusing to get out, a block of resistance washed right out of my mind, and I suddenly relaxed. I felt my shoulders drop and my face relax, and I fell into a bliss I had never known before; it was one of joy and the deepest peace possible. I knew that my life was never going back to the way it was. It simply was not. The breathing and the affirmation were only making it more tolerable.

The logical me was not at all happy with that realization. I felt like I had just fallen out of my comfort and assurances and was heading into an unknown and unstable reality.

Jill and I hadn't talked since I told her about her mother's stroke. She had gone home to be with her folks. I missed her and wanted to call her and talk to her about what was happening with me. But I didn't want to interfere with her being with her mom. That wouldn't have stopped me for most of our relationship because we were all family.

How had it come to this?

And as if that wasn't enough, the tight wrapping of my job was coming undone. During my third week back at work, I arranged two plea bargains that granted defendants shorter prison terms in exchange for counseling and some remedial education. My boss, Frank Conklin, the district attorney, liked prison time. He believed criminals would always be criminals and that our job was to put every one of them away for as long as we could. Strangely, I now saw through this new prism that at one time I'd wholeheartedly embraced, but now I saw his attitude from a different perspective, and it seemed too simplistic, calloused, and often overly punitive.

17

On Friday of that third week, Frank called me into his office, pointed to a chair in front of his desk, and stared at me over the top of his glasses. "Keegan," he said, his voice tight, "please tell me what the hell is going on with you."

I knew why he was upset. "Frank, neither of these guys has a record of violence. They're both addicts with little education. I believe maybe they can straighten their lives out."

"Oh," he said with a head jerk, "so now we're turning dirtbag criminals into Boy Scouts. That it?"

I knew I was in trouble. "No, Frank, that's not what I'm saying. Please." I paused, looking around his office at his diplomas on the wall, his pictures with Ronald Reagan and George Bush. "Frank, I'm just starting to think that some of my past convictions might have done more damage than good. That's all. I know a lot of those guys need to be in prison, but maybe not as many as we're sending. Sometimes I think we're making felons out of people who aren't even there yet."

He pushed up out of his chair, put both hands on his desk, and leaned toward me. His voice was tight. "Keegan, this isn't you." He bit the words off. "This is not the prosecutor I know you to be."

He straightened up, took a breath, and adjusted his tie. "Now, listen to me," he said, "and listen good. You're working for me! You got that? I'm the DA here, and I say our job is to convict, not to convert. The public defenders can try to get people off or get them less time. That's their job. We're supposed to be arguing *against* them." He glared at me. "You hearing me, Keegan Tate? If I say this department will come down hard on crime and criminals, you can damn well bet your butt that that's going to happen!"

I was surprised by his anger. It seemed to me that suddenly I was disappointing everyone.

He turned away from me and looked out the window. "Something screwy's going on with you, Keegan. I don't know what it is, but"—he turned back to me—"you damn well better get it figured out, and you'd better do it fast."

I stood up and looked directly into his eyes. "You're right, of course. I haven't been myself, but I'm trying to pull myself together. I really am."

"You're a damn good prosecutor, Keegan," he said, his voice softer now. "You've got great talent and a great conviction record and a great future here. There's no reason you can't make it happen." He turned back to the window. "Thanks for coming in."

As I reached for the door, he added, "If you need some time off, let me know. I'll handle it for you."

"Thanks, Frank. I'll be okay."

He was right, though. I had changed. I saw people differently and saw them on a much deeper level than I ever had. Sometimes good people do stupid things, and while they needed to be held accountable, they should also be allowed to straighten themselves out and get their lives back on track. When we lock good people up and treat them like thugs, they too often become thugs. I saw that and wondered why that fact had never been important to me before.

18

A case landed on my desk the following Monday that completely undid my career. A white man in a Market Street bar was beaten nearly to death by a twenty-two-year-old black man named Adam Wright. The victim, Jared Lang, was in the hospital in critical condition.

I usually looked forward to these cases as a chance to get another violent offender off the street so they couldn't hurt anyone else. But when I read the police report, something didn't seem right, so I decided to do some legwork. I went to the bar where the fight had occurred, introduced myself to the bartender, and asked if we could talk. He pointed with his chin to a table in the corner, then came over a few minutes later with a pencil and pad. I ordered a sandwich and coffee.

When he returned with my order, I asked him about the fight. He shrugged. "Things happen in bars. That's just the way it is."

I stopped him and told him I was the prosecutor on Adam Wright's case and had some misgivings about it. He studied my face, then turned to look around the bar. Almost empty. Then he looked back at me, leaned forward, and put his hands on the table. "Now, listen here. I don't want to get pulled into court on this, but still, I'm not real happy about what's going on with Adam right now."

"So you know him?"

He pulled out the chair across from me and sat down. "The kid's a janitor in that office building across the street." He jutted his chin at the building I could see through the window. Adam comes in almost every night after work to talk baseball over a couple of beers. That kid's sharp as a tack; he knows the batting average of damn near every player in the leagues. And he's friendly to everyone. He's usually got the whole bar laughing." He shook his head and chuckled. "Man, that kid does love to laugh."

I leaned back in my chair and frowned. "So how does a guy like that do what he did? He almost killed that guy. It makes no sense."

"This Jared, the guy that got beat up? Now, he's a real piece of work, that one. I've tossed his ass out of here more than once for pushing people around. I should have tossed him out that night, but I was busy and didn't get how serious it was getting until it was too late." He looked around at the bar again, then back at me. "That night, Adam went to his regular place over there at the bar, and he ordered a beer, just like always. Then old Jared, who's been drinking long enough to be tanked, starts in on Adam. I yelled down the bar and told him to cool it or he was gone. I told him twice, but he ignored me and kept harassing Adam. The next thing I know, I saw him say something to Adam. He said it so quiet I couldn't hear him, but a guy who was sitting close to them said Jared had been on Adam about his ugly black face, and then he slammed his mother.

"Adam tried to ignore him. I know that kid; he was just going to finish his beer, get up, and leave. But then Jared shoved him up against the bar real hard. Adam came back at him fast and pushed Jared away. But then Jared smashed a fist into Adam's face, knocked him to the floor, and started kicking him.

"Then it was like Adam went crazy. He came up off the floor in a heartbeat and ripped into Jared with a rage like I've never seen before. By the time we pulled him off a few seconds later, Jared was out cold and bleeding bad."

He looked around the bar again and then back at me. "So now that good kid's in jail and maybe going to prison. Is that right? Is that the way our system's supposed to work?"

Back in the office, I ran a background check on Adam Wright. He was being raised by a single mother who had regular work as a maid in three Pacific Heights homes. In high school, Adam played shortstop on the baseball team. One night after a tough game against a visiting school, he was grabbed by three white kids from the losing team who beat him unconscious and allegedly raped him with a broomstick. The attackers produced witnesses who provided alibis, and they went free.

Adam had been an honor student up to that point, but then it all changed. He became quiet and distant. He wouldn't talk to anyone. He was beginning to find a place where he could be okay and have a couple of beers with friends. But inside of him was a sleeping volcano that erupted in the bar that night.

I decided to visit Adam in jail. As the bartender had said, he was a quiet and polite kid. His skin was almost black, and his eyes were golden, holding me in their warmth.

He told me he had asked to call the injured man and apologize, but his request was denied. So he sent his apology by mail. His attorney told me the young man was devastated by what he had done and couldn't understand how he was being charged with attempted murder when the man attacked him first. He also couldn't understand why the boys who had molested him as a teenager had been set free. He figured it was because he was black and they were white. I didn't know, but I could see that it might have been an inescapable conclusion for him.

"Is it because I'm black, Miss Tate? People get off when they're white, right? And guys like me go to prison. Is that fair?"

"No, I don't think it's fair, Adam. But you damn near killed that guy. If they hadn't pulled you off, you might have."

He looked down at his hands. "I know, I know. I lost it. He was calling me names and trying to get me to fight him. He even called my mom a black whore. I was trying to leave when he decked me. I am sorry he's hurt so bad, but, ma'am, he started it."

"I know. I'll talk to your attorney and see if there is something we can do."

19

I went to see Frank and asked if we could lower the charge to third-degree assault. I knew I was baiting the bear, but what the hell?

He stared at me for a long moment. He looked as if I had spit at him. "So here we go again," he said, his voice flat. "You're a prosecutor, Keegan. You're a deputy district attorney, not a damn social worker!" The way he looked at me made me feel like I was being stabbed. "What in the hell do you think you're doing, asking me to go easy on a guy who damn near beat another man to death? That punk belongs in prison, and what, you want to pat him on his little head?"

"Frank, can you please listen to what I've learned about this defendant?"

"No, Keegan." He leaned back in his chair. "I won't listen." He picked up a pen and twirled it under his chin. "As of right now, you're off this case." He tossed the pen on his desk and put his hands behind his head, his elbows out. "I'm taking you off this and all other cases for a while. You go home for the rest of this week and consider whether you still want to work here."

I looked down at the patterned carpet for a long minute. Then I stood up and looked at him. "I'm going to need more than a week, Frank. I'd like some additional time off."

"How long?"

"I don't know. A month?"

He waved me off, no longer meeting my eyes. "Be back in this office in a month, ready to be a prosecutor again. Or don't bother coming back."

I spent the next three days in a fog. I slept in every morning, spent hours exploring the beach, watched old movies, and even thought about getting a kitten. I was doing anything I could to get grounded, but the two realms of reality I was living between didn't blend worth a damn. The career I had worked so hard to create was dissolving, and I was devastated. I felt like I was losing my job and my life. What would I do with myself? How would I pay my bills and my mortgage?

I often fell back on Tia Ana's slow, even breaths and the affirmation: *I am loved, and I am safe.*

Then during one long, sleepless night, it occurred to me that if I wasn't getting the right answers, maybe it was because I wasn't asking the right questions.

20

I waited for my prescription, leaning against the brick wall outside the pharmacy, my eyes closed as I turned my face to the warm autumn sun. I opened my eyes to see a small dark-haired girl sitting on a bench directly across from me. She was swinging her legs and watching me.

"Hello," I said.

"Hi," she said. "I'm sorry you're lost."

"Lost?" I laughed. "I'm not lost. What makes you say that? Are you lost?"

"No, silly, I'm right here."

"Well, then," I said, "you're the silly one because I'm right here too."

She closed one eye and studied me, then shook her head. "Nope," she said, "you're not here. Not here at all."

Her quick response surprised me. "Well, if I'm not here, where am I?"

She shrugged. "Don't know. Just know you're lost."

"You know something? You are a very interesting young lady."

At that moment, a woman came out from the pharmacy, her arms full of packages. "Okay, honey," she called to the girl, "time to go. Let's get in the car."

I froze. The woman's voice sounded exactly like the one that had said *Find the Three*. It was Johanna's voice! I looked at her as she walked away. I wanted to call out, to go after her, but I was frozen in place. I watched as she buckled the child into the passenger's seat, then went to the driver's side. Just before the car pulled away, the back passenger window rolled down and I heard the mother say, "Johanna, tell the nice lady goodbye."

The girl waved and blew me a kiss. "Goodbye, Keegan!"

And then I was in tears . . . again.

That night I learned that Adam Wright had committed suicide in his cell.

21

Without Noah's directions, finding Cassie's Place took me nearly an hour. I parked across the street and sat in my car, staring out the window, asking myself if I really wanted to do this. Did I really want to start up the craziness again? Then I laughed at myself. Start it up again? It had never stopped! I looked across the street to the café and wondered if Tia was even there. Finally, feeling lost and nervous, I got out, locked my car, leaned against it, took the prescribed deep breaths, and said softly to myself, "I am loved, and I am safe."

Finally, I crossed the street into the alley, and as I raised my hand to knock, the door opened. "Come in, come in, my niece. I've been waiting for you!"

My voice sounded tiny. "You've been waiting for me?"

And then I was in her arms, sobbing. I was no longer embarrassed to be crying in front of her. I knew I had come home.

She held me until my tears stopped and the world began falling into place again.

"Come on now," she said. "Your tea's hot. Oolong, isn't it? And I've made us some lunch." She headed toward the kitchen.

"Tia, I have to tell you what happened this morning," I said, my voice breaking.

She turned to face me from the kitchen doorway. "My niece, please be still now. You're safe. We'll eat first, and then we'll talk. I'm so proud of you. You've come through the roughest part."

I sat at a table and waited. She returned with deep crockery bowls of fresh tomato soup and grilled cheese sandwiches made of a thick, rich dark bread.

We ate in silence, and the food blessed and relaxed me. When we were both finished drinking tea, I picked up the conversation where it had left off. "You said the roughest part?"

"Yes, the parts where you kept denying who you are, ignoring your soul calling. I know; that time was tough for me too when I was beginning."

"Tia, I thought you said I could go back to my old life."

"No, dear," she said, shaking her head. "I said I didn't know how to put the genie back in the bottle. Remember?"

I looked down at the table and nodded.

"Tell me what happened."

I told her about Johanna at the pharmacy, Frank, and my job. I told her about things I was learning about myself. I told her how it felt like my old life was slipping away. I told her about my dreams of flying and being naked amidst throngs of clothed people, dreams I had not remembered until I began telling her about them. And then my eyes filled with tears again, and I told her about Adam's suicide.

"So now, my niece, do you still think you can return to your old life?"

I hesitated momentarily, then shook my head. "I can't go back. I tried, I tried hard, I really did, but you know, somehow I just don't fit that life anymore." I shrugged. "Or maybe that life doesn't fit me anymore. I looked at her, sitting across from me, calm and assured. "So I'm into this new reality, right? Now, tell me, what the hell am I going to do? Become a beach bum?"

"Would that be so bad?"

I looked at her. "You're kidding me, right, Tia? I'm not at the end of my life here. I might still have some value to the world. I'm sure not ready to throw in the towel."

"Why not?"

"Why not? Because . . . because I'm being pulled by something I don't understand." I laughed. "What you called my soul calling. Tia, I'm filled with hunger and a passion I don't even understand. I have to be doing something that matters, something of value." I was still laughing and didn't know why. "I don't even know what I'm saying!" I told her.

"So you don't understand it. Do you think it's possible that things might open up for you if you let go of your need to understand?"

"What? What would open up?"

She repeated my question back to me. "What would open up? Keegan, you already know the answer to that question. But you are stubborn, aren't you? And your stubbornness is a wall you've built around your mind that demands you to understand before you let anything new in. You're standing on the beach, and the tide is coming in around you. Pretty soon it will be over your head, but there you stand, refusing to accept it because it doesn't match what you think the tide should be. You read today's tide chart, and this doesn't match. So there you stand; here you sit. Same thing."

22

The tide was a great example because I felt like I was being overwhelmed by a consciousness that was expanding in me, threatening to dislodge everything I held dear. Tia was watching me, probably reading my thoughts.

"This tide rising around you," she said. "is not something you can put in a classification. It is goodness and creativity, Keegan. It's goodness and creativity, and it's yours. It's your own grace awakening inside you. Do you think you can maybe relax and trust for a bit? Let things unfold naturally?"

I studied her, thinking about her words, becoming aware of my righteous, artificial wall of self and seeing how it had me trapped. I looked into her eyes and said, "This tide, Tia, that's the problem. If I let it come in . . . Well, I have no idea how to swim in this sea."

She tilted her head in a way that I would get used to when she was about to say something that would change my life. "Well," she said, "you sure won't learn until you get into the water, will you? And then you might be surprised because maybe you already know how to swim. Who knows? Maybe you'll find the greatest joy and peace you've ever known. Then maybe you'll be swimming for the rest of your life. You think?"

She watched me trying to put it together, fighting the instinct to understand. Then she said, "Tell me, my niece, what other choices do you have right now?"

I dropped my head and closed my eyes. I had spent my life depending on logic as my foundation, my safety net. Now this tide was picking me up, turning me around, and nothing made sense as it used to.

Tia continued to watch me.

"Honestly, Tia . . . I'm in anyway, aren't I? I'm in right up to my neck. And I'm sure seeing that my old way of thinking isn't working too well here. I guess little Johanna was right— I guess I'm lost."

"Or"—Tia lifted one shoulder—"maybe you're found."

I sighed. "Okay, okay. I'm tired of whining. Let's get on with it. Parachute or not, I'm out of the plane."

Tia threw her head back and laughed. "Then you better learn to fly. You think you can?"

"I have no idea, but I've got a flight instructor here, and you'd better teach me because I'm free-falling down and down."

She smiled. "No, my dear Little Bird, not down. You're not falling down; you're falling up. Up and up. You're being lifted by pure grace."

I smiled so wide my face hurt. "I'm learning to fly?"

"Oh yes, indeed you are. Now let go of your self-doubt."

"That would be letting go of a big part of my life."

"No," she said, "it would be letting go of a big part of how you see your life."

23

I came back from the beach, left my sandy shoes on the porch, and walked into my sweet little home, practicing my breathing, repeating my affirmation, and feeling wonderful. Never had I felt as alive than that moment in the shower when I finally decided to let go.

It wasn't until I'd made tea and sat down to read my mail that I noticed a brown envelope that had been pushed under the door. I must have walked right over it, unless it came when I was in the kitchen. I picked it up and tore it open. Inside was a single notebook paper with a scrawled note: WATCH YOURSELF BITCH. I'M COMING FOR YOU.

I was stunned. I sat down on the floor, right where I was, and read it again, then I wadded the paper and threw it across the room. I was shaking when I got up and moved to sit on the couch. I leaned forward and put my face in my hands. "Keegan," I said aloud, "will you please stop being such a wuss? Some nutcase is trying to get to you, and you're letting them do it."

My mind was darting back and forth like a frenzied housefly, and I was having a hard time breathing. I picked up the phone and dialed Noah; he would know what to do.

He answered on the first ring. "Keegs? I don't believe it. You're calling me?"

"Yes, Mr. Policeman, I'm calling you." I tried to smile. "Noah, I'm in trouble. I need your help."

"I'll be there in fifteen minutes. You okay till then?"

"Yeah. Yes, I think I am."

He hung up, and I went to make more tea. My hands were

still shaking. What the hell, Keegan?' I thought. You've been dealing with crooks and killers for years,

"Yeah," I answered out loud, "but I've never seen myself as a victim."

I felt ashamed of my fear. I'd always thought I was tough and could handle a personal threat with courage and dignity. Yet here I was, trembling over a stupid note.

I heard a knock and met Noah at the door. "My God, Keegs, you're white as a sheet! What the hell is going on?"

I handed him the crumpled-up paper. "This was pushed under my door."

He picked up the note by one edge and gently opened it. He read it, went to the couch, sat with it in his hands, and looked at me. "When did this happen?"

"I went to see Tia. It was here about a half hour ago when I came home."

He raised his eyebrows. "You went to see Tia?"

I nodded. "Yeah, I did, and we talked for a long time." I looked into his eyes, holding him in my gaze. "Noah, I'm back in."

He stared at me with what looked like disbelief.

"I . . . I guess I was never out. I just thought I was. Noah, will you please accept my apology for abandoning you?"

"Of course I will," he said gently. "Thank you."

I looked at the note in his hand. "I hate to admit it, my friend, but I'm really afraid. Someone out there wants to hurt me or maybe even kill me."

He watched my face with admirable calm. "I know," he said. "I know you're afraid."

I sat beside him, and he leaned closer to me. "And that's exactly what this scumbag wants: for you to be terrified. He wants you out of your mind with terror, Keegs. He'd have already done it if he wanted to hurt you physically. He wouldn't be sending you notes."

"Noah, this guy knows where I live!"

"Yes," he nodded, "and that's exactly my point: he knows where you live, but he sends a threatening note instead of ambushing you. Can't you see this, Keegs? This butthead's toying with you like a cat with a mouse."

"Well, I'm feeling like a mouse right now, and I'm also more than a little ashamed of how I feel."

He put his arms around me and pulled me into his chest. "Hey, Keegs, we're on a new journey right now. You're not alone; we're in this together. And I think we need to get used to things not being like they were. I think we're in for some surprises, maybe some good and some like this one." He took me by the shoulders and held me at arm's length so he could look into my eyes. "Just know I'll always be here to watch over you. Always."

I collapsed onto his chest again. Now I wasn't sobbing. I was grinning as I never had before.

He pushed me away again. "And that little scumbag who wrote this note? Hey, he's not a problem. Oh yeah, he wants to be a problem, but he's not. Chances are good this clown will never do anything more than write notes, and he'll write them just to get to you."

I pushed away to retrieve a tissue from the coffee table and dabbed my eyes. "Well, his first shot hit the mark, didn't it?"

Noah put his arm around my shoulder. "Yeah, maybe it did, but you know what? That was probably his best shot because now he can't surprise you anymore. Remember, he wants to keep you afraid. And now you won't let that happen, will you?"

I shook my head.

"Now you've got his number," he said. "Now he's dealing with the real Keegan Tate."

I leaned against him, smiling. "You sounded like Tia just then."

"Well, that makes sense because I've been talking to her a lot."

"Well," I said, "speaking of adventures." I pointed to the note on the coffee table.

He picked it up by one corner. "I'm going to check this for prints in the morning. Then I'll talk to someone who knows about handwriting and threatening notes, and maybe we'll get a lead. Meanwhile, Keegs, I want you to keep a low profile."

"Am I in house jail?" I teased.

"No, not at all." He got up, went to the window, and drew the curtain aside to peek out. "Just keep your eyes and ears open. This clown could be anywhere. Most likely, he won't show himself." He turned back to me. "Like I said, if he wanted to hurt you, he's had his chance. It looks like he just wants you terrified."

"But why? What the hell have I done to get this . . . nutcase after me?"

"You know the answer to that as well as I do, Keegs."

"You mean it could be someone I helped convict? That's no help at all. It could be any one of dozens of people." I stood up and went to him. "And you know something, Noah? Even though you'd think those guys would go after their prosecutor, that's rare. By the time they get out of prison, their anger has pretty much faded."

"Good," he said. "Good to know. Now, can we put this note in a clean plastic bag?"

"Sure." I went to the kitchen to find a small storage bag. Noah called after me. "Keegs, I want you to spend some time thinking about who this could be. It's probably someone you know."

I returned with the bag. He slipped the paper inside and zipped it closed. Then he put a hand on my shoulder and looked me in the eye. "Now, if you get even the slightest idea of who this might be, you'll call me, right?"

"That could be a lot of wild goose chases," I said.

He lifted one shoulder. "I don't care if there are dozens. You call me."

He went to the door, and I followed him. "Okay," I said. "Meanwhile, please let me know what you find out about prints."

He reached the door, then turned to look at me again. "Promise me you'll be careful."

"Hey, Noah, I'm a trooper. And yes, okay, I'll be careful."

His presence lingered long after the door closed behind him, and I was smiling as I rinsed out our cups, wondering how I could be smiling when someone was threatening me. It made no sense, but I didn't care. Something peaceful and happy was awakening inside me.

24

It was a hot, late summer day in San Francisco. I drove up to Mount Tam right after dawn to hike the Verna Dunshee Trail. I watched the deer come out of the brush in the early morning and begin nibbling leaves, glancing my way occasionally. From the overlook, I could see the city and the bay. The water mirrored the deep blue sky. I breathed in the clean morning air, more at peace than I could remember ever having been.

I returned to my car and drove down to the café, feeling like I had when I came off the bridge that day, like I was floating on a river of grace.

Tia met me at the door and looked at me, her eyebrows arched. "You're sure?"

I hadn't said anything, but of course she knew. I nodded. "Yes, I'm ready to get on with it."

"Then are you willing to surrender to me for ten minutes?"

"I am."

"So," Tia said, "if you are ready, put your hands in your lap, lean back, close your eyes, and breathe in and out gently through your nose."

I did not ask where she was taking me. I simply breathed and let my thoughts dissolve into the sound of her voice.

"Hold each breath for four heartbeats, then let it go. When you do, feel your body fall deeper and deeper into relaxation."

I drifted with her voice into empty space, leaving my thoughts behind me.

"Continue breathing and falling away. Let yourself float

away . . . away." Her voice faded with each word. She was silent for a long time, then softly said, "Let yourself be wrapped in a blanket of grace."

Not long ago, the words "a blanket of grace" would have made no sense. Now they sent me into a deep bliss.

After more silence, she said, "Picture a little spot of consciousness like a small glowing light about ten inches above your head. Focus your attention there. That is your Higher Mind."

When I reached that place, she said, "Now ask your Higher Mind whether your life as an attorney is your true life's mission or was it simply a pathway to your life's mission."

I observed my life through my Higher Mind without judging. I saw myself growing up, attending school, then attending college and law school. Finally, I saw my life as an attorney. And then as a prosecuting attorney. I saw clearly that it was all valuable but in the past; it didn't matter anymore. My life had opened into a new chapter, maybe even a new book. I felt my old identities fade into quiet photos of a once-lived life. Then they slipped away completely, and I was free.

When I finally opened my eyes, Tia was still sitting across from me, watching. On the table was a pot of tea, two cups, and a plate of cookies. I couldn't talk. I was still somewhere else.

She spoke. "You see, you are not an attorney anymore. That was an identity, a suit of clothes, a lawyer suit that you wore to the office and court. You wore it day and night in your mind."

The room was so quiet I could almost hear my tea cooling. I had just watched my life unfold through a completely new lens. And still from within me came a protest: "I didn't think I was pretending to be an attorney, Tia. I was one."

"And a good one, too; no doubt about that. But is that who you are now, an attorney?

"No."

"Then who are you?"

I had always seen myself as an attorney, a woman, a cook, a beachcomber, an avid reader, and a tea connoisseur, and up to now, I had thought of myself as a thinker as well. I realized now that Tia was asking me to open a door in my mind to a room I'd kept closed my entire life.

"Tia," I said, "my mind is empty. I don't know who I am, and I don't know which direction to go."

"What about the Three?" she suggested.

I sighed. "Tia, what the hell does that damn Three have to do with who I am?"

"That's good," she said, nodding. "That's the question you needed to be asking."

"And the answer, Tia?" I asked. I knew I sounded frustrated, but I was hanging by my fingertips onto reality and saw no place to go. "I'm trying here, I really am, but I don't need more questions."

"Little Bird, questions contain the answers; you must pay attention."

"To what? I should hang out with the question until a good answer appears? Is that what you're saying?"

She smiled at me. "More tea?"

I watched her as she poured fresh tea into my cup. We might have been discussing rose cultures instead of questions that challenged who I thought I was. Yet she knew—I was sure—that I was adrift in a sea of contradictions.

It suddenly occurred to me: *she knew what the Three was!*

25

She watched my face as realization awakened in me, then picked up the teapot and disappeared into the kitchen. I heard water running and dishes clanking. When she came back and placed the teapot on table, she leaned forward with her hands on her chairback and looked at me. "Little Bird, if I tell you what you want to know, it's going to be words, just words without meaning. Each of the Three is an element of awakening. The awakening has to come first, then the words. Can you slow yourself down and see how this works? If you can, this is going to be a lot easier. Each of these Three will be a seed planted inside your mind, planted inside your soul."

"A seed?"

"Yes, a seed. That's what Johanna did: she planted seeds in you."

I looked at her for a long time, and then something struck me as funny and I laughed. "And you can't tell me anything, can you? So we could be talking about three years, three cans of beans, or three little pigs. I don't even know where to start."

"That's where you are now," she said. "You're at the start." Then she laughed. "Finally!"

"And that's all I'm going to get from you? That I'm at the starting point?"

"I'll give you one small hint and no more. Ever. You ready?"

"Oh yes, I'm ready!"

"Be you!"

The room fell silent, and something shifted inside me. *Be you?* I'd spent my entire life being me or thought I had. But could it be that that me was only part of me?

We were silent for a while as I sipped tea and pondered: *be you—be me.* My deeper mind gently opened as I sat with this wizard lady and drank tea in that dark, silent café. Somewhere a clock chimed three times.

"Tia," I said, "you've talked about a light several times. What is that?"

"The Light," she answered, "is the source of all things, material and nonmaterial, in all dimensions. Different people call it by different names—I'm calling it the Light— but none of us is correct because no one can name that constant, eternal presence. We can only come close."

"Okay, maybe that was a dumb question. It's just that, right now, I feel like I'm free-falling through space, and my instinct is to grab onto anything that seems solid. Light doesn't seem too solid right now. I don't think that's going to save me."

"Well, is free-falling through space really so awful? Isn't that what freedom is?" she asked.

I thought about that for a minute, then surprised myself by laughing. "Truthfully?" I said. "Sometimes I'm so happy, I feel like I'm glowing."

"And?"

"And, well . . the world feels more balanced."

"So not so awful, unless you're hiding from truth, and then life gets messy."

"Well, I've finally decided I must find the Three, even though it's still a crazy mystery and I have no idea how to go about it."

"I understand," she said. "Here's a lesson I learned a long time ago, and it's saved me many times: when I accept whatever I am up against, its energy flows with mine, and it becomes my friend."

She sipped her tea, watching me so intensely that I felt like a butterfly pinned to a corkboard. "Acceptance," she said, "is the key to it all. But you'll have to deal with that block inside you before you can get to that place. You know what that block is?"

I shook my head.

"It's your self-doubt. You automatically cling to self-doubt because you think it's keeping you safe when it's actually keeping you trapped in an old identity that doesn't work for you anymore. Self-doubt is the furry little head of your ego, your self-identity. Its job is to fight change, so it pushes for all it's worth to keep you from changing. It keeps telling you that you can't. Self-doubt."

I looked away, dismayed. "Is it always going to be like this?"

"Oh no," she said. "Once you get over these few bumps in the road, you're going to find your vision, and then your power will come to you. Then nothing can stop you."

"Well, hey," I said with a laugh, "sounds like I'm drafted into metaphysical boot camp."

"Indeed you are! And I see you're not thrilled about it. Get thrilled! Get excited about living your precious life outside the box of ego. Get excited about becoming you."

She reached for a cookie and took a careful bite, then held it away and smiled at it. "It's just a choice, you know, Little Bird. It's a simple choice. That's what life is: choices and their results. Nothing else. Your life is opening into grace and joy, transforming into more fun than you ever dreamed possible. But between now and then, you'll go through some changes. And if you resist them—and again, that's your choice—then it's going to be a lot harder for both of us."

"You're saying I have a choice? What choice did I have over being recruited into this?"

"Simple: you chose throughout every month of your life to become the Keegan that you are. You even had a choice today, and you made it—you came here."

My brain was buzzing, and being an attorney, I was looking for a loophole. That's what a lawyer does: looks for a way around any inconvenient truth.

I leaned back in my chair and looked into the darkened part of the café. "You know, right now, when I look at myself, I see a victim. And that doesn't fit me because a victim I'm not."

26

I closed my eyes and went back into that place she called the "Higher Mind," and I saw clearly from there that I had come to a crossroads. And I saw it was time I made a choice and committed to it.

I sat up straight again, looked into her eyes, and sighed deeply. "Okay," I told her. "I'm in. I'm in all the way."

"Good," she said, clapping and smiling. "So what do you need from me right now?"

I sipped my tea and thought about that question. I was not swimming but dog-paddling across the entire ocean. That's how it felt. I had only a vague idea of where I was going and didn't know if I'd ever know. I only knew I couldn't go back. And besides, the mystery of the whole thing thrilled me. "How about something to boost my lagging self-confidence?" I asked.

"Like an affirmation?"

"Yes, that would do nicely. Please."

"If I give you one, are you willing to say it two hundred times a day for thirty days, each time with conviction?"

"Two hundred times a day for thirty days? Are you kidding?"

"Two hundred times, said each time with mindfulness and conviction. And if you miss a day or even part of a day, you return to day one and start over."

My mouth dropped open, and I stared at her.

"Big commitment, yes?"

"A giant commitment!"

"Bigger than the commitment you made to law school?"

I shook my head slowly. "No."

"And that was truly a life-changing commitment, wasn't it?" I nodded. "It was."

She raised her eyebrows. "So this is your new school, the path to your new life. And it's a really steep path."

She looked at me in silence. "And it will be steep and rugged until you commit, commit your heart, mind, and spirit." She smiled. "And then it won't be hard at all."

"Tia, I'm ready. I'm committed. Two hundred times a day for thirty days?" I watched her for a moment, watching me, waiting for me. "Okay, I'm all in!"

"Good. Then here's your affirmation: *I am open to a greater truth.*"

"I am open to a greater truth," I repeated.

An hour later, I headed home, repeating my new affirmation all the way.

27

I was still repeating "I am open to a greater truth" as I drove back to the top of Mount Tam, back to my own aerie above the scurry and bustle of the city, where I could see out over the vast blue ocean, out over the city and distant hills, where I could see into forever.

I followed my special trail to my rock, and I sat with my back against it and looked west toward Hawaii and Japan. For a while I sat there, soaking up the peace, feeling the mountain pulsing beneath me. I then opened my sack lunch: a PB&J sandwich and hot tea.

As I ate, I let the great space of sky and sea wrap around me. I breathed in the sweet bay trees, the firs, and the redwoods, and watched a doe and two spotted fawns venture out to graze. To the south, giant thunderheads were stacking up and moving my way. I wasn't concerned, though; this was my place of enchantment, and those clouds were miles away.

Then as Noah had asked, I started looking back over my life as a prosecutor to try and see who might want to hurt me. I'd put a number of criminals behind bars, but revenge from convicted felons happens very seldom, and I just couldn't take it seriously. It must have been something else—maybe a case of mistaken identity. The person who had left the note must have confused me with someone else. The more I thought about that possibility, the more convinced I became that it was so.

Now what to do about it? I called Tia from my perch, and she agreed to meet with me again. I said I'd be there in about an hour.

By the time I got to the café, the thunderheads had arrived

in the city, and it had started to rain. At first it was just a sprinkle, but by the time I parked, it was a downpour. I waited in the car for a few minutes, hoping it would slack off, but it was only getting heavier, so I got out and ran to the café door. By the time I got there, Tia had the door open. I was soaked. I darted inside, laughing hysterically.

Tia put her hand on her cheek. "Well," she said with a laugh, "I can't call you Little Bird anymore, can I? You're now Little Duck."

"Tia, if I'd parked any farther away, I'd be Little Fish."

I pulled off my wet jacket, and Tia handed me a towel, then retreated to the kitchen. I dried myself as best I could, then wrapped my hair in the towel like a turban.

When Tia returned, she brought two mugs of hot chocolate. We sat at our usual table. I took a drink of the thick, rich beverage. I took another sip, and a strange feeling filled my head and moved down, enveloping me. I was as light as air.

"What did you put in this chocolate?" I asked her. "Magic mushrooms?"

She reached for my hand, and her eyes were dancing. "The only magic here is you, my niece." She nodded at the cup in my hand. "You're going to get used to having these experiences now because they're going to be almost a daily thing with you."

"I was up on Mount Tam when I called you, in that place where my mind gets clear. I said my affirmation for half an hour and then tried to figure out who the maniac is who's after me. Noah wanted me to go back over my life and see who popped up. So I did. I looked as hard as I could, and you know what? Nothing popped up. Nothing! I have absolutely no idea who he is."

"And so you came here to ask me?" she teased.

"Sure. Why not?" I quipped though it wasn't completely true. "I really came because you can move beyond the obvious.

I must find out who this is before he hurts me or someone else. So I came so we can talk about this stuff, and I'll maybe get a clue."

"This stuff?" she asked, her eyebrows going up. "So that's what this is called. I've always wondered."

I put down my mug. "When I went up on the mountain this morning, all I could think about was how I was in danger. But sitting up there in the quiet this afternoon, watching a hawk glide along on the wind, I realized I don't need to know who's after me. I don't have time for that. I don't give a damn who or what he is. At the same time, there's a crazy person out there who might hurt me or someone else. I don't want to be stupid. So I decided to come and talk to you. Maybe you can help me move past this dilemma." I sat back in my chair. "There. That's what I came to tell you."

Her deep brown eyes held my gaze. "My niece," she said, "Johanna knew who you were, and she chose you for this path. If it wasn't yours or right for you, you wouldn't have been there in that instant, wouldn't have stopped, and wouldn't have heard her last words. On some level, you were already ready and in a place of acceptance. This situation with the crazy person? It's a growth step for you, and it will be a big one. The question to ask yourself is, do you think you might give up if it gets harder?"

I shook my head vigorously. "Tia, that giving-up ship has already sailed."

"Okay, good. Then let's talk about the person who wrote you the note."

"You mean the person who wrote someone the note but maybe not me?"

She looked at me without saying a word, but her meaning was clear.

"You think that note was meant for me?"

"Little Bird . . ."

"Dammit, Tia! I thought I'd gotten rid of that fear."

"What, by denying it?"

I unwrapped the towel from my head and draped it over the chair next to me. "Yeah. In truth, I guess I just thought that since I couldn't figure out who sent it, maybe I could just ignore it."

"And would Noah think that was a good idea?"

28

We continued talking for over an hour, and when we finished, I headed home. I couldn't remember feeling more grounded and balanced. Whenever I had a conversation with Tia, even when it felt prickly, I left grateful to be alive.

I picked up a bake-at-home pizza, popped it in the oven when I got home, kicked off my shoes, and poured myself a Merlot. Then I turned on the local news, where the main story was about a four-year-old boy—the photo showed a tiny kid with blond hair and a huge smile dressed in overalls—who had gone missing down by Daly City.

By the time the pizza came out of the oven, my mouth was watering. I put three pieces on my plate, refilled my wineglass, and returned to the couch. I propped my feet on the coffee table and turned on my all-time favorite black-and-white movie, *To Kill a Mockingbird*. Still, when the pizza was gone and Gregory Peck was being called to deal with the rabid dog coming up the street, I realized I was no longer paying attention. Something was bugging me.

I turned off the TV and slipped into bed to read, but I couldn't focus. Finally, a little after nine, I gave up, turned out the light, snuggled under the covers, and felt the world dissolve as I drifted asleep. Then in startling clarity, I was in a room with the lost little boy from the news. I reached out to him, but he couldn't see me. His face was wet with tears. Behind him was a blonde woman smoking a cigarette and playing solitaire.

I was instantly awake. I jumped out of bed and checked

the time: one fifteen. As I stood in my dark bedroom, the only light coming from the illuminated clock dial, a rush of emotional energy swept through me. I felt like I was being lifted off the floor, away from my body. My awareness sharpened, just as it had on the bridge, and I was floating, carried in a current outside my rational mind. Yet I felt peace, that same deep peace that had so moved me when I was with Tia Ana that afternoon.

Then I felt the presence of that little missing boy. He was in the room with me; I could almost see him.

What does this mean? I asked myself. This boy has nothing to do with me! It's just another aspect of my changing consciousness. Let it go!

"Bless you, little sweetie!" I said aloud as I walked into the living room and looked out the window, trying to settle my mind. I took two melatonin, returned to bed, and tried to read again. Eventually, I turned off the light.

It was no good; my eyes would not close. I got up again, made a cup of chamomile tea, and turned on the news. They were still talking about the boy, but now I paid closer attention. As the story unfolded, I slipped out of myself into an untethered space and found myself not watching his story so much as being in his story. I was with his parents and feeling their agony and fear. I felt the boy's tear-streaked face against my neck as I held him.

In a burst of certainty, I knew I could find him, though I had no idea how. I put down my tea, turned off the TV, and tried to see him in my mind. It wasn't working. Finally, I realized that I was using my intellect when my connection with him was way beyond intellect, way beyond logical thinking. I remembered Tia saying *The heart knows rather than understands.* So I stretched out on the carpet and let my mind go blank, moving my consciousness from my head into my heart. Whenever I felt thoughts elbowing their way in, I repeated my affirmation—*I am open to a greater truth*—and my mind opened into a stillness, a peace, and I was only conscious of the little boy.

And there he was! His face was streaked with tears. I pulled him close, ruffled his blond hair, and rocked him. Then I slowly pulled back until I could see the room he was in. Again I saw the blonde woman on a couch behind him. At first I thought she must be a relative. But as I watched her playing cards, smoking, and putting on nail polish, I realized she didn't care a whit about him; she was his watchdog. I drew farther back until I was outside, looking at a middle-income tract house surrounded by others like it. The house number was 1391. I lost focus before I could see a street name. And then the vision was gone.

I called Noah. He answered on the third ring, sounding wide awake.

"Thank God you answered. I need to talk to you right away."

"At three in the morning? It must be important."

"You know that little boy who's missing?"

"Timmy Johnston? Yes."

"I know where he is."

"Keegs, now listen . . ."

"No, Noah, you listen. I saw him tonight. I saw the house he's being held in, and I saw the woman who's guarding him."

"I'll be there in fifteen minutes."

I was dressed and ready, standing at the curb when Noah pulled up. His car was filled with his woody scent. I got in and watched him in the dim light of the dash, wanting to tell him how good it felt to be near him. Instead, I sat with my arms crossed and looked straight ahead, trying to stay focused on my mission. We sat in the car with the engine running.

"You really think we can find this kid, Keegs? You say you saw the house?"

"I saw the house number: 1391."
"Did you see a street name?"
"No, I couldn't pull back that far."
"Pull back?"

29

I told him what I'd seen. He nodded, pulled out his notepad, and started writing. He ran a hand through his hair. "Was there a driveway, maybe a car?"

I closed my eyes and brought up the image. "Yes! A dark car was parked in the driveway in front of the garage. The house number is above the garage door."

"What is the house number again?"

"Thirteen ninety-one Bancroft." I looked at him, startled. "Noah; I just said Bancroft!"

"That must be the street name."

"Okay," I whispered. "I'm surrendering. I'm really surrendering to this now. I'm letting go." I took a deep breath. "The address is 1391 Bancroft."

We drove to the precinct station, parked in the lot, and Noah led the way through the glass doors, past an officer at the front desk, and through the maze of offices until we reached his desk. He pulled up his chair and turned on his computer.

"Let's see if we can find this place. We'll search for any city in a hundred-mile radius with an address of 1391 Bancroft."

I focused on staying in peace while Noah searched for the address. An agonizing half hour later, he sat back, frustrated. "Dammit," he said. "There are no addresses of 1391 Bancroft in any nearby cities."

"But there has to be, Noah. I saw the house."

"Well, it's not showing up in this database."

"So maybe it's a new housing area, and the street isn't in the database yet."

He stared at the monitor, stroking his chin, then picked up

the phone and punched in a number. "Hey, Buddy, I need a favor. I need to find a street or road named Bancroft that was added anywhere in the Bay Area since our location software was last updated . . . Good. Get back to me as soon as you can. It's important."

Noah turned back to me. "Can you go back to where you saw the house?"

"I can try."

I closed my eyes. It took me a few minutes to remember that trying didn't work. I grimaced. "Noah, I need to do something, and it's going to look a little crazy but humor me, okay?"

He nodded, then leaned back in his chair, his fingers laced behind his head.

I lay on the floor between his desk and the one next to his and closed my eyes. After I stopped feeling foolish, I stretched and started to slow my breathing, repeating silently, *I am open to a greater truth.* With each breath, I focused on Timmy, filling myself with love for him. After several minutes, I was there.

"Okay, I see him now," I whispered.

"Is he okay?"

"He's so scared he can't even cry anymore. He's wet his pants."

"Is the woman still there?"

"Yes, and someone's talking to her. A man."

"What's he look like?"

"I can only see his back. He's a small guy with thinning black hair."

"Can you see what he's wearing?"

"Yeah, a dark jacket and brown pants."

"Good. Okay. Now, can you go outside?"

I took another breath and backed away from inside the house. "I'm outside."

"What can you see that will help us find this place?"

I looked carefully, but my desperation was blocking my vision. I shook my head. "I'm sorry."

"It's okay. Is the car still there?"

"Yes. No, wait. Now there are two cars."

"Can you describe them?"

"One's the dark sedan that was there before. Now there's another one behind it. I think it's brown."

"Can you read the license plate on the second car?"

"I'm trying, but it's too dark."

"That's okay, Keegs. You did well. Come back now."

I let the images dissolve, then sat up slowly. I felt empty, like my mind was drained. I rubbed my eyes and looked at Noah. He was smiling at me.

"What?"

"Keegs, I want you to do something for me, okay?"

"Sure."

"I'm going to ask you a question, and I want you to blurt out the first thing that comes to mind."

I shrugged. "Okay."

"What was the license plate number on the brown car?"

"PFT 412."

He beamed at me.

Then I started crying. I couldn't help myself. "My God, Noah. Oh, my God. How did I do that?"

"Same way you got the street name," he said. Then the phone rang, and he answered it. "Yeah, okay . . . Great. That's great. Good work!" He looked over at me, his eyes sparkling. "We've got the street. It's in San Mateo." He picked up the phone again. "Get me San Mateo PD!"

30

A few days later, I met with Tia again at the café. I had so many more questions. As we settled at our usual table, she poured steaming apple cider into my mug.

"Yes," she said as if reading my mind. "You're right. It is enlightenment we seek. But enlightenment isn't a destination, you know. It is not some fantasy place at which we finally arrive, not some level of spiritual mastery or stage of completion. Enlightenment is the path—the journey. It's the journey into forever. You never arrive. It's an ongoing process during which you keep expanding and discovering."

"You know," I said, "it sounds like you're quoting from *Alice in Wonderland*."

She nodded. "In my view, that's a very enlightened parable."

"Okay, then, here I am on this path, and you're my guide. But I've never heard you say I was on the path of enlightenment. How come?"

"What's in a name?" she answered. "'Enlightenment' is just a word that got assigned to the path, no more than a bunch of letters strung together to make a sound, but they don't say a thing about what it really is."

"Well, what would we do without names?"

"Names. Every time a spiritual path or philosophy gets named, it seems someone turns it into a religion. And then that path into forever disappears."

"Disappears?" I leaned back in my chair. "How can religion make a path disappear?"

"Listen," she said. "Lao Tzu was a spiritual master five

hundred years before Jesus was born. Five hundred years! Lao Tzu guided people along this path until he was eighty years old. Taoists now honor him by practicing over and over what they recall of his teaching. But he was not teaching words, was he? He was teaching consciousness; that is the only true Taoism.

"Now Jesus. He was a Jew, right? And he was also on his path of enlightenment. He invited other Jews to walk that path with him like Lao Tzu did. His work and the sacred information flowing through him were still expanding when he died. Then a man who had never even met him established a religion in his name, and it came to be called Christianity, and again the sacred path was boxed in by a set of policies that one must follow. It was organized into an institution, and the institution became more important than the path. Buddha walked this same path about three hundred years later, and his followers created Buddhism."

"Whoa!" I said. "I never thought those guys were on the same path."

"Well," she said with a shrug. "They were, and they weren't. They each saw the path through their own filters."

"Filters?"

"Yes, filters they'd had since childhood, filters rooted in them by their individual cultures. And even if they'd been in one culture, there would still be differences."

"Differences? How?"

She went to the kitchen without answering, so I followed her. She filled the kettle with water and put it on the burner.

"Tia, those religions were different because Lao Tzu, Jesus, and Buddha had different philosophies, right? But now I'm hearing you say they're all somehow the same."

She opened the refrigerator and took out a coffee cake. She set the plate on the counter and stood over it, staring at it without seeing it. Finally, she turned to me. "Look, my niece,

I'm your coach and your guide. I've been following and teaching this for more years than you've been alive. So yes, I know a few things. But my job here is not to make you my clone or even my follower. My job is to show you how to expand your own consciousness."

"But, Tia, come on. You are my teacher."

"Oh, that's true, but I'm not teaching you to be like me, am I? I don't want you to be like me. I want you to find your own path. I want you to find and recognize the incredible you."

I thought about that, then asked her, "How can you guide me if you don't see my path?"

She turned to me. "Dear niece, I don't need to know your path because I know you."

"Really? Okay, well, maybe you do. Maybe you do. But I don't know how because I barely know myself."

She opened a drawer, took out a knife, and began to cut thick pieces from the cake. "Tell me, can your left eye see itself?" she asked.

I laughed. "What a goofy question. Of course not. Neither eye can see itself."

She rested the knife against the counter. "Why not?"

"Because it's the eye doing the looking. It can see a reflection in a mirror, but it'll never see itself."

"And neither can you see yourself," she said, "because the *you* that you'd be trying to see is the one doing the looking."

She placed healthy portions of cake on two plates, poured the boiling water into a teapot, and placed them all on a tray. "Come," she said, and led the way to the table.

I followed her, thinking about what she had said about my left eye not seeing itself. If my eye couldn't see itself, then I couldn't really see myself either because I was the eye trying to see itself. It changed something inside my mind. If I couldn't see myself, how did I even know I existed?

31

We sat together and ate the moist cake. I looked at her. "Then if I can't see myself—"

"You see others, right? You look at the life around you and see that you are part of it all and how it's all a part of you. My niece, you'll eventually see that there's nothing you see that is not you."

As we ate in silence, her words woke up parts of my mind that I had not known existed. And it created a hunger inside me. I wanted to know more, to know it all, and I wanted it right now. I felt like I did when I was a little girl learning to ride my bike. It kept tipping, and I kept trying because I wanted so badly to take off, to be wheeling along in the wind, feeling free. Now I wanted the same thing—except I wanted to fly.

"Tia, you were talking about those spiritual leaders and their followers. If people had simply followed the examples of their teachers and stayed on those paths rather than building shrines, would our world be different right now? Could we all be living in harmony?"

"Well, that's hard to say because I think there will always be those who follow their leaders like sheep because then they don't have to think or be personally responsible."

"But those followers, they weren't the ones who created the organizations, were they?"

"No, they weren't. Some saw the opportunity to make something concrete happen, to dam up the river of truth and make a lake they could say was theirs and claim that their lake was the whole truth. They called people to come and swim in their lake and become one with it."

"Is that so bad? Sure, the crusades and other battles were fought in the name of religion and did a lot of damage, but is that the religion's fault?"

"Little Bird, it's not a small thing. More than forty-five million people have so far died in wars fought in the name of religion. Forty-five million! Do we think for even one minute that that's what those spiritual leaders wanted?"

I thought about that. Forty-five million people were dead because their religious beliefs differed. That was nothing less than slaughter. It made me feel sick.

Tia must have noticed the pain on my face because she said, "And yet all religious people are not in that camp. Many in every religion are on spiritual paths and are doing only good. Some won't fight and kill, no matter the cause. They have taken control of their spiritual lives and are following in the footprints of their masters. And as they do, they discover that the path of enlightenment is exactly that: a path. And each person's path is slightly different."

She studied me. "Tell me, my niece, what impressed you the most this morning up on the mountain?"

I closed my eyes and thought back. "A beautiful red-tailed hawk soaring above me. It glided so close to me I could see the colored bands on its wings. So beautiful. He was free and . . . and so very confident."

I paused, remembering. "And the golden leaves on a tree on my right shimmering in the light with radiance, such radiance. The shimmering took me to another place, opened a window in my heart. I fell into the deepest joy ever. It took my breath away. Oh, and I saw a doe with her two spotted fawns. The quiet grace of their movements and the caring between them moved a quiet grace in me."

I paused again. "And there was a sailboat down on the bay, its brilliant white sails leaning against the dark blue water."

I opened my eyes and looked at her. "And then I called you."

"And those experiences, were they the truth?"

"Oh yeah," I nodded. "They were truth—real truth."

"And if you took me up there this afternoon, could you show me those things?"

I saw her point immediately and shook my head. "No, of course not. It wouldn't be the same."

"And can you ever have those same experiences again?"

"No. I guess . . . those were once-in-a-lifetime experiences."

"And since you have been with me here today, have you had once-in-a-lifetime experiences?"

"Yes, of course I have. So your point is that truth isn't static but changing. But again, it's staying the same. You're the same right now. The restaurant's the same."

"I'm the same?"

I stared into the darkened part of the café and thought. Something was swimming around in my mind, and I was trying to corner it. Finally, I saw it. "No, Tia, I suppose you've been changing since I came in here, and I guess you are changing now. That almost makes me dizzy!"

She nodded and smiled. "Good for you. So now you know that no two things can ever be the same. Because it's all a river, isn't it? The river of truth I talked about before. Even a solid rock is constantly changing. More slowly, of course, but changing just the same. Life is a river of creation where everything is in motion. Physics has proven that everything around us"—she pointed around the room—"the walls of this restaurant, the floors, the tables. Everything is made of particles that cannot be seen individually but that are in constant motion. This table"—she touched the table—"is more than ninety-nine percent space." She squinted at me. "Ninety-nine percent! You learned that in school, right?"

I laughed. "Oh yeah. Subatomic waves and particles, all moving and behaving according to how we view them. Is that where we're going?"

32

She gave me a wry smile. "Okay, so now we're on the same wavelength. We know everything is in motion, including your body, brain, and mind. And whether that motion expands or contracts is dependent upon whether you are following your Light. It's really as simple as that."

"My light."

"Your Light."

She sat very still and studied me. As she did, I watched her face change. It morphed into the face of a young girl, then it became a boy's face, then a man's, then a very old woman's before returning to the face of the Tia I knew. I looked at her, stunned: she was all those people? I felt myself slipping into a dimension beyond the one I'd called my mind. It was a dimension that would be hard not to love.

I stood up to go to the bathroom, and Tia busied herself in the kitchen. When I came out and we returned to the table, I asked, "Tia, if following the Light is a choice, why aren't more people doing it?"

"Because as human creatures, we're terrified of change. We fight like hell to keep our reality stable and secure. We want familiarity's safety, and most refuse to see beyond that. But that's not you, is it, Little Bird? You're here to grow. You're here to reach beyond what you thought was possible."

Her words "fight like hell" surprised me; they were so unlike her. She had made her point, though; she was fighting like hell to make sure I got it.

We sat silently for a time. Then I asked, "Do you think Jesus and Buddha would be disappointed in their followers?"

"One thing they would certainly agree on is this: Buddha didn't want his followers to become Buddhists but to become Buddhas. And Jesus never once encouraged people to become Christians. He wanted them to become Christs."

We paused to eat lunch, chatting about more mundane things. When we finished, we pushed our plates to the center of the table. Tia picked up the thread of our previous conversation. "You know now that Johanna chose you for this gift?"

I wrinkled my brow. "Tia, how could you possibly know that?"

"Because of how deliberate and focused she was. Johanna never did anything without a deliberate and conscious purpose."

I suddenly got it and opened my eyes wide. "Tia," I exclaimed, "you knew Johanna!"

"Oh yes," she nodded. "Johanna is my friend."

"But why in the world didn't you tell me?"

"Well, because I didn't want to influence your relationship with her. I wanted it to be your own."

I shook my head, baffled. "How could you have influenced my relationship with someone dead?"

"Oh," she laughed, shaking her head, "you're not yet seeing this clearly at all, are you? Johanna's not dead, child—she's here with us right now!"

I watched her skeptically, then I got it. "Oh, I get what you're saying. Dead people aren't dead; they're just sleeping or something, just resting in peace."

She studied me silently for several minutes. "Little Bird, Johanna's not sleeping. And she's not dead."

"Tia," I said, and looked at her skeptically, "Noah saw her dead body. He saw it."

She raised her eyebrows and nodded. "Yes, I know he saw her dead body. But did he see her? He saw the body she left behind, but he didn't see her being dead."

"There's a difference?"

"Oh, most certainly!"

"Now, Tia, this is a bit hard to swallow."

"Well, don't hurry it. Let it come to you as it will. And it will!"

I was in that foggy area where my skepticism was much stronger than my clarity. "What? Let what come to me? The belief that people are really alive when they're dead? What kind of nonsense is that?"

"So you're finding it hard to believe."

"Some things are so far out they are beyond belief, Tia."

"But I'm not talking to your beliefs, niece. Your beliefs are simply viewpoints, opinions. No, I'm asking you to swim deep into yourself, deeper than your beliefs. Into your knowing. There's a big difference."

I sat back in my chair and looked into the distance. Once again, that feeling came over me that this path was the yellow brick road. It felt illogical and even absurd. I looked at Tia. The only reason I wasn't getting up and heading for my car was because of my trust in her. I looked around the café as if I might find answers lurking in a corner. I had already tried to flee this new life once and failed, yet it was still scary to abandon everything I knew as truth and replace it with illusory ideas. Not to mentally understand was my biggest challenge.

"So, okay," I said to Tia, "Johanna's alive, and she chose me, right? Then why is she not in touch with me?"

She raised her eyebrows as if not believing how thick I was. "Maybe it's because you're not open to her. Maybe it's because her being alive doesn't fit with your consciousness, so it's impossible to get you on her wavelength. You automatically disregard her, don't you? Is it maybe because you're a bit afraid of her?"

I said nothing, but I could feel the pressure building inside me.

Tia continued. "Until you get how much she loves and cares for you, you're closed off from her and closed off from her guidance."

33

"Okay, look, Tia, I get that you can communicate with people beyond the grave; I see that. But please don't think I'm just being stubborn when I say I can't. I'm just not there."

"But my niece, you *communicate daily* with those you think have died."

I tried to understand. "And how am I communicating with people I don't see, hear, or even believe in?"

She sighed. I realized I was testing her patience.

"Can you please just stop that incessant motor of your brain long enough to see a greater truth? There is no death, Little Bird. There is only the eternal here and now in endless dimensions. When people leave their bodies, they don't go anywhere because there isn't anywhere to go."

When I didn't respond, she tried again. "When you were in school, when you learned about the time/space continuum, did you believe that?"

I thought back. "Well, I tried to, and . . . Yes. Yes, I guess I did, in a kind of abstract way, but not in any way that affected *my* life. Now then, what does me talking to dead people have to do with the time/space continuum?"

And as I said those words, things became clearer. If all time and all space are right here at this moment, then everything that ever has been or ever will be must also be present here and now.

I leaned back in my chair. Tia was watching me with a slight smile. She knew I was starting to get it. But I was free-falling into places where my logical mind had no footing. I took measured breaths and let it come: all nature was in this instant change. Constant change, always unfolding, always amazing. Never nonexistent. Everything changes, but nothing dies. Ever.

"Oh, my God, Tia, I'm getting it!" I started shaking. "Johanna *is* right here with us. She has to be."

"Welcome home, Little Bird. You're waking up."

I felt a current flowing through my mind, dissolving my old beliefs and carrying them away. "This is exactly how I felt on the bridge," I said. "Is Johanna doing this to me?"

"No, dear, no one can do this to you. You alone unfold your soul. Until now, you've been a child afraid to swim into the pool's deep end."

"But it's natural to be afraid of such a big change, isn't it?" I asked.

"Sure, and don't push that scariness away—embrace it."

I couldn't help smiling. "And now I'm going to embrace fear; that'll be the day!"

She drank the last of her tea, pushed her cup and saucer away, leaned back in her chair, and looked steadily into my eyes. "My niece, listen carefully to what I'm about to say because you've reached a major turning point in addressing your fear."

I leaned in closer. I trusted this petite woman in her flowered apron.

"Fear is neither good nor bad," she said. "It's neither negative nor positive. Fear is energy—like electricity. And like electricity, it can be used to light or destroy. We can't pretend it doesn't exist because it does—fear does exist. And if it exists, it's a part of nature, isn't it? A constant. Fear is also a constant. And like electricity, it can either benefit us or destroy us. It is our choice—always."

"But, Tia, energy's only sometimes controllable, isn't it? Think about lightning."

She sat up straighter. "Little Bird, we're not talking about lightning here. We're talking about the energy inside you, the energy of fear. You alone have control over that energy."

"You think I'm in control of the scary things outside me?"

"The scary things happening outside of you are just things. It's the fear inside you that you have control of. When you think your fear is about something outside you, you let yourself feel invaded, then you cringe, and there goes your self-confidence. Now, tell me you see that."

I shook my head. "No, Tia, fear is fear. One can't just ignore it."

"Oh, I'm not saying to ignore it. I'm saying to harness it. Fear can be empowering. How else can someone lift a car or tractor off an injured person? That's fear power, isn't it? It happens regularly. We need to welcome it. We need to learn how to channel fear energy into serving our purposes. That's what it's there for. It's with us as constantly as our skin. If we stop fighting it and let it empower us, we can change our lives; we can do amazing things."

What a change it would be for me to see my fears as positive rather than negative and to learn how to use that energy.

"Thank you," I said. "I'm seeing it. Now how do I go about harnessing it? Because right now, fear still feels dangerous."

She looked at me for a long moment. "Is love energy?"

I looked down at the scarred table, considering her question. Then I looked up at her. "Yeah, I guess it is. It must be because it causes reactions, just like fear causes reactions. So yes, love has to be energy."

She nodded. "Love is not good or bad. We interpret it in a thousand ways, but love is energy. And you're right: it's the same thing with fear. It's actually the same exact energy, just interpreted in different ways. Love and fear—neither good nor bad. Just energy."

"Yes. And I have a choice of how I use the energy of either of them. I see that."

"So if you push love away, that energy becomes loneliness and unworthiness. That energy now diminishes and paralyzes you, making your days dark and helpless. Right?"

"Right."

She looked at me for a long moment. "So when we push fear away, it converts into anxiety and self-doubt. In neither case does energy disappear; it just converts to the negative. And guess who converts it?"

I laughed. "Well, the individual of course—me."

"So we agree that repressing the energies of fear and love creates anxiety, self-doubt, loneliness, and unworthiness. You see any similarities there?"

I thought for a minute. "Wow, the effects are the same!"

"So if we see fear and love for what they really are—the energy of the universe, the energy that propels a planet around a sun, the energy that is gravity and electricity—we see that fear and love can be sources of our personal power, our ability to create miracles."

"Have you seen any of those miracles?"

"Many times. But let me tell you about two women in England who, with the help of an elderly man, lifted a one-ton car off a boy pinned underneath. And in Oregon, two teenage girls lifted a 3,000-pound machine off their father, who was being crushed underneath. In both cases, the energy was the fear of someone they loved being killed or injured. Their fear and their love were the same thing."

I stared at the empty plates on the table but saw only the inner workings of my mind. Accepting fear's constancy and seeing it as an attribute would mean it was not what I thought it was. I had kept that lion caged inside me, and now I was being asked to set it free and let it become my friend and my power. If that was so, I had to accept that fear is not negative because it's also love—love energy. And with that thought, I began to feel a new self-confidence.

Tia watched me process that new knowledge, then as I reached for my purse, she said, "We're in a transition place now, and it will be good to keep going. Can you be here tomorrow at ten o'clock?"

34

I had a pleasant night. No terrorist notes under my door, a brief chat with Noah, and spending time with my book, my tea, and my thoughts. Creating miracles? I had begun to see that we create miracles every day, and we do it easily without recognizing them as miracles. Just making breakfast is a miracle because we're bringing into reality something that didn't exist before.

I was at Tia's a little before ten, and she was waiting for me. We sat at our usual table with a pot of tea and a plate of cookies between us.

I took a bite of cookie. "I never thought I'd be doing this, Tia: finding a new me. Yet I can't remember ever being so peaceful or so unafraid."

She studied me. "Then what's that question flapping on the clothesline of your mind?"

"I need to better understand this journey that I'm on. I call it a journey because I'm leaving my old self behind. Can you help me understand it better?"

"I know that's what you think you need: to understand. Needing to understand a thing before you can accept it will keep you stuck like it keeps most people of the world stuck. Understanding has its place. But it can become an obstacle in spirituality because the deepest truths are beyond understanding."

"Beyond understanding?" I laughed. "That I just don't understand."

"It's the difference," she said, smiling, "between head-mind and heart-mind awareness. Understanding is studying a flower to learn about its genesis and place in the physical world. Knowing is simply being one with the flower so it blooms inside you—as you."

I shook my head. "That makes no sense to me."

"Of course it makes no sense, Little Bird, because you're still trying to understand it. Understanding is overrated as a means of wisdom. Tell me, do you understand how the carburetor on your car works? Or how signals come through space to your TV?"

"No, but that's a separate issue, isn't it? We're talking here about *knowing* if something is true. Don't we need to understand a thing before we can know it's true?"

"Good question," she said. "And here's your answer: when we *know* a truth, we have an understanding of it greater than if we'd tried to intellectually understand it first. In this sense, knowing precedes understanding and produces deeper and clearer mindfulness. And of course, then understanding is expanded. Does that make sense?"

"But, Tia, I've dealt with lots of people who claimed they knew something, and they were dead wrong."

"That's because they didn't really know, did they? They believed, and that's very different. They thought believing was the same as knowing. Now we, you and I, know better than that, don't we? We know a belief is a fixed viewpoint, like being certain of your god or political party. Knowing, on the other hand, is not fixed. It's the river, the constant weaving and expanding of deeper and clearer realities of truth."

"Then how about this, Tia: I'm sitting here right now, looking at that wall. I believe it is there, and I also know it is there. Aren't the two the same?"

"If you're fixed on it being a wall, then it's a belief. If you're observing it as a wall yet open to it being something else, that's knowing."

I scoffed. "Hey, come on, it's a wall! What else can it be?"

She looked at the wall, then turned back to me, smiling and tipping her head, "Well, now, it could be a wall, or it could be an illusion. True, right now, it looks like a wall and feels like a wall. But 'wall' is just a four-letter word, a concept, isn't it?"

"That wall is a concept?" I looked at her, not hiding my disbelief.

"No, but the word 'wall' holds a concept for you. Are you the one seeing the wall right now?"

"Yes."

"Then it's your concept."

I sighed. "Oh man, I'm reaching here. I really am."

"Relax, niece. You're close now. We know that material things are made of subatomic particles, right? And subatomic particles are invisible, right? So that means that wall is invisible. Are you with me? And if the wall is made of invisible ingredients, then what are we seeing? Albert Einstein, Niels Bohr, and Max Planck, the world's greatest physicists, all proved that we turn the invisible into the visible by observing it. So then doesn't all physical reality seem to be made of consciousness?"

"But I can clearly see that wall. If I go over there, I can touch it. And that's trusting my senses to tell me that something is so. Yet if I understand what you said, my senses have no intelligence. They're just messengers."

"Right. Good for you! You just won the lottery. So if that wall is only space, what are you touching?"

I considered her question. "Well, for one thing, the wall feels like it has structure. But is it only solid because of consciousness? If so, it's got to be more than just my consciousness because I'm not the one constructing that wall. It has to be a universal consciousness."

"Universal consciousness. My goodness, you're bright!"

"I'm not smart; I'm just guessing."

"No, what's happening now is that you're knowing instead of understanding."

"So that wall is the result of consciousness?"

"Yes. And consciousness is unlimited, is it not? Both in time and space."

35

I fell quiet, allowing this new way of thinking to get traction in my slippery mind. It was a stretch for me because thinking of physical reality as being created by the presence of consciousness was beyond belief. And yet belief and truth are not the same, are they?

Tia watched me process. "I see your mind humming along, trying to assimilate, and that's okay. Don't slow your progress by matching your new discoveries to your old way of seeing. If it is true, let it be true, and let the change happen within you. You will eventually accept knowing, which paves the way to true understanding."

"Is knowing in another dimension, Tia?"

"Yes, it's in the fourth dimension and beyond. But don't try to understand that because if you do, you'll be looking at those other dimensions through the lens of this one, and they are just not going to fit. They won't make sense. Then truth will be lost."

"Tia, how can I know this is not all fantasy, not something our imaginations are just making up?"

"Oh, you'll know," she replied. "You'll know when you're there because you'll see clearly that you're in a place where realities are born. You'll be in the Creator Mind."

"Creator Mind?"

"Great Spirit. That vast wisdom from which all of creation springs."

I leaned forward and put my elbows on the table. "I'm trying to get this, and I think maybe I'm getting there slowly. It's a totally new way of"—I started to say *thinking*. "It's really a new way of *being*, isn't it?"

"Yes, a new way of *being*."

"Tia, what's it like to be in that place? That place where this reality is being born?"

She leaned back in her chair. "Trying to describe that state of being is like trying to describe the taste of an apple to someone who's never had one. It just won't work. You have to experience it."

"So you can't tell me anything about that realm of consciousness?"

She shook her head. "It can't be calculated or organized or especially understood in the way we think of understanding because it's beyond that, and it doesn't conform to what we think of as worldly logic."

"I keep running up against that, don't I?"

"You're doing just fine. What you still need to surrender to is that this reality we sense is the expression of something you can't name. That's your challenge: to become one with it without needing to understand it."

I looked down at the table. "So all my years of schooling were a waste, weren't they? Because they were all about understanding."

"A waste? Oh, my goodness, no!" She shook her head vigorously. "They weren't a waste at all. They taught you how to search for answers and think on multiple levels. You developed the ability to look beyond the obvious. Never discount the miracle of your education. It awakened your brain, the most magnificent creation in the universe. Say, would you like to hear some numbers about your brain?"

"Sure."

She excused herself and returned to the table with a neatly folded piece of paper. She was beaming. She sat down and unfolded the paper. "Your brain has over one hundred billion neurons, nerve cells, which may be the number of stars in the Milky Way galaxy. And each of your neurons has about forty thousand synapses—the connections between cells—for thinking and imagining. So to know our capacity for realization, we multiply the hundred billion neurons times their forty thousand synapses, and we have a number greater than all the stars in the universe." She pointed at me. "That's *your brain*, my niece. Right here, right now."

The numbers boggled my mind. "Tia, thank you. I'm amazed."

"Well, it amazes me every time I think about it. And here is the best part. As great as the brain is, it is not your master. It's your servant. Your *spiritual knowing* opens the door for the brain to really work instead of simply replicating what's already stored there."

The significance of what she said moved me to a new place of awareness. I had to find my balance again. It was impossible to imagine more thinking connections in a single brain than stars. I was beginning to see that there might be absolutely no limit to a person's potential. And yet so few of us know how astounding we are. I spent nearly forty years not knowing. We dwell in our perceived limits of mind, our self-doubts.

As I pondered in silence, I felt freed from the confines of my long-held beliefs and self-limiting identity. I was free to be the real me.

I knew it would take time for this consciousness to change all my thinking, but already I was breathing easier and feeling peace.

36

Five days after Tommy Johnston had been returned to his parents, I found myself with no particular plans. Then I remembered a pub in Half Moon Bay that had the best fish and chips I had ever had. The forty miles would be a pleasant drive, so I grabbed my coat. As I walked to my red Mustang, I noticed a gray car parked half a block down. It was not a neighbor's car because I would have recognized it. Or perhaps some neighbor had bought a new car or had a visitor. I paid no more attention. The windows were too dark to see if anyone was in it.

When I pulled away from the curb, the gray car pulled away too.

I drove down Sunset, then headed south on Skyline Boulevard. In the rearview mirror, I saw that the gray car was still behind me. If I slowed down, it slowed down too. If I sped up, it accelerated. I thought I might lose them at the cloverleaf when I picked up Highway 1, but a mile later I looked, and there it was, about a quarter of a mile behind me.

Remembering the nasty note, my stomach clenched. Something wasn't right. I felt my body tightening with tension. Mile after mile, that sinister gray car stayed on my tail.

But why was somebody following me? Surely they wouldn't go to all this trouble to hurt me, if that's what they wanted to do, because they could have done me in when I was walking to my car. Unless they needed to get me out on the road where there would be no witnesses.

"Stop it!" I said to myself aloud. "Just stop it! This is pure fantasy, and you're letting it poison this beautiful day."

After watching the car for almost a half hour, I stopped checking the rearview mirror. Whoever it was knew I had seen them, and they were obviously just trying to terrorize me. And as much as I hated to admit it, it was beginning to work. I recalled the original affirmation—*I am loved, and I am safe*—and began repeating it aloud until I settled down. I put on a jazz station and put the gray car out of my mind.

Then I saw a semi-truck with a trailer pulling out onto the highway from my right. I hit the gas and raced past the nose of the truck as it merged. The driver blasted his horn and shook his fist at me. But it worked. Now there was a semi between me and the gray car.

I kept my foot on the gas to put some distance between me and the semi, knowing that my pursuer could pass him and slip behind me again at any moment.

Then I saw a turnoff to the right, almost completely hidden by trees and shrubs. I made the turn and pulled in behind a large hedge. I watched in my side-view mirror as first the semi, then the gray car sped by. I waited five more minutes before I pulled back onto the highway heading south. The smart thing might have been to go north, back home, but I was in a fish-and-chips state of mind, and I refused to be bullied.

I relaxed again as I drove along the coastal highway. To my right was a beautiful view of the deep blue sea. The radio was tuned to soft jazz. The day seemed perfect again. As the road wound up and along with a high point over the sea, I was writing a song in my head when I saw something off to the right that made my heart stop: a red Mustang that looked just like mine teetered on the crumpled remains of a guardrail.

A small crowd had gathered where the car had come to rest. I parked across the road, got out, and leaned against my car. As I did, I was flooded with compassion—I had to go help. It was an odd feeling that would have worried me in days gone by, but my mind was crystal clear, and I was anchored in self-confidence. Still, I could not do whatever I was being called to without help, and as I walked across the road, I felt filled with assurance. I didn't question it or where it came from; I just accepted it and went on, right through the crowd of onlookers, climbing over the ruined guardrail without giving it a thought. Again I realized the car was the same make, model, and color as mine.

This was no accident.

As I neared the car, I heard a small voice whimpering from inside. I took a deep breath and was again with Johanna on the bridge.

"Don't get any closer, lady!" a man behind me yelled. "Do not touch that car; it's barely balanced there!"

I turned my head and looked at the man. He wore a dark suit and tie. I knew the look well; he was a lawyer or insurance agent. I turned my head back and moved forward, placing my feet carefully because I was walking on a steep slope. I got as close as I could without touching the car. A man was slumped against the steering wheel. Through a back window, I saw a little girl strapped into a car seat. Her face was white, and she was gasping between sobs.

"What's your name, honey?" I called out twice before she answered.

"Becky," she said, her voice small and shaky.

"Well, Becky, my name is Keegan, and I have good news. I'm going to get you out of there."

"Oh, please, please help me," she sobbed. "Please. I'm scared."

And then I was suddenly hit with a suffocating wave of fear. "This is ridiculous," a voice inside scolded. "Keegan, you're in way over your head here, and you don't have one damn clue what the hell you're even doing! You need to get your butt back across that railing and go home. This is not your business!"

I stood there, unable to move, sure that if I stepped any closer, I would die. My heart hammered in my chest, and chills ran up my spine. I was losing my confidence. But then I looked at Becky's face, and my fear dissolved.

37

Nothing mattered more than that little girl. It was not courage; it was simply that my safety was no longer the issue. And in that moment, I was also no longer alone. I was surrounded by a powerful presence, and I realized that the presence had been around me my whole life, guiding and protecting me. I had simply been too busy focusing on myself and my career to be aware of it. Becky's face converted my fear into love, and the same danger that had begun to paralyze me now motivated me.

The slope down from the car was steep for about two car lengths, then dropped almost vertically down to a rocky shoreline below. The force of the car's impact had torn the rail and dragged it forward nearly three feet; the back tires were caught on the railing and were all that kept the car from sliding down the cliff. The suited man behind me was right: the slightest nudge might tear the rest of that rail away and send the car careening to the rocks below.

Becky was on my side of the car, but the slope was too perilous for good footing. The other side seemed safer. I moved carefully around, over the rail, and around the back of the car until I was at the back window. Becky was watching me from across the seat.

The door was locked, which barely paused my progress. I picked up a rock the size of a softball and called out to Becky, "Close your eyes, sweetie." Then I hit the window with all my might. To my surprise, it shattered into bits and completely disintegrated. I reached in, unlocked the door, and pulled it open, causing a weight shift that moved the car a few more inches toward the cliff.

"Becky, I'm coming in to get you now. Okay?"

"I'm scared!" she sobbed, her lips trembling.

"I know, honey. But it's going to be okay now."

"Lady, you're going to kill yourself and everyone else in that goddamn car. Now get the hell out of there!" the suited man barked.

Then I heard a woman call out, "You go right on ahead, dear. We're all right here, praying for you." Then she added, "And, Leo, you shut the hell up!"

I kept my weight close to the back of the car as I slid in beside Becky and reached to unclasp her seat belt. The car lurched again, twisting to the left, but then she was in my arms, clinging to me. Her warm little body against me brought me to tears.

"Is my daddy okay?" she whimpered.

The man was slumped behind the wheel, maybe dead. "I'll get your daddy, honey. But let's get you safe first."

But when I turned to crawl out the way I had come in, I saw that the car had twisted, and the open door looked down the steep slope. We'd have to go out on the other side.

I inched my way back across the seat, holding Becky close to me, feeling her breath on my neck and her heart beating against me. When I reached the door and started to open it, I realized that the weight shift of the opening door might send us down the cliff. As I pushed it open slowly, I saw a woman standing on my side of the railing. Her face was streaked with tears.

"What's your name?" I asked her.

"Vera."

"Vera, if I reach Becky out to you, can you take her?"

Without hesitation, she stepped forward and extended her arms.

"Becky, here's my friend, Vera. She is a nice lady, and she's going to take you over to where it's safe."

"No!" Becky clung tighter to my neck. "Don't let me go. Please!"

"Becky, listen to me. I need you to be brave now so I can help your daddy. Can you do that? Can you be brave for your daddy?"

She hesitated only for a second, then let go, and I lifted her as far as I could. Vera took another tenuous step forward, and then Becky was in her arms. The crowd cheered.

I left the door open and turned to look at Becky's dad, buckled into his seat, his head resting against the steering wheel, still unconscious.

I took a deep breath and closed my eyes. After a moment, my scattered thoughts settled, and I was again aware of that sweet presence. I reached around and unfastened the seat belt, then I hesitated. Becky's dad seemed to not be a big man, yet there was no way I could pull him into the back seat. I closed my eyes again and breathed. I said out loud in a low voice, "I am open to a greater truth. Let go now, Keegan, let go and trust."

I inched my hand forward and around the left side of his seat, found the tilt lever, and released it. The seat back dropped toward me with a jerk that lurched the car downward another inch.

"Anyone out there have a rope?" I called over my shoulder.

A nearby voice answered. "Ma'am, you'll need to come out of there now."

I turned to see a uniformed fireman a few feet away. Behind him, a fire engine's red lights flashed. I had not heard it arrive.

"I just need a rope to tie around him," I said. "Then I'll come out."

"How do you know he's even alive?"

"I can hear him breathing."

"Okay, then, you come on out of there, and I'll come in and get him fastened up."

"What's your name, sir?"

"I'm Ed. Now please, ma'am, just give me your hand and let me get you out of there."

38

"Well, you see, Ed, here's the thing. Every time I move even slightly, this car slides forward more. That rail will probably not hold me getting out and you getting in. Now, I'm already in here, so let's work together, shall we? Can you just get me a rope so I can tie him up?"

"No, it's not that easy. You'll need to fit him into a rescue harness, and that's got to be done in a certain way."

"Well, Ed, then you'll have to show me how because I'm not leaving here until he's hitched up."

He stood watching me for a long moment.

"Come on, Ed, you know this is the only chance he's got."

"Okay, then, I'll stay here and talk you through it."

Another fireman handed him a jumble of straps, and Ed reached out to hand them to me. "There are two harnesses here. The first one is for you. No arguments now! We'll get yours on first, and then I'll help you with his."

He talked me through putting on the harness, then attached a ring fastened to a rope that ran back over the railing, probably to the truck. I gingerly reached over and around the seat back to get the harness on Becky's dad. I couldn't see what I was doing, which might have seemed impossible, yet I felt completely calm. Nothing mattered to me but getting that harness on right. I had to twist around the seat and lift him partway up to get straps under him. I could feel the car grinding forward now, inch by inch. I knew time was running out.

When I finished and hooked a rope to the harness ring, Ed handed me a cervical collar. "Can you get this around his neck? We don't know if his neck is injured, but if it is, this might prevent further injury."

As I reached for the collar, the car twisted and slid downward, and I was sure that only one wheel was still behind the bent rail. I put the cervical collar around the man's neck as quickly as possible, wondering if I did it right, but we were out of time. The car was now shifting with every beat of my heart. I glanced back at Ed, who was now about eight feet away, his face tight with concern.

"Ed," I said loudly, thinking he might not hear me from where he stood, "I'm afraid when we pull him out of here, he's going to get caught up on this door jamb."

"That's a risk we're going to have to take. Ma'am, please get out of there—right now! The car's moving!"

It did slide then, forward and down, until it felt nearly vertical. I knew the man could not be pulled out through the door at this angle, even though he was in a safety harness and hooked to a rope. I gripped his harness with both hands, braced my feet against the seat in front of me, leaned back, and pulled with all my might. I felt the car lurch, heard a screech, and then it fell away. The next thing I knew, I was lying on the rocks, feeling every one of them. I heard crashing as the car banged its way down the cliff.

Becky's dad lay on the hillside just below me. He had come to and was moving an arm. It was over.

The crowd applauded as I climbed over the guardrail and pulled off the harness. Then their attention turned to the rescue crew as they carefully maneuvered Becky's dad up over the rocks.

I headed for my car. The man who'd tried to stop me when I first climbed over the rail was hurrying after me. "Lady, hang on just a minute. Please, hang on."

I stopped and turned. "Yes?"

He took my hand and shook his head. "I can't believe how

brave you were out there, especially after the hell I was giving you. Will you forgive me? I was just so damn scared!"

"It's okay," I told him. "You know what? We were both doing what we thought was best. There wasn't any script for us to follow."

He shook my hand and thanked me, then returned to his group. I got into my car, made a U-turn, and headed for home, checking in the rearview mirror to make sure I wasn't being followed by anyone who might want to talk. The last thing I wanted was a conversation about what had happened. My mind was hollow. I was completely empty and my hands were shaking. How could I possibly discuss that powerful yet peaceful presence that had surrounded me and guided me?

39

I was no longer worried about the gray car that had been following me; he'd done his dirty deed for the day, having run a car off the road that looked identical to mine.

My little home felt different when I walked in. My precious space, furniture, and pictures were warmer and more alive, and they welcomed me home.

I went to the bedroom, stripped off my clothes, and got into the shower. I stood crying under the hot water until my tears ran out. Then my mind empty, I was at peace.

I called Noah, reaching him just as he was going off duty. Within minutes, he was in my house, hugging me.

I went to the kitchen and made a pot of double strong oolong tea—it had become his favorite now too. He came up behind me. "Guess who's getting famous."

"What are you talking about?"

"Oh, you haven't heard about the woman in the red Mustang down by Pacifica who saved a man and his daughter from going over a cliff?"

I turned and stared at him. "Have I no secrets?"

"Not when you do something that spectacular. They're looking for you, lady. And when they find you, you'll probably get a medal."

"They won't find me, and I don't want a medal."

He laughed. "You are one weird lady, Keegan Tate!"

I put the tea and cups on a tray and added shortbread cookies as I thought of how to explain the gray car.

"Noah, that wreck wouldn't have happened but for me."

He frowned. "What are you talking about?"

I carried the tray to the living room, and Noah followed me. After we were seated, I told him about being followed and that I was sure the man ran the red Mustang off the road, thinking it was mine. He looked down into his cup as he listened. "Now," he said, "we're moving to a new level." He looked up. "You didn't, by chance, get a license number?"

"No, he was never that close."

"Of course not. He's too smart for that."

We sipped our tea in silence. Finally, Noah said, "This guy is not some nut, Keegs. He's a pro."

I studied his face. He looked worried. "Should I put my worry hat on now?"

He sighed deeply. "We're way beyond worry, Keegs. We're in action. I'll get a patrol car to cruise by here, and we'll watch for that car or anyone suspicious." He looked at me with a tenderness that melted me. "And you need to call me like you didn't call me today when you were being followed."

I started to explain, but he put up his hand. "I know, I know. It didn't seem that important, but now we know differently, don't we?"

I nodded, once again hearing the tumbling, crashing car that only by a miracle didn't have Becky and her dad in it.

"Will you tell me about it?"

I snuggled against him, took a deep breath, and told him every detail.

40

The next day, I told Tia what had happened. She listened carefully, occasionally asking how I felt at a given moment. When I finished, she said, "You're now seeing the power of heart-mind and brain-mind working together as one."

She took our mugs into the kitchen, leaving me to think about that, then returned with a plate of warm blueberry muffins.

"I'd like to hear more about heart-mind," I said.

She took a bite of muffin and chewed it slowly. "Well, let me tell you a story. A group of patients in severe pain was given morphine, which brought immediate relief. The next day the same patients were injected, only this time they were injected with a neutral substance. Yet the pain relief was almost identical to the day before. Does that make sense?"

I studied her. "Of course, it makes sense. That's the placebo effect. Everyone knows how that works."

"Oh," she said, and raised her eyebrows. "Then please explain it to me because I don't understand it."

"Come on, Tia, you know. It has to do with ... with ..." I stopped, unable to grab the thought as it swept through my mind. "Okay, maybe I don't understand it well enough to explain it, but a doctor or psychologist could."

"Oh?" she asked. "My dear, scientists have been trying to understand the placebo effect for years, but they still don't have a grasp of it. But it doesn't seem that hard, does it? When we feel like something will heal us, it has a healing effect. It's that simple. And did you know that when people are told that it is a placebo, quite a large percentage of them are still made

better? Now, how could that be? How can we possibly understand that?"

She studied me as I considered her words.

"Here's another story," she said, putting her elbows on the
table and leaning forward. "A woman we both know was
called on the phone by someone thought to be dead, and now
that woman suddenly has profound spiritual powers. Now,
that's truth, isn't it? And yet how does it make sense?"

I had no answer.

"Understanding comes from your head, Little Bird.
Knowing comes from your heart. We've talked about that
before, and it still comes up, and it will come up until you
make your knowing greater than your understanding. That
distinction will be crucial as you travel your path."

"So are you saying that everyone should just make understanding second?"

She considered what I asked. "That's a good question. Let
me explain. When we put understanding first, we are most
often looking at and trying to understand the box the shoes
came in while being unaware of the shoes inside. Understanding the box, which is the construct of a thing, does nothing for understanding the heart and purpose of the construct,
which is the shoes. The first is a concept, and the second is
truth. It is simply learning to see beyond the filters of ego. Then
we realize that there are things we can *know* that we cannot
understand because they are in a different dimension."

"But, Tia, our lives are also guided by facts, are they not?
Facts are the seeds of truth."

"Niece, facts are merely temporary snapshots of the river
called truth as it flows by. And yes, they're good pictures, but
they are each only slivers of truth. A picture of a river is not
the river, is it? Nor can it come close to telling the river's story.
Just so, facts are valuable slivers of truth, but without the
whole, they just don't add up."

"Wow, what a mind shift this is!"

"That's a good term because we're not talking about *what* we think but *how* we think. Beginning in kindergarten, we were taught to ignore our hearts and follow our heads. Now we must relearn that, learn to balance intellect with consciousness. To do that, we must learn how to trust and what to trust. Trust is another word for faith. The great masters all taught it. Jesus said that faith can move a mountain. Buddha said faith makes impossible things possible. Trusting your consciousness—trusting your heart—releases an enormous creative power. It is the sacred power of the universe."

"What, then, we ignore our intellects? Our brains?"

"No," she laughed, shaking her head. "Ignore our brains, and we drift around smelling flowers and never get anything done. We need both consciousness and intellect, and we need them in harmony. Then when they're balanced, they tell us which to follow."

I closed my eyes, trying to absorb her words.

After a few minutes, she asked, "You took physics in college?"

"Yes, and I loved it."

"Then you know that when scientists discovered how subatomic particles behave, all the old theories and laws about physical reality were blown away."

I grinned. "We talked about that the other day when I found out that wall was made of space."

"That's right. Photons, electrons—none of them behave like the physical reality we think we understand. Even Einstein was frustrated, wasn't he? He said, 'God doesn't play dice with the universe!' He was trying to *make sense* of the new reality, to *make* it fit into his intellect."

"But then he finally started thinking in a new way," I said.

"Yes, he did," she said, and nodded. "And, Little Bird, so can we."

"Okay. All right. I get that. But why do I feel there's a bigger point creeping in here?"

"Oh, aren't you the smart one! Sit with that question a minute while I make some more tea."

I waited, absorbing the wonder of the world opening before me.

Tia returned and filled our mugs. Then picking up where she left off, she said, "You and I are dealing with the very same unfolding of truth that Einstein went through. We can't find a new truth when we insist on thinking in an old way, can we? We need to ask better questions."

I laughed. "Better questions, better answers."

"And when we're only focused on answers," she said, "we too often anchor them as truth."

"How is that?" I asked.

"We find an answer, any reasonable answer, and stop searching. But that answer is often incomplete; it's just the first step. It might take digging for an hour or even a lifetime, but that's our journey. It is in the seeking of deeper answers that we continually unmask the truths of ourselves and of the reality we live in. We've become explorers, my niece. We've become spiritual pilgrims, following the questions and letting them challenge us and pull us forward, always forward."

I shook my head. "I'm going to need to give this more thought. If I can wrap my head around it, it will change how I think."

"And that's what we want, isn't it?" she asked. "That's how you'll stay on track with your purpose." She watched me for a response.

41

I smiled. "I love this stuff, Tia. I do." Then my smile faded. "But all this altered reality business has some real-world problems too. Like, I'm probably going to lose my job."

"Your job?" She reached out and touched my arm. "Little Bird, you can't see by now that you've already lost that job? It's no longer yours."

My heart fell, and I sat back in my chair. "What are you saying, Tia?"

She leaned forward. "Tell me this: has your prosecuting attorney job been at all the same since Johanna?"

I answered without hesitation. "No, of course, it hasn't."

"So what's changed?"

I swallowed a lump and stared at her. "I guess I have."

"And so?"

"But, Tia, I love my job. It's a job I trained years for. And not only that—I need the paycheck."

Tia smiled. "Oh, my niece, you've trained for years for the job you're now moving into. And money?" She laughed and shook her head. "Money will never be a problem for you, dear one. You will have all the money you'll ever need."

My mouth dropped open in astonishment at that statement.

She saw my shock and said, "Little Bird, please stop fighting this."

"I'm trying."

"Look into my eyes."

I looked into her deep brown eyes and felt bathed with compassion and warmth. That presence was coming around me again.

"Inhale, let your breath out slowly, and let yourself go with it."

I did as she asked, and as I did, I sensed the room sliding away. I fell into a deep space in which I was Tia as a child, leading a dappled horse into a pasture.

Tia's voice came to me through my trance. "His name is Lobo."

Then I felt myself aging as Tia into an ancient, wrinkled woman. I wore a tattered red and blue robe and stood at the rim of a canyon at daybreak, my wrinkled arms outstretched, embracing the sunrise. Time and space were one, and we were both flowing with it, never born, never to die. It was truer than anything I'd ever known. It was our home.

The old woman spoke. "Don't look away now. Take slow, deep breaths. What is your affirmation?"

"I am loved, and I am safe."

"Good."

Then I was back with Tia in the room, but it was not the same room or the same Tia. The walls were flowing like liquid, as were the tables, the chairs, the paintings, and the curtains. Before my eyes, Tia morphed between child and ancient again and again. Then it all stopped, and we were back in the café, our mugs of tea on the table.

I gasped and leaned forward with both hands on my chest, feeling my heart's slow, deliberate thumping.

"My niece, that was a small sample of where you're going. Bit by bit, you're going to master that journey."

I stood up from the table and looked around the room. Everything had stopped flowing, but no longer were they hard, immovable objects; they were alive and a part of me.

"This is so beautiful. Why can't I experience this all the time? Why do I have to work at it so hard?"

"You don't have to work at it so hard. But you do because your old ways of thinking have smothered your spiritual wisdom, your ability to flow with the river. Not to worry, though. The weights are starting to fall away. Be patient."

"Can't I just go there now and stay there?"

"No," she answered. "There will be time enough for that after you leave this life. What is being born in this time and place is true consciousness. You're going through a birthing process."

"Birth pains."

"Pains if you resist. If you surrender and accept the journey, you'll flow and become more balanced with each new step."

I sighed. I was sighing a lot these days. "Tia, this path must have been so much easier for you."

"No, not really," she said. "Oh, well, I indeed had this gift as a child, but I didn't value or appreciate what I had. Then when I was about your age, the feeling became so intense I couldn't fight it anymore. So I surrendered, and I just let it have me. It became beautiful when I finally let go. And then I couldn't have stopped it if I wanted to, any more than you can now. Once you *have* chosen, you *are* chosen."

"I don't think I'm at complete surrender yet. I'm still an attorney. And I'm falling through space."

Tia smiled, her eyes crinkling. "*Falling up* through space, learning to fly. You know, you were an attorney, and I was a schoolteacher—both were interim assignments, temporary identities. You graduated from law school to become an attorney, and then Johanna touched you, and you graduated again. Only this time you became you."

I thought on that for a while, then asked, "Does everyone have a Johanna?"

"Oh sure, absolutely! Every person has a Johanna who appears several times during their lives, and they usually ignore them because they don't *make sense*. But anyone who is a searcher and doesn't give up just because things don't

make sense will eventually find the path. You are now dancing out of your nest and spreading your wings!"

"Yes!" I said with a laugh. "I feel it. I'm learning to fly!"

We sat for another hour, drinking tea and talking. Tia was
so far ahead of me, yet I knew I was now on my path.

When I got up to leave, she casually asked if I had seen
Noah.

"Yes, we spent an evening together after the car wreck. But
then you know that."

She smiled.

42

It was early afternoon when the phone rang. Noah's voice was strained. "Keegs, can I come over? Right now? I need you."

"Of course. Come on."

My heart became concerned. Noah never asked to come over when he was on duty. Something must be very wrong. I put on a pot of tea and set out scones on the coffee table just as the doorbell rang. He slipped soundlessly inside. His face was white, his features tight.

I took his jacket and hung it on a hook by the door, then turned back to him. He fell sobbing into my arms. I held him for a long time.

Finally, as his sobs subsided, I said, "Come sit, Noah. There's hot tea and fresh scones." I led him to the couch and sat beside him. "Have you even eaten today?"

He looked at me, still dazed, and shook his head. "No, I don't think so."

"Well, start eating now. We can talk while we eat."

"Okay." He managed a small smile and picked up a scone but only stared at it as if wondering how it had gotten in his hand. Then he looked at me and said, "Keegs, I killed a girl this morning."

A cold wind blew up my spine. I took a breath. *I am loved, and I am safe.*

"My God, Noah. My dear, dear man. Can you tell me what happened?"

He put down the uneaten scone, closed his eyes, and leaned back on the couch, his shoulders hunched to his ears. "This girl went up to a stranger in the Marina District and stabbed him.

I was headed down Divisadero when I got the call, and right away, I saw a girl off to my right who matched her description. I pulled over, got out, and followed her. She was young, Keegs, a teenager dressed in jeans and an old army jacket. I figured she was too stoned to know I was right behind her. When I got up to about three feet away, I told her to stop. She acted like she didn't hear me, so I told her again. And then she whirled around, faster than you can imagine, swinging a butcher knife at my throat. I jumped back, pulled out my gun, and yelled for her to drop the knife. But she looked out of her mind, Keegs, like she thought it was all some game. She sprang at me like a cat, thrusting her knife at me. She must have had some training because she knew what she was doing with that blade."

"You weren't hurt?"

"Well, I was stepping backward, stumbled on a raised pavement, and went down on my butt. Then she was right on me, slashing me with that knife."

"Noah!"

"Oh, Keegs, it's four stitches; it's no big deal." He showed me the bandage on his arm. I hadn't noticed it when he first took off his jacket.

"What happened then?"

He covered his eyes with his hand, and I saw his shoulders shaking. I went to him, put my arms around him, and he reached his arms around me. His head was on my shoulder when he said, "I shot her, Keegs. I shot her in the heart. And then I watched her die." He moaned, a sound that came from deep within him.

"My God!" I murmured, tears streaming from my pierced heart.

"I tried to save her, Keegs," he sobbed. "I tried, but it wasn't any use." He shook his head. "No use at all."

I held him, and after a long time, he finally pulled away and said. "I'm okay. I just need to get through this."

I had not hurt like this since my brother died. I felt the world collapsing inside me. I breathed and repeated to myself, "I am loved, and I am safe." I focused on loving Noah with all my heart and gradually became calm.

"Do you know what drug she was on?" I asked.

"No, the tox screen isn't back yet." His eyes were red, and he seemed to be as empty as space.

"So what happens now?"

"Well, I turned in my gun, and I'm on paid leave. That's standard procedure when an officer shoots someone."

"Is there . . . is anyone saying that you—you maybe made a mistake?"

"No, not at all," he shook his head. "Everyone knows I did the right thing. I had no choice—it was her or me. A woman across the street saw what happened and gave a statement. She said the girl would have killed me if I hadn't shot her."

"Noah, grab your jacket while I change my shoes. We're going to the beach."

We walked silently along the shoreline, listening to the surf and the gulls. Then Noah stopped and looked down at the sand. "Keegs, I don't do real well asking for help. I never have. But today I came right to you."

I moved to stand in front of him. "So what's changed?"

He looked into my eyes, and without him saying a word, we both knew.

We turned to face the sea, standing with our arms linked.

Finally, Noah said, "You know, that girl should be going out with her friends tonight. Instead, she's in the morgue, and I'm the guy who put her there." His voice was tight. "There's no way around that, Keegs."

I walked around to face him. "Now, listen to me, buddy. You're you, you're not her. You didn't make her decisions; she made those. Drugs or hatred or whatever, they were her decisions, her choices, hers alone. And you made your choice.

It was the right one or you'd be dead. If you'd failed your duty today, how many others would have died by her hand?"

He looked into my eyes, then over my shoulder at the sea.

I sighed. "Oh, I know you've got all this, but I want you to keep it foremost in your mind. Now, you're never going to forget this day, but let's just keep its parts in balance. Okay?"

He was still staring out across the ocean. "How'd you get so smart?"

"I think it's love."

"I was in the war, but I've changed since then—really changed."

"Maybe not, Noah. Maybe you've expanded. Maybe you've become more."

He nodded, then looked down at me. "You're right. I've expanded. And if I keep this in perspective, it will expand me too. I'm accepting it now." He raised his chin. "It hurts like hell, but I'm accepting it."

We continued walking in silence, and as we turned to go back, we held each other close. And I knew that this man would be with me forever.

My bed was barely bigger than a twin, but we were so tightly entwined that night, it didn't matter.

43

One week later, as I began to fall asleep, a beautiful scene appeared. I was on a white beach, walking partly in the water, and I was happy. The air was warm with a gentle breeze, and I was one with the sky, sea, and sand—with life itself. In the distance, a familiar solitary figure moved up the beach toward me. I couldn't see who it was, but the golden peace around me expanded, and we connected. I quickened my pace, anxious to see who it was. The connection grew stronger with every step, yet the distance between us stayed the same. I began to run, but still, I came no closer. The distance between us on that expanse of long white beach remained the same.

I slowed to a walk, and as I tried to place that familiar figure, I also became aware of someone following me. I looked back and saw no one, yet I couldn't shake the feeling that someone was there. Between the presence behind me and the one before me, I felt enveloped in tremendous love. I closed my eyes, feeling surrounded by grace and realizing again that the presence I was feeling was that same one that had guided me in the car wreck and had been with me ever since, loving and protecting me. I wondered again how I had never noticed it before.

I focused again on the figure in front and stopped, no longer trying to catch up to him or her. The figure also stopped and turned to face me.

We stood watching each other for a time. Then he or she waved a hand and vanished, simply disappeared. And at that moment, the presence around me also dissolved. That wonderful assurance was gone, and I felt empty and abandoned. Somehow that person on the beach and that warm presence within me were one and were vital to my existence. And now they were gone.

Unable to continue, I collapsed on the sand, overwhelmed by the loss.

I awoke weeping, feeling desolate and alone. I cried for what felt like a long time, fully knowing it was a dream and knowing also that it wasn't.

Finally, I managed to slow my breathing and speak my affirmation, but I could not go back to sleep. I lay awake, wondering how a simple dream could affect me that deeply. I felt I'd lost a vital part of myself and that dear person on the beach. It was someone I loved with every fiber of my being and without whom I was sure I could not go on. I tried to convince myself it was only a dream, but the feeling of loss did not go away. I pulled out my journal and recorded every detail. When I finished, I put the journal aside, rolled over, and fell instantly asleep again.

Yet when I got up the next morning, a sadness lay over me like a shadow. I feared that my dream was so real that it would now become part of me. I made my tea and sat down to read what I had written. The dream became a reality as I read, and I was again on that beach. I knew then that I would never rest until I knew who that person was. There was only one way to find out.

When I arrived at the café, Tia Ana was waiting for me. We sat at our usual table, mugs of hot chocolate steaming. I gave her my journal to read the entry, but she pushed it back to me, saying, "I want to hear it in your voice."

I took a sip of chocolate and began reading. Soon tears blurred my vision. When I looked up, Tia was leaning back in her chair, her eyes closed, and she was smiling.

I waited.

Finally, she asked, "So who was that on the beach?"

"I have no idea," I exclaimed, shrugging my shoulders. "That's why I'm here, Tia. I need your help to find out. This was not just a dream. This was real. And now it's a part of me." And yet somehow I knew it had always been part of me. Only last night I finally got to see it.

"So who was that on the beach?" she asked again.

And again I shrugged.

She leaned forward, peering into my eyes. "And yet, Little Bird, you *do* know!"

I sighed. "Well, then, I guess it was you."

"Oh no," she said, shaking her head and leaning away. "No, it was not me. And I won't say who it was. That you must discover for yourself."

"Why won't you just tell me, Tia? Why do you always make me figure out everything on my own? Aren't you my teacher?"

"Yes, but my job is not to fill your head with me but to help you discover you. It would be a great disservice to tell you what I see. There is a universe in you, dear niece, more vast than you can imagine. You are being called, and you must follow that calling. The beach and the presence—those are your teachers. I am only your guide."

I bit my lip. "I thought I was moving forward with this spiritual stuff. Today I feel like I'm back in kindergarten!"

44

"Kindergarten?" Tia's voice had an edge I felt and hadn't heard before. "Where are you getting that nonsense?" she asked. "You have made great strides, and you're well along your path, and now you're questioning your progress? If you think you're back at the start, that's where you'll be. You are not owning your wins right now, are you?"

"Owning my wins?"

"Yes," she said, her voice still with an edge. "Anchoring your wins, your achievements as a growing self-identity. Who you see yourself being and becoming. If you make progress and don't own it, don't feel it, then you don't grow." She looked hard at me. "You want to grow, don't you? If you don't own your wins, how can you possibly grow? You'll slide into feeling unworthy, and then just as you said, you'll be back at the beginning. That's not what you want, is it?"

I sat quiet, watching her. I'd sparked something in her I'd not seen before. Her kindness was still apparent, but she was firing from the hip. And this seemed like new information. I'd never thought owning my wins was important. It sounded to me like what someone full of themselves would do.

"I never saw it that way, Tia."

"Think of it as your spiritual bank account. You admit it to yourself when you gain wisdom and expand your consciousness. You celebrate the *you* that is waking up. You anchor your wins in your mind, and they become part of your growing self-identity."

"This makes so much sense. How is it I never thought of it that way? I felt that celebrating my wins would be boastful."

I started laughing. "When you say it now, it makes so much sense."

"When we don't accept ourselves as constantly elevating, expanding souls, registering and owning every one of our individual wins, then what's the point of all this?" She raised her arms and waved around the room. "Unless we are crisply aware of where we are from where we started, we have yet to start. That negligence sabotages us, keeps us stuck in one place. That thinking of celebrating oneself as arrogance is itself a form of arrogance. Real humility is being honest about who you are and what you accomplish and acknowledging that you are a marvelous being in a marvelous universe."

I nodded in agreement, knowing I'd need to work on this. "How can I anchor my progress?" I asked her.

She leaned back in her chair and smiled. "Gratitude."

"Gratitude? Tia, I need something more powerful than gratitude."

"Well, good luck in finding it. Because I don't know anything more powerful. Gratitude's the foundation of higher consciousness; we don't move an inch in that direction without it. You want more self-confidence?"

I nodded.

"Well, without gratitude, self-confidence does not exist."

I sat quietly, looking into the darkened area of the restaurant and thinking about the ways I'd been blessed. Had they been shrugged off without my gratitude?

"You know what? I have been grateful for the good things in my life, Tia. I look back and see myself being grateful, always."

She looked at me as if she were waiting for more. When it didn't come, she said, "Niece, I'm not talking about being thankful for this thing or that. I'm talking about gratitude for everything, for every single thing everywhere, in all time and space. I'm talking about a state of mind, a way of living. In that place, we're automatically banking our wins and celebrating our progress."

I stared at her, my mind searching. "You're saying gratitude as a state of being? A constant?"

She raised her eyebrows and nodded.

I leaned forward, my elbows on the table. "But what does that have to do with my dream? With the person on the beach and that strange presence?"

"Would you like more hot chocolate?"

I laughed. "Oh, Noah was right. You are an evil woman. You're not going to answer that question, are you?"

"I will tell you this: if you keep your heart open and try to see every instant of life as a blessing, you will expand your ability to love. And if you will stop thinking everything to death, stuffing everything that happens into that little intellectual box of yours, you may find yourself in a brand-new paradigm."

"Paradigm?"

She grinned. "Should I have said consciousness?"

"No," I said, and laughed at her childlike grin. "I like paradigm just fine."

She regarded me kindly. "Paradigms, stages of reality. It's all a river, you know, a river weaving and always changing. And we need to change with it."

45

Early the next morning, I went to the beach, set my backpack on a towel, and waded in the surf, letting it sweep around me and pull at me. I stood there, thinking that this too was a paradigm, one that, at one time, I would not have accepted. And as I stood there, I said, "This is real. Keegan. Just because you sit on the sand and ignore it doesn't make it less real. Can you now just be one with it?"

I stood in the frothing, cold water, the great sea from here to Asia, almost six thousand miles of clean, open, alive ocean, feeling its presence, its life. I stayed until my legs were numb, then pushed through the waves back to the warm sand. I pulled out my thermos of tea and sat cross-legged, staring out across the laughing sea.

The sky and the sea were close to the same color that morning; there seemed to be no horizon, just one gray with no seam. If I were to step off the sand into that grayness, I might free-fall in the endless sky.

I lay back on my towel and wondered again about the lone figure in my dream. Who was it?

After a while, I sat up and finished my tea, stowed the thermos in my backpack, and lay back on the sand again, losing myself in the timeless motion of the sea and sky. If only I could drink in all that wisdom.

Then I felt a warm furry body beside me and sat up. A dog had come to sit next to me, pressing so close that I could feel the heat of its body. I propped myself up on my elbows and looked at him.

He looked back at me with one brown eye and one blue eye. "Hey, buddy. Are we cousins or something?"

He wagged his tail, stretched his head forward, and licked my cheek. Without even thinking, I leaned forward and licked his too, then laughing at my crazy impulse, I took out my water bottle and rinsed my mouth, spitting into the sand. Then I took a long drink while the pooch watched.

"Oh, all right, since we're cousins." I poured water into my cupped hand, and he lapped it up.

"Did Tia send you here to teach me more lessons?"

He wagged his tail.

"That's what I thought."

I wanted to hug him to me, but instead, I honored his space and turned back to the sea. "Yep," I said. "Well, you're the exact guru I need right now."

He leaned against me until I could no longer resist. I put my arm around him and pulled him close, and his warmth went inside me. It was delicious. Together we looked out at the sea, up at the sky, then out at the sea again.

Something new, warm, and beautiful was growing inside me. I turned to look at him, seriously wondering if maybe he was more than a dog. He sure seemed to have the gentle and patient wisdom I was seeking.

"Thank you for sitting with me, oh wise one. Now, tell me who sent you?"

You did! I heard the words in my mind as clearly as if they had been spoken.

"What did you say?"

His tongue hung out, causing the corners of his mouth to turn up. Was he smiling at me?

What if I truly had brought him here somehow? And if I had, then maybe I was bringing everything else to me, like the figure on the beach in my dream. But if that were true, did that mean that the special presence that had been awakened around and in me was also my creation? I looked back at my new friend.

"What the hell are you doing to that dog?" a familiar voice behind me demanded. I didn't turn around.

"Well," I said, "his owner won't give him water, so I have to."

Then I turned my head toward the voice and tried to look charming. "Would you like a kiss?"

"After you've been kissing that dog? I saw how close you two were. So . . . well . . . okay, I'll make an exception since it's you."

"Sorry," I replied. "On second thought, I'm only into dogs today."

"Arf!"

And then I was in Noah's arms, feeling his strength and warmth and knowing I would love him forever.

"I didn't know you had a dog," I said, pulling back to look at him.

"I don't," he said. "I have no idea whose dog that is."

46

I met with Frank on a Friday afternoon two months after Johanna's death, and I got right to the point. "Frank, I'm going to need more time off."

He studied me from behind his desk, his hands forming a steeple under his chin. "What's going on?"

"Well, I ... I've got some things going on, some problems to work out after the strange things that happened in my head after that death on the bridge."

He leaned back in his chair, clicking a pen impatiently. "Oh yeah? What kind of strange things?"

I decided to be honest with him. "Something pretty weird is happening to me right now. I'm not losing my mind or anything, but all the same, my life is changing. I see things and know things that normal people just don't see and know."

"Like what?"

"Like right now, you're worrying about your son in law school."

The pen stopped clicking. "Who told you that?"

"No one told me. No one had to. That's what I'm saying. I found a little boy who'd been kidnapped. The police couldn't find him, but I did. Don't ask me how because I don't know. All I know is that things come to me out of nowhere, and when they do, they're right. Frank, whatever's going on is pretty darned big, and I can't ignore it."

He leaned forward over his desk again. "So it was you who found that kid? I heard it was some psychic."

"Yeah, well, I'm no psychic."

Frank put down the pen and stared at me, considering. "Keegan, I don't know what to say to you." Then he stood and turned to look out his window. "Okay. You get this thing straightened out." He turned back to me and spoke gently. "And if you want to come back, the job will be here waiting for you. I'll get some paperwork started now. You're going to be okay financially?"

"Yeah, I think I will."

"Good." He stretched out his hand. "You stay in touch."

I was surprised to hear Frank's understanding and kindness. Maybe because I knew about his son? Well, miracles— I guess it was time to get used to them.

47

The next morning, I ran along the beach for what seemed like hours. It was one of those rare days when the sun warms the air and gulls are keening and wheeling overhead above a sapphire blue sea. I got home sweaty and happy to find a notice stuck in the door from the post office. I had missed a delivery.

I showered, ate a toasted sesame seed bagel smothered in avocado and cream cheese, and then headed for the post office. As always, it was packed, but I waited patiently, savoring the bliss of my morning. When I finally got to the window, I signed for a certified and registered letter from Anthony Margolis, an attorney in Oakland.

I returned to my car, tore open the envelope, and pulled out a single page. Mr. Margolis was writing to tell me that I was mentioned in the will of Johanna Gooding and that my presence was requested at the reading.

My mind stopped. I could no longer feel my body. I felt like I was falling, not down, but up and up, into an expansion of who I was. As I lifted higher, I was aware of a dimension beyond imagination that cannot be described except to say I felt freer than I ever had. An all-knowing presence surrounded me. Was it me in another realm? Maybe. Whatever it was, I was not controlling it. This was a presence and a wisdom far beyond my control, and it was pulling me up like a hot air balloon.

After a while, still in an all-aware vacancy, I looked again at the letter. Could my life possibly get any stranger? I had never met Johanna Gooding. I had only spoken to her on the phone after she had supposedly died. She didn't know me and could not have known me when she drafted her will, yet she named me in her will? I was again sliding into a warm embrace of— what? The universe? Nothing made sense. And yet making sense was somehow becoming less and less important.

I picked up my phone. "Hey, Noah, you got a minute?"

"For you, I do. And if you're calling me, I guess there's a problem."

"Can we meet for lunch?" I asked.

"I'll pick you up at one thirty."

When Noah arrived, I got in the car and showed him the letter. After he read it, he handed it back. "Keegs, I know we've been over this already, but you're sure you never met Johanna before that day on the bridge?"

"I'm sure."

"Then we're now playing on a whole new ball field, aren't we?"

"Yes, and I don't know how to play."

Tia was waiting for us at the café. She brought us hot tea, then read the letter. When she had finished, she closed her eyes, and when she opened them again, she gazed at me. "My niece, it appears you've inherited a good deal of money."

I had no words.

"You *are* going to see this attorney, right? And hear the reading of the will?" Noah asked.

I found my voice. "Well, of course I am. I have to, don't I?"

"Then I'm going with you. That is, if you want me to."

"Oh yes, I do. God, yes. I need you there, Noah."

Tia pushed herself up from the table. "You two come with me now; it's time I showed you something."

We followed her through the kitchen, breathing in a thousand wonderful smells, then up a carpeted stairwell into a large room rich with Native American rugs scattered over polished hardwood floors. Oil and watercolor paintings hung on the adobe-colored wall. The one nearest me depicted wild horses running beneath a dark, thunderous sky across a plain dotted with low trees and bushes. From the far wall, the afternoon light splashed through.

"Sit now." Tia motioned to a well-worn leather couch, then walked into another room. Noah's presence next to me was magnetic; I felt his warmth opening and moving into my very being. He put his hand on the sofa between us and rested it against my leg, waking up something inside me. In another moment, our hands would have joined, and I would have felt his deliciousness filling my whole body.

But Tia returned, and Noah moved his hand away, leaving the space between us empty. Tia sank into an elegant tapestry chair across from us and pulled out a candle and a small wrapped bundle from a blue leather bag. "I made this candle years ago using beeswax and some herbs I like. I burn it at special times, mostly when I'm alone." She smiled at us. "Today, I'm stepping outside *my* box."

She held the small bundle toward us and opened it to what looked like a fat cigar of dried hay tied with string. She asked if we knew what it was.

Noah and I looked at each other, then back at Tia, and shook our heads.

"Oh, you children!" she exclaimed, laughing. "You will come to know this sacred plant very well. It's sage, and it's connected to thousands of years of spiritual oneness in our human family." She looked at the sage as if it were an old friend. "Centuries of sunny days and starry nights, of rain and snow and windswept plains are in this. Holy people were using this wonderful sage for blessings and cleansing long before the birth of Jesus." She looked back at us. "Different herbs from Mother Earth are used to bridge the space between this world and the next, and this one is my favorite because it works for me. Now let's see how it does for you."

She set the candle in a small clay pottery dish and placed the bundle of sage and a small box of wooden matches next to it.

48

"Do either of you meditate?"

Noah shook his head.

"Not really," I replied. "Though I've been to some special places with you, Tia."

"Well, then, it's time you two made a life practice of meditation."

"Why?" asked Noah.

"Because," she said, "meditation will clear away any mental rubbish you have and connect you to the Divine." She looked at the sunlight streaming through the window and laughed aloud. "And it makes the journey fun." She looked back at us, her eyes ever so gentle. "If your journey isn't fun, you've gotten on the wrong plane."

Her smile in that enchanting, silent room was surreal. "You two have been exploring other dimensions, and it's been a bit confusing sometimes, hasn't it?"

I leaned forward. "It seems to me that I'm spending most of my life now following some magical path that I'm not allowed to understand."

Tia watched me thoughtfully for a moment. "Ever been to Bali?" she asked.

"Nope." I shook my head.

Tia waited.

Finally, I saw it. "Oh, I won't know Bali until I go there."

"Exactly! And if you two look closely now, you'll see that what you thought was reality a year ago has changed. You two are in the blessed state of becoming."

I opened my mouth, but she held up her hand. "No more questions now. We can philosophize all day and not get anywhere."

We both nodded that we understood.

"Now, tell me, do you both feel safe here?"

"Safe?" I asked. "I feel like I'm in your sanctuary."

Noah laughed. "I may never leave."

She leaned back. "Get comfortable, then. Still your minds and follow my directions, and all your questions will soon be answered."

I relaxed my muscles while my mind drifted into semi-sleep.

She spoke again, her voice soft. "Breathe ever so gently in through your nose and hold that breath for four counts, then let it go. Don't push it out; just let it go. Think of a quiet, sunny beach with a wave reaching up high on the sand: that's your inhale. The wave pauses for a beat of four, then relaxes back into the sea."

Then she was quiet, and I was immersed in the room's stillness.

After a few breaths, I felt myself expanding into the space around me. Then there was silence.

The next time Tia spoke, it sounded like she was much farther away, her voice as soft as music. "Take another deep breath and hold it ... hold it ... hold it ... Now let it go and let yourself fall away ... fall away"—her voice faded more— "fall away."

I felt myself leaving my body, like what had happened on the bridge. I became hollow and empty, just as I had then. I felt again that warm presence around me. And then I was the presence. I was a new me.

I heard Tia's voice, and it was part of the presence. "There is a light above your head now. Focus your mind and heart there and *be* there, in the pure Light of your Higher Mind. If your awareness slips back into your head, breathe it into your Higher Mind again."

I breathed slowly and deeply and felt myself drifting over my head and into peaceful purity with each breath. Each inhale was of the sweet fragrance of sage. Each exhale was pure joy.

Tia began to chant, her voice high and clear. She continued for some time. And then there was silence. And I was without thought in a place I'd never been, in permanent *now*. Time and space were constants, and I was immersed in pure bliss. Only peace, safety, and freedom existed.

When she finally spoke again, Tia said, "My children, let go now and drift back to this room. Take your time. Let it happen at its own pace. Bring back with you the good you experienced."

49

I had no idea where I was when I heard her words. I was not asleep, yet I had traveled far. Coming back, at first I could not feel my body and noticed that I was not breathing. For how long? When I opened my eyes the room seemed strangely darkened. Could that be from the meditation? The flickering candle had melted down but yet burned on the table before us, revealing shapes and shadows on the wall beyond. I glanced over at Noah; his eyes were open, but still unfocused. Then I turned to look out the window and was amazed by what I saw.

"Tia, how can it be dark already?"

"My dears, where you were was only a few minutes. But time in this dimension here moves much faster. You two have been gone for three and a half hours."

I looked at Noah, staring in puzzlement at the darkness around us. I nudged him. "You okay?"

He looked at me, still not quite focused. "Sure, but ... I just ... Yeah, I'm okay."

Tia got up, stepped into an adjacent room, and returned with two steaming blue mugs. "Now, let's have some tea and talk about your crossing over." She placed the mugs on the low table before the couch and sat in the tapestry chair across from us. "You two just left your body-minds and became pure spirit," she said. "Oh, how I wish you could have seen the Light surrounding you."

"Like the Light I saw around Keegs that day?" Noah asked.

"Yes," she said, and nodded. "Exactly like that. And this

time, your two lights blended. I will let you figure out for
yourselves what that might mean."

She leaned toward us. "Cup your hands in front of you
now as I brush the sage smoke in your direction. Gather it in
your hands and wash it over your face, head, and body. Let it
enter your body and bless you, inside and out."

The sage smoke washed over us.

"Welcome to your new world," Tia said softly. "Your journey home has finally begun."

"Will we do this again?" I asked.

"Oh, sure you will, and often. I am sending you each home
with your own magic bag. You'll find everything you need to
replicate what you just experienced, including my blessing."

The bags were made of a soft material that was smooth to
the touch. Inside were a bundle of sage and a beeswax candle.

Noah blew out a great breath. "I have no idea where I was,"
he said. "I felt nothing but peace and a deep happiness."

"I felt the same," I said. "I don't think I've ever been so
filled with joy. I wish that could be me all the time."

"What you just experienced was not inconsistent with
who you are. What you experienced was the eternal you, the
you behind the body and mind you thought was you. It is the
real you. And from now on, that must become the *you* of your
daily focus, the *you* who is in the world." She opened her
arms. "You don't want to be there only in meditation. You
want to be there all the time. It is who you are."

We talked awhile longer, feeling embraced by the room
around us, floating on its deep, beautiful peace.

Then Tia stood. "Well, our supper is ready. Shall we eat?"

"Supper?" Noah asked. "You cooked supper while we were
gone?"

"That I did. Doesn't it smell good?"

It was delicious. I ate two helpings of the rich vegetable
stew with freshly baked bread. Afterward, we sat together,

wrapped in silence, listening to rain pattering on the window.

Finally, I asked the question that had brought me to the café that day. "So what do you think my being in Johanna's will means?"

Tia put down her cup and stared into it, considering. "We are now dealing with something I've only seen once."

Noah looked up. "This has happened before? Somebody left something to someone they didn't know?"

Tia looked at him. "Noah, my son, Johanna *did* know Keegan. She knew her well. She also knew you, knew that you would find each other, and knew what that would mean. She knew every single bit of it."

Noah shook his head. "Come on. How is that even possible?"

"Oh, nephew, you have no idea yet what is possible."

50

The sky and bay were gray, and I fell into the creamy fog that slid down the flanks of Mount Tam, down through the hills of Mill Valley, and out across the bay, enshrouding all but the hilltop of Angel Island. The folds of East Bay's green hills still lay in shadows, darkening homes whose windows would become multicolored diamonds at sunset. Oakland cannot compare with San Francisco's international charm; few cities can. Where else is there such enchantment, such a melding of sorrow and opportunity? This is Willy Wonka's playground of steep hills, cable car music, aromas of chocolate, wine, coffee, and the constancy of challenges. Those bothered by the constant intensity are more comfortable across the water in Oakland.

Noah and I drove across the Bay Bridge the morning of Johanna's will reading and found a place to park close to Robert Margolis's law office. We crossed the street and walked into an elaborate lobby, where we were met by a smiling gray-haired receptionist dressed in a business suit and wearing blue-rimmed glasses. She greeted us with a gentle smile, then led us along a carpeted hallway to a conference room, where wide windows looked out over the harbor.

We were the last to arrive. Four people stood drinking coffee and talking at one end of a polished walnut conference table. Mr. Margolis stepped forward and introduced himself. He looked exactly as I had pictured him: medium height, hairline receding at the temples, neatly trimmed beard, meticulously dressed in a chocolate-colored suit, cream-colored shirt, and blue tie. He introduced us to Johanna's daughter and son, Bernadette and Clement, and to Clement's daughter, Angela.

I had dreaded meeting this family whose property I was here to take. But if they were at all resentful, they hid it well. Their faces were kind. Noah seemed to be as surprised as I was at the gentle atmosphere. We had been anticipating a wall of dark resistance. Instead, we felt very much accepted.

"Please help yourself to coffee or tea," Mr. Margolis said. Noah poured coffee for both of us, and we settled into comfortable leather chairs across from Clement and Bernadette. Angela sat in the chair next to me.

Mr. Margolis started the meeting. "Ms. Tate, we read the will pertaining to the others yesterday. We arranged today's meeting to discuss the details of your portion." He donned a pair of reading glasses, removed a document from a folder, and placed it on the table before him.

I couldn't wait any longer. "May I say something before you begin?"

Mr. Margolis looked at me over his glasses. "Of course, Ms. Tate."

I looked around at the family. "I want to apologize to you all. I know this has to be uncomfortable. But I want you to know that I'm ... I'm not trying to—" I searched for the right words. "I'm not trying to take something that isn't mine. That's not who I am. I didn't know your mother. While it's true that I ... talked to her while she was ... when she died, I'd never met her. And now here I am, inserting myself into your lives at a most vulnerable time. I came here today to meet you and to thank you, and to tell you I don't want or need anything from your mother's estate."

Mr. Margolis removed his glasses and cleared his throat. "Thank you, Ms. Tate. And now, if I may continue, I think things will become clearer for you."

I looked at Noah. He nodded slightly.

Then I looked back at Mr. Margolis. "Of course," I said. "Please go ahead."

Mr. Margolis glanced around at the faces and picked up the will again. "The decedent, Johanna Gooding, left the majority of her estate to her two children, Clement and Bernadette; to Clement's daughter, Angela; and to Angela's daughter."

He looked over his glasses at me. "As I said, Clement, Bernadette, Angela, and I discussed that part of the will yesterday, Ms. Tate. Today we're here to honor Mrs. Gooding's wishes on your behalf."

He nodded, flipped a couple of pages over, and began again. "And to my dear Keegan Tate, who very kindly listened to my last words and heard the message from my heart, I leave the remainder of my estate."

He set the will back on the table, removed his glasses, and met my eyes. "And that, Ms. Tate, is Johanna Gooding's gift to you."

I was stunned. "But ... but how can that be? Johanna didn't even know me." I looked at each family member in turn, seeing only smiles on their faces. I was in a dream, and nothing was real.

The three Goodings exchanged glances with one another, then Angela put a hand on my arm and I looked into her eyes.

"Ms. Tate, Keegan," she said, her voice soft, "you don't need to worry about us. Our family is very well off. We have everything we need. Now, this was Grandma's wish, and every one of us wants to honor that wish. And frankly," she said, "we expect you to do so too."

I looked at her with curiosity. Her voice sounded vaguely familiar.

"But, Angela, I only ever talked to your grandmother on the day she died." I gestured over to Noah. "This man, dear Noah, was with her. I was a hundred yards away. She spoke to me on the phone, but I didn't know her."

Clement leaned forward and smiled. "You know her now, though, don't you?"

I thought for a moment, then nodded. "Yes, I guess I do."

I looked at Angela again, and then it hit me: she was the mother of the little girl who'd called me Keegan!

"Angela! You have a daughter named Johanna, don't you?"

She leaned back, looked around the room, and laughed. "Oh, my God, I am so busted!"

51

"What's the story? What happened?" asked Bernadette.

Angela told the story, and everyone laughed.

"Little Johanna inherited her grandma's gifts, that's for sure," said Angela, still smiling. Bernadette came around the table and knelt beside my chair. She placed her hand on mine. "Keegs," she said, looking into my eyes, "we talked about this among ourselves before you and Noah got here this morning, and we know what you are feeling right now. And we also know who you are. We've known for a long time. Mama talked about you a lot. And yes, we understand how confusing this must be right now, but it's not confusing to us. Please try to understand. Mama knew what she was doing. She would not have chosen you unless she was sure."

Noah leaned forward. "Was your mother that clairvoyant?"

Clement laughed. "Clairvoyant, Noah? Well, yes, she was clairvoyant, but she was so much more than that."

I shook my head. "Forgive me, but none of this makes sense. I've got questions that I don't even know how to ask. My thoughts and feelings are all just a big jumble."

"And we understand that," Bernadette said. "We've each been pretty much there ourselves." She looked at the others. "And do you know what we did and what we do? We accept. We just accept what is. We stop trying to figure it out. We quit trying to understand. We simply follow the Light, and we surrender, and we accept what is."

I heard Tia's voice in my head. *The Light is the source of all things material and nonmaterial.*

Goosebumps covered my arms.

Clement addressed me from across the table. "Can you please be patient, Keegs? Be patient and let this unfold?"

Angela pressed my hand in hers. "You will come to know what it is. Be patient and trust my dear grandma."

"But, Angela, she—"

"She what? She died in a car wreck? And now you can't understand how such a holy woman would allow that?"

"No," I said with a shrug. "No, I really can't."

Clement got up and came around to my chair, leaning against the table next to Bernadette.

"Keegan and Noah," he said, looking at each of us in turn, "please hear me. You are now both members of this family. You're now a part of us. In fact," he said, squinting his eyes in thought, "you've been part of us for quite some time. And we're all thrilled to have you with us and to know that Mama's work is going forward through you. If you'll trust her, you will see everything unfolding in perfect form. We know a little about how this works. We've all been where you are."

"Well," said Noah, "it's sure a reach."

"It will become less so," said Clement, "when you can embrace rather than resist. We resist not because something is dangerous but because it's different. When you embrace it, the fear becomes something else, maybe love. Now, can the two of you keep your minds and your hearts open and let these changes develop?"

Angela spoke again. I was still getting used to how much she sounded like Johanna. "Grandma used to tell me, 'You are always looking for answers, and it's a waste of your time. Why don't you try looking for better questions?'"

Better questions. Tia's voice again!

I looked around the room. "If it's not too painful, can you explain why your mother died? Obviously, she didn't have to. Did she?"

Clement shrugged. "She was in charge of her life and knew exactly what she was doing. She taught us that there is no such thing as death, that life is eternal. She talked to each of us in the last few weeks before the accident, preparing us. We didn't know then that that's what she was doing. Only later did it become clear. Did you know that she was ninety-seven years old? She seemed ageless to us, but we know now she felt it was time to pass the torch." He nodded at Noah and me. "To pass it to you two."

Noah spoke up. "How are you three handling that so calmly now?"

Angela answered him. "It was and still is painful for us. We all loved her. And yet we know she's not dead. She is with us right now, right here in this room."

The family walked us outside, and we said our goodbyes on the sidewalk. That's when I began to see that something remarkable had just happened: we'd been adopted into a family that had lived their entire lives where we were just beginning.

Noah and I drove back across the Bay Bridge, the late afternoon sunlight casting shadows, too filled with our thoughts and feelings to talk much, until halfway across the bridge, I broke the silence. "Right there, Noah," I said, pointing. "That's where I stopped my car."

About a hundred yards later, he said, "And here is where she died." As we passed, I suddenly felt a weight lift from my chest.

I looked back at the place where my life had changed on that Friday afternoon and felt blessed. I felt Johanna's presence and heard her voice again. I remembered the magnificent streams of Light. And now I knew what she had been saying to me.

I wiped tears from my face. Noah glanced over and said, "We may never know why Johanna put you in her will before she died. Not one bit of this adds up in the way we normally think, but I keep hearing Bernadette's voice saying *We just accept what is*. And I think that's what we need to do too."

52

We drove without speaking for a while. Then I looked at Noah. "I wonder how much it is. Am I awful to be thinking that?"

"No," he said. "I'm wondering that too. Margolis said it would take a week or so to get it squared away, but the family says they're well off so it could be a lot. Maybe even fifty thousand or more."

"Oh, my God, Noah. You think so?"

He shrugged. "Well, Keegs, right now, anything seems possible."

We drove the rest of the way home in silence. I tried to get my mind straight. I was being asked to accept a new way of thinking and a new way of being. What would it take for me to accept it all? How could I find acceptance?

And then there it was, as clear as a bell: the first of the Three. It came as suddenly and clearly as a morning sunrise breaking over a mountaintop. *Acceptance!* That word alone started dissolving a block inside me I hadn't even known was there; it was a chunk of resistance fighting to keep things in a predictable order that I could understand so that I could feel comfortable and safe. I looked around me: at Noah behind the wheel, the other cars, and the people in them. I saw them for the first time in my life without judgment. I simply *accepted*. It was such a simple concept, but it had so much meaning. I worked it around and saw that acceptance was more than a concept. When I looked at it from my experience of being one with everything, it immediately became forgiveness and gratitude for and of all. I noticed I was taking slow, deep breaths and that my heartbeat had also slowed. I felt peaceful.

"What are you smiling about?" Noah asked.

"I found the first of the Three," I said.

"You did? What? Right now? What is it?"

"Do you remember our first meeting with Tia?"

"Yes, it was that afternoon you met her."

"And she said something that day that I just blew off. Maybe you did too."

"And that is?"

"Acceptance."

"Acceptance?" He drove on in silence, then said again, "Acceptance."

I was waking up to a new reality. I had told Tia once that I wasn't a victim, but as long as I was judging reality, I was always a victim. I couldn't change what I didn't accept. Couldn't change what I didn't forgive. I must be grateful for everything exactly as it was and exactly as it was not. Only then would I be in the driver's seat of my life.

"Acceptance," Noah said again. "And yes, I remember that first day and that first conversation with Tia. She told us that acceptance was the first step. She told us! And still we didn't get it."

"Ah," I said, and laughed. "'When the student is ready, the teacher will appear.' We just weren't ready."

"And we discounted it as idle conversation."

"Tia knew where we were going before we did."

"So now, Noah, can you see acceptance as the first of the Three?"

He glanced over at me. "Well, it has to be, doesn't it? Nothing good can happen with us unless we're empowered to be the best us we can be. Acceptance is just that, isn't it? Feeling empowered by surrendering."

"Sounds like a contradiction, but it makes such sense.

When we are completely accepting, the universe is one with us."

"Tia said something else that day that I've always toyed with in my mind. She said, 'It is the way it is—it is the way.'" He looked over at me, excited. "It is the way it is; it is the way! Not the way I want it to be, not how I planned it, but how it is. That's my foundation."

I was right with him. "That's acceptance, isn't it? Knowing that what's happening is supposed to be happening."

"Yeah, and sometimes that's going to take a lot of surrendering."

"Like what?"

He thought for a moment. "Like when I shot that girl. It's a bit of a stretch to say that was supposed to be happening."

"I agree. But when it happened, it instantly became the past, didn't it? It happened, and then it was the truth. And unless we accept truth, we're lost."

He was quiet. "For days and weeks, and even now, I'm still resisting it."

"Resisting it or grieving it? I think we do need to grieve, but not in resistance to what is or what was. So which is it? Are you in grief or in resistance?"

"Thank you, oh wise one," he said, and smiled. "It's grief; no doubt about it."

"Good, then you're in acceptance of it."

He nodded. "For sure. It's what has passed, even a second ago, that is now truth. The opposite of truth is untruth. When we're not in truth, nothing very good can come our way."

53

We were silent as we thought that over. Then Noah said, "If we look at it like a finished thing, like it's done and can't be undone, then we have to see that it is the way it is, and nothing will ever change it."

"So when we are not in acceptance, then what? I guess we're in rejection, or at least resistance. Resistance to what is. That's pretty futile, isn't it?

"Yes, and that's when we get caught up in a jumble of *what should be or could be or could have been*. We're not accepting the truth, and there goes any clarity we might have had."

"And with it goes our creative ability."

"This acceptance is life-changing!" he said.

"Thank you, Johanna!"

"You said 'There goes our creative ability.' How do you see that?" he asked.

I turned to him. "Well, I think that creativity is an expression of what we experience. And if we are acceptance, then our genius doesn't get diluted."

"Diluted?"

"Yes, by our judgments and beliefs. Tia taught me that beliefs and judgments are illusions; they're not real. We only hold onto them because they bolster our egos. When I'm in acceptance, I'm beyond those things. I'm one with truth, with reality. Then the energy of reality—Tia would call it the grace of the universe—can flow through me and I can create."

"Not all artists are in acceptance."

"No, not all of them; only the geniuses."

"Oh, you wise one!"

I grinned. "I'm seeing right now that by admitting *the way*, we are open to possibilities we couldn't see otherwise."

"It is the way it is—it is the way," he said thoughtfully.

"I sure wish I'd been taught this in grade school!"

"Tia saw this day coming and set us up the day I met her," he said, laughing.

"Hey, buddy, what's so funny?"

"I don't know. It's just when I feel you being with me, I'm taking in things about life I'd never truly appreciated before."

"Like what?"

"Like the color of the sky and your nose—things I never really took in before."

"You're taking in my nose?" I asked, rubbing it.

"Baby, I'm taking in all of you." He was still laughing.

Truly, I hadn't needed to ask what he was laughing at because that joy bubbled in me as well. I was in paradise with the man of my dreams. And much of it was because I was in acceptance. I was seeing the beauty of life in a way I never knew was possible.

So," he said, "I realize that what I'm feeling is gratitude."

"Gratitude..." I remembered Tia saying that gratitude was the foundation of higher consciousness, and here it was again, this time finding a home inside me. Thankfulness wasn't just a concept; it was, as she had said, a state of being.

As we talked, we agreed that gratitude and forgiveness were the soul of acceptance, and that without acceptance, life was empty. I couldn't see this before because I always filtered everything through my judgment. Accepting was letting go of judgment.

As Noah pulled the car up in front of my house, he seemed a step ahead of me. "In tai chi," he said, "we learn to not resist what comes at us. We accept it. We let it flow through us so that the strength of anything coming at us becomes our strength. Acceptance is just that; it allows us to be one with all universal energies."

"So now my challenge is to stop judging and *become* acceptance."

Noah hugged me. "You got this, Keegs."

54

The phone rang while I was putting away my lunch dishes.

"Ms. Tate?"

"Yes?"

"Will you please hold for Mr. Margolis?"

Here was the call I'd been both hoping and dreading and for which I was in no way ready. The first week after the meeting with Johanna's family, I'd kept the phone within reach every minute. After two weeks, I realized it could be months or longer before I heard from Margolis. I had gone back to my usual routine and pretended not to care.

Margolis came on the phone. "Good afternoon, Ms. Tate. I hope you are well. I'm calling to let you know that the estate has been settled. All parties have signed the probate papers, and all relevant taxes have been paid."

"Okay," I said.

"Now, if you don't mind, I need your bank information to transfer these funds."

My mouth was suddenly dry, and my hands were shaky. I asked Mr. Margolis to wait while I found my checkbook. I got a glass of water on the way to pick up my purse; I needed time to think more clearly, but I couldn't keep the man waiting.

"I'm back. Thanks for your patience, Mr. Margolis."

"Oh, please call me Anthony."

"Well, if you'll call me Keegan."

I gave him the bank information and my account number,

"Good. Then I believe that does it, Keegan, unless you have any questions."

I didn't dare ask how much money it was; I was embarrassed by the fantasy of the fifty thousand dollars that Noah had suggested it might be.

"No, no questions. At least not right now."

He hesitated, then asked, "Keegan, are you still uncomfortable about this?"

"Well," I said, "I guess I'm not hiding it too well, huh?"

"No, I don't think so. Because if you felt this money was rightfully yours, you'd have asked by now how much it is."

I felt my cheeks getting hot. "You're right, Anthony. It still feels almost like I'm doing something a little dishonest."

"Okay, I can help with that. When Johanna and I created this codicil, she said you would feel this way and asked me to give you a message."

"She did?"

"Yes, she did. Because while it's true that you didn't know Johanna, she sure knew you."

I sighed. "Yeah, that's what the family said, but it's still puzzles me."

"Then give me a minute to explain. Over the years, Johanna Gooding and I became close friends, and I can tell you that Johanna knew you quite well, Keegan. She knew that you grew up in a small town in Missouri, received full academic scholarships in college and law school, and worked as a prosecuting attorney in San Francisco. When we discussed this codicil, she predicted you would feel uneasy and maybe even frightened by her caring for you. She foresaw this very moment. She said that when this time came, I was to ask for your patience and trust. That's exactly how she said it: 'Ask her to be patient and to trust me.' She said you would eventually understand. She also said—and I wrote down her words exactly as she said them to me—'Tell Keegan that acceptance will set her free.'"

I couldn't speak through the tears filling my eyes.

"Keegan, Johanna trusted me to ensure her wishes would be honored. Will you just be patient and trust her?"

"Thank you, Anthony. Thank you. Yes. Okay, then, I will accept this gift, and I'll do my best to honor her wishes."

"Now then, do you want to know how much money you'll be receiving?"

"Yes, I do, Anthony."

"Keegan, you are receiving six million, seven hundred and eighty-five thousand dollars."

I pulled the phone away from my ear and stared at it as if it was responsible for what I was hearing. Then I held it up to my ear again, but I could not speak.

"Are you all right, Keegan?"

My voice shook. "Would you mind repeating that, Anthony, so I can write it down?"

55

After he hung up, I stared at the paper in my hand. I had thought I was in acceptance, but this was over the line, way, way over the line. I began sobbing. Before Johanna, I hadn't cried in years, but now I seemed to always cry. As I wept, I felt sorrow draining from my heart until I felt empty. And then I felt like something new was building in me, a joy, a me I'd never known before. Scary!

I wiped my tears, grabbed my rain jacket, and ran for the beach, my great healer. With rain pattering on the hood of my jacket, I made my way across the sand, breathing in the new life that had been handed to me. My poor confused heart didn't know whether to race or beat softly. I was waking up in a transformed state, in a transformed world. I felt the vibrations of everything around me, and my thoughts were tumbling like storm clouds in the wind. I could not focus.

But hey, I was rich! And Johanna was right: it did scare me because I didn't know how to be rich. Within ten minutes, my life had changed from a successful young attorney to a multi-millionaire. I tried accepting that I had over six million dollars in my bank account, and it was all mine. It made absolutely no sense.

I peered through the rain that had now become a downpour and saw a solitary figure approaching. This time, I knew who it was. "Hey, buddy," I yelled, "what in the hell are you doing in this rainstorm?"

Noah yelled back, "Looking for a duck."

"Well, sweetheart," I said as we drew near, "you have found yourself a very rich duck!"

"I know," he said. "I know all about it. That's why I'm here. I need a loan." He wrapped his arms around me.

"Don't you want to know how much it is?" I asked, leaning my head back so I could see his face. "Don't you?"

"Nope," he grinned. "I don't need to because I already know. It came to me in a dream."

"Oh, sure it did, Mister Smartypants. Okay, then, how much is it?"

He raised his eyebrows and looked at me like he was Einstein. "I dreamed that Margolis called you today and told you he was going to transfer money into your account. You asked him how much, and he said six million, seven hundred and eighty thousand dollars."

"You dreamed that?" I gasped, stunned.

"Yep. I saw it in a dream. And I'm right, aren't I?"

I shook my head. "Sorry, my dear, but your dream was wrong."

"Really?" He dropped his head to look at the sand and frowned. "I was positive. I even wrote it down."

"Well, you're way, way off, buddy. It's six million, seven hundred and eighty-*five* thousand dollars."

Then we laughed and laughed and wrapped ourselves together in the falling rain. We were the only two people in the world.

56

As soon as the funds came through, I paid off my mortgage and car loan and walked out of the bank, feeling like a weight had lifted off me. I was debt free, and I was a homeowner. I had never imagined this day.

I took Tia and Noah to Nob Hill Club at the top of the Intercontinental Mark Hopkins for dinner, then spent the next two weeks practicing acceptance. I was continually learning that acceptance was a more subtle process than I'd first thought. I was learning more every day about the difference between accepting and *being acceptance*. When I accepted something, like Noah's shooting incident or the car wreck on the cliff, I was making a choice. But *being acceptance* is a platform, a foundation. The questions were gone. *It is the way it is; it is the way.*

Noah and I spent a morning nestled in the porch swing. The day was clear and bright with a cool, refreshing breeze. "Do you think this money would have come to me," I wondered out loud, "if I hadn't been working on acceptance?"

"I've been wondering that same thing," he answered. "I've come to the conclusion that miracles can't happen unless we're open to all of life. I've been doing an affirmation I made up, and I feel it's changing me."

"What is it?"

He closed his eyes as he spoke. "I feel myself changing every time I say this affirmation. *I am welcoming everything in my life.*"

"I like that."

He went on. "Until now, my life has been either accepting

or rejecting. When I wasn't in acceptance, I was in rejection, and there was no third option. When we reject any part of our lives, I see that we are shutting down the good that can come our way."

"Like millions of dollars." I grinned.

"Exactly!"

"Johanna is still doing this, isn't she? She showed us acceptance just as we drove by where she died the day we went to the attorney's office. This unfolding pattern is too coincidental to be anything else."

When we went inside for lunch, the sun had disappeared behind black and heavy storm clouds blowing in from the south. A shuddering bang of thunder was followed by drumming rain on the roof. Wind rattled the windows.

I had just finished clearing our lunch dishes and poured two cups of tea when the phone rang.

"Hello?"

"Is this Deputy District Attorney Keegan Tate?"

"May I ask who's calling?"

"My name is Patricia Styles. I'm an ER nurse at San Francisco General Hospital. We have a woman here we can't identify. We're hoping you can help. We found your business card in her wallet."

I was puzzled. "You found my card but didn't find her ID?"

"Yes. In fact, your card was the only thing in her wallet. I tried calling the DA's office, but they said you're on leave. This number was on the back of the card."

I tried to think who the woman could be. "Can you describe this woman to me?"

"She looks to be about thirty-five or so. Red hair. She's still unconscious."

"Oh, my God. That's Jill McDonald. I'm on my way."

I hung up and turned to Noah. "That was San Francisco General. Jill's in ER. They found my card in her wallet."

Noah picked up his car keys and grabbed his coat. "I'm driving."

How could a day of such peace and joy be suddenly shattered? I chewed my nails as Noah drove until I remembered to breathe again.

We parked and dashed into the hospital, where we were shown to her room. The woman's head was wrapped in bandages, and what I could see of her face was covered with cuts and bruises. One eye was hidden under a bandage, and the other was only a bruised slit. I would not have recognized her except for her hair and hands.

"Are you related to Ms. McDonald?" the gray-haired nurse asked.

"No. Actually, we're closer than that. Jill was my college roommate, and she's my best friend. We're like sisters."

"Then this must be awful for you," the nurse said, looking at Jill's still form on the bed.

I fought back tears. "What happened?"

She shook her head. "We really don't know."

"Well, is she . . . is she going to make it?" I asked fearfully.

The nurse looked at me with kindness. "It's really too early to know. When she wakes up, we'll know more."

"But . . . will she wake up?"

She put a hand on my shoulder. "And it's also too early to know that. I'm sorry."

She turned to leave, then at the door turned back, "Do you happen to have her family information? We need to contact them."

57

I hadn't considered Jill's parents. This would be a blow to them. "Her mom recently had a stroke," I said, "so this isn't a good time for her to hear that her daughter is—" My voice cracked. "If it's okay with you, I'll call her parents."

"Yes, please do, and have them call us after you talk to them."

Noah, who had been listening, stepped forward. "Ma'am, where can I get information about when she came in and where she was when she was found?"

"I'm sorry, sir, but we can't give that information to anyone except her family."

Noah showed her his badge. "I need to know what happened."

The nurse sighed. "I was told it was an auto accident." She looked at Jill and shook her head. "I have my doubts about that. And so does the doctor. Her injuries just aren't consistent with an auto accident."

"Yeah," Noah nodded. "This looks more like a beating."

I gasped. The idea of Jill being beaten hit me in the gut.

"Does she have injuries that aren't visible?" Noah asked.

"I'm sorry. I really can't say more. I hope you understand."

"Of course," I said quickly. "I'll call right now and get Jill's parents to make me her advocate."

I went out into the hall and called Jill's parents. Her dad picked up immediately. When he heard my voice, he called out to his wife. "Nancy, get on the phone," he said. "It's Keegan!" While we waited, he told me, "You must be psychic,

Keegan. We were just talking about you at breakfast."

As soon as Jill's mother picked up the other line, I told them as best I could what had happened. Jill's mother broke down in sobs. Jill's father said solemnly, "Keegan, I don't know what to do. The doctor said Nancy can't fly and has to stay quiet. I know he won't let her fly to San Francisco."

We talked for another few minutes, and he agreed to call the hospital and make me her legal advocate. I promised to speak to them every day. I knew it might kill her mother if Jill didn't make it.

It might kill me too.

I stepped back into Jill's room. Noah was still grilling the nurse. "I just need to know how she got here. Who brought her in?"

The nurse picked up Jill's chart from the end of her bed and studied it. "She came in at 11:40 this morning." She put the chart down. "We were told that someone found her in a yard. That's all we have."

The nurse left the room, and I looked at the bandaged, battered face I loved so much. "How could anyone have done this to her?" I asked no one in particular. Then I turned to Noah. "I need to get myself together. Can we go sit somewhere?"

"Shall I take you home?"

"No, no. Let's go find the cafeteria."

We found a corner table, and Noah brought me a cup of tea, then watched me stir in cream and sugar. "You becoming a sissy too?"

"What?"

He pointed at the empty cream container.

"Oh." I looked down, unable to enjoy his effort at a joke.

He put his hand on mine. "Keegs, are you going to be all right?"

I shook my head. "I don't know. Dammit, Noah, I love

that lady with my whole heart, and it's killing me to see her like this. I don't remember ever feeling this much pain."

He squeezed my hand. "Remember, Keegs: acceptance!"

58

We sat together in silence, gathering our thoughts, trying to tie things together as hospital workers drifted in and out of the cafeteria to pick up coffee and snacks or to sit for a quiet meal. Many of their faces were solemn; they were faces that looked at death and heartbreak every day. That afternoon they were all saints to me. I wondered if the pain they saw bled into their personal lives. But how could it not? Because to work as a healer, one must be empathic. But being exposed to suffering every day had to make them stronger.

I felt Noah watching me and looked at him. "Let's talk about this," he said quietly.

"What can we talk about? We don't even know what happened."

He put his hand on mine. "Keegs, listen to me. We're in my jungle now. I know this territory. You need to trust me. Do you trust me?"

"Yes, of course I do. With my life."

"And with Jill's life?"

I hesitated for only a second. "Of course. Completely."

"Okay, then." He took a small notepad from his coat pocket, opened it to a new page, and clicked his pen. "The first step is to write down everything we know."

"Okay. Number one: Jill was brought in at 11:40 this morning."

He wrote that down. "Two: whoever brought her in said they found her on a sidewalk or in a yard and claimed she'd been in a car wreck. Three: whoever brought her in appears to have vanished."

"And four," I said, "her injuries don't match those of someone who's been in a wreck."

He studied the list, tapping the pen on his chin. "Anything else we can think of?"

"Yes: will she survive, and if she does, will she be mentally okay?" I clasped my hands on the table. "When Jill's mom had a stroke, I could see it all so clearly. I knew she would recover. So why can't I see now whether Jill will be okay?"

He looked up at me and raised his eyebrows. "Maybe because you're also the victim here. Maybe you can't access that plane of wisdom when you are emotionally involved. Maybe you and I both need to remember acceptance."

I looked around the cafeteria to see if anyone was listening to our conversation. "Noah," I said in a low voice, "if you and I are now these . . . these special people, can't we use our abilities to move beyond our emotions and help her heal?"

He dug out his cell phone. "Let's ask."

While he explained to Tia Ana what had happened, I got up to refill our cups. When I came back, he was smiling.

"What?" I asked.

"Tia knew all about Jill. She's been filling her with Light for the past three hours, waiting for us to call."

I looked at him quizzically. "How did she know?"

He shrugged. "She wants to see us right away. Let's get going."

59

Despite the heavy rain, we made it to the café in record time. Tia met us at the door and wrapped her arms around me. "My dear niece, I am so sorry for your pain. But it's going to be okay." Keeping her arm around my waist, she led us to a table where bowls of soup, plates of sandwiches, and a pot of coffee were set out.

Noah sat down, but I could not let go of Tia that easily. I needed her strength.

"Tia, you're saying it will be okay. What in the world makes you say that?"

She pushed me back to arm's length, jutted her chin, and looked into my eyes. "Jill doesn't look so good right now, and that's true, but she'll be fine. I promise. She's going to be even better than fine. She's going to be wonderful."

"Wonderful?" Noah jumped up from his seat. "Auntie, if you'd seen her . . ."

She brushed him off with one hand. "Sit back down, both of you." Her voice was stern.

She pulled out her chair, sat, and leaned into us. "Now listen, you two. You need to get on the team here."

"But," I interrupted, "if you could see how bad she is."

Tia raised her hand to stop me. "I've already seen her, Little Bird. I know how she looks, and yes, that's a challenge, but it's a challenge for us, not for her. She's not looking at herself. Deep inside herself, she is as completely whole as ever. *And* she is going to recover. *She is.* And then . . . then something wonderful is going to come from this."

I was not buying it. "Am I missing something here, Tia? How in the hell could anything good possibly come from Jill being beaten almost to death? Tell me how."

She leaned her arms on the table and looked at both of us. "That's why I wanted to see you two right away. We have to get our hearts in harmony here. Today we're all moving into a broader level of consciousness. No more waiting; we must do it now. So today you're going to discover something that will change your lives."

She motioned to the food on the table and told us to eat. And while we did, she said, "You two listen now to your old auntie." She reached to pour us fresh coffee, watching us with steely eyes. "Everything that happens," she said, "happens with purpose. Not for a purpose, but with purpose. That's your lesson to learn today: purpose!"

I was not happy with that. "Oh yeah, Jill being nearly killed has a purpose. That's what you're saying? Because that's just nonsense." I knew my voice was harsh, and I didn't care.

Noah looked at me with surprise.

But Tia was gentle. "Be still, child. Just be still and listen. You can't digest this while you're broadcasting. Just eat; you're going to need your strength. And now, both of you, clear your minds and your judgments about what's happening. And please be still."

Noah and I looked at each other sheepishly and began eating. Later I thought about how, on that stormy afternoon, she was feeding our bodies and our minds both.

Then she began, her voice a soft cadence that demanded listening.

"The instant something happens," she said, "no matter what it is, at that instant, it becomes real, does it not?" She looked at each of us in turn. "Does it not?"

We looked at each other, then nodded.

She continued. "It's real, so then it's a part of creation, of truth. Isn't that so?"

We nodded again.

"And since what happened to Jill is now truth, it has a place in our universe. It cannot be undone. Now, listen closely because it's easy to misunderstand this. Every event comes with opportunity. If we're not too traumatized or dogmatic in our opinions, it has information that could teach us something."

"What?" I asked, still upset. "Now Jill's tragedy is a teaching moment for us?"

She paused. "Are you in a place to learn, Little Bird?"

I looked down at the table, abashed, and began crying.

"I just don't see why she has to go through this," I blubbered. "It isn't fair!" I hit the table with my fist. "It isn't fair."

Noah put his arms around me, and I sobbed into his chest and felt Tia's warm arms. I let go of the emotions I'd been holding since I saw Jill.

When I finally stopped, I went to the bathroom, blew my leaky nose, and washed my face. When I came out, there were fresh scones and hot tea waiting. How in the world does she always do that?

"We okay?" she asked.

"I'm okay," I smiled. "Thank you both." I put a hand on Noah's shoulder as I sat.

"This was really a good thing to happen right now," Tia said, "because it shows how our emotions, if not expressed, can block what we need to be doing. And what is that which we are to do? To make miracles out of messes."

"So," asked Noah, "you're saying that what happened to Jill had some ethereal purpose to fulfill?"

"No, I'm not saying things happen with an automatic purpose to be fulfilled. I'm saying that once an event is done, it's done. And then it opens doors to new opportunities, always. But when we're living in reaction to the event, we get swallowed by resistance and miss those opportunities."

"What opportunities can possibly come from Jill's situation?" Noah asked in frustration.

60

"Give me a moment, son, and it will become clear to you. This universe, both visible and invisible, is made of energy. Right?"

We both nodded.

"And every event is loaded with energy when it happens. Otherwise, it couldn't happen. Right?"

Again we nodded.

"So when we encounter an event, our energy tries to align with that energy, and if we allow it, our energy increases. Make sense?"

We both agreed.

"But until we react to it—and this is the tough one for people to get. Until we react to it, it has no meaning and no purpose."

"An event, unless we react to it, has no meaning?" I asked.

"That's right. The event is neutral until someone reacts to it."

"I'm reaching for this," Noah said.

"So, my son, the most profound event that ever happened in this universe: the Big Bang. What new information from that event now guides your life today? What energy empowers your mind?"

He shook his head. "None of it."

"Right. So no matter how immense the event, unless it affects your current consciousness, it's neutral."

"Oh, I got it," he said, and smiled. "Events themselves are neutral. That's amazing!"

"Exactly. Now, today we're reacting to our dear Jill's situation, and the question for each of us is: what will we create out of this? How will we use its information and its energy to create something we want?"

"How about purpose?" I asked. "Doesn't everything happen for a purpose?"

"No, it doesn't. Everything that happens comes with information and energy to allow us to form and follow a purpose. The meaning of something only becomes clear to us when we take action in response to it."

"Wow," said Noah. "My head is ringing. Yet I do think I'm getting this, and it's totally rearranging my thinking. One thing, though. We were talking about the Big Bang. It surely was followed by events that could be called its purpose. Yet no one was reacting. What about that?"

Tia laughed. "Imagine for a moment that the Big Bang was not an event but was itself a reaction to an event. Then you see the domino effect of actions and reactions."

"But I thought someone had to be acting and reacting in order for purpose to be established and followed."

She was still smiling. "There was a consciousness there, acting and reacting, don't you think?"

His eyes opened wide. "God?"

"Well, yes, that's one name for it."

"Now, the two of you have a lot to discuss together. Right now we are creating the purpose of this situation." She looked at each of us in turn. "You're spiritual warriors, more powerful than you yet know. What happened to Jill is now history. What happens from now on is up to us. This is the time not of Jill's destruction but of her rebirth."

"Jill's rebirth?" I said.

She smiled. "She is going to be on this team now. Just wait and see."

Noah had stood and walked away, hands in his pockets.

"We change the future by changing how we see the present,"
he said.

"I couldn't have said it better," Tia replied.

61

"Okay, so then what can we be doing for Jill right now?" I asked.

"We're doing it. We three are communicating with her right now. Even in her unconscious state, she's hearing our thoughts. They're flowing into her on the river of our love. What she needs to know is that we see her strong and well."

"In the now," I said.

"Yes, in the now," Tia said, and nodded.

"There is only now!" I exclaimed.

"Yeah," Noah said. "That's pretty obvious, isn't it?"

"Well, it was never this clear to me. Not until right now. I'm talking about being in this exact instant. I'm talking about being alive and being fully aware of this reality—this moment—this instant."

Then something shifted in me and I felt like I was moving through space, seeing and knowing as I never had before.

Tia watched me with a gentle smile.

My mouth fell open. "Tia," I whispered, "I'm in the second of the Three: right here, right now. This is number two!"

Her eyes shone as she nodded.

I turned to Noah. "What are you feeling?"

His eyes were closed and he was shaking his head. "My God, my God," he said. "Something strong is waking up inside me right now that's real, a lot deeper than words. Like . . . like, wow, like my life is suddenly expanding!"

"Then we're in this together, Noah, waking up in this new reality, this world we've never known before."

Tia sat back in her chair, her hands folded on her lap, and looked from one to the other of us.

"You knew this was going to happen today," I told her. "You knew it."

She replied, "Several weeks ago, you discovered acceptance. And have you become acceptance?"

"Not completely, but it's easier every day."

"Why do you think it's easier?"

"Because I'm more in the present."

"You see how they support each other?"

"Yes, I see that. Acceptance and the here and now are one thing." I sat back and closed my eyes. "Oh, dear Johanna," I said under my breath, "How can I ever thank you enough?"

And Johanna's voice answered, "Be you!"

My eyes popped open. "Did either of you hear that?"

"Hear what?" Noah asked.

"I just heard Johanna say *Be you!*"

"In response to what?"

"I asked her how I could ever thank her enough."

"And she said *Be you*? Perfect answer, don't you think?"

"The perfect answer for both of us, Noah."

"So now that you see how the power of each step makes the others stronger, it's becoming fun, isn't it?" asked Tia.

"But you know," said Noah, "that Johanna chose Keegs to find the Three. That's beautiful and I love it, but what's my place in this?"

"Oh, come on. Johanna didn't just choose Keegan; she chose both of you."

"I don't see that."

"Okay, your job isn't to be on patrol. Right? You're a lieutenant. You're not a patrolman, right?"

He was watching her and nodding.

"Then how did you find yourself the first on the scene of Johanna's accident?"

"I was in an interdepartmental meeting with Oakland PD and on my way back."

"Just coincidence?"

"Well, maybe. I don't know."

"And how did you just happen to be in Golden Gate Park when you met Keegan?"

He rested his chin in his hand and closed his eyes. After a bit he said, "I was in the office that morning and I was frustrated by something I couldn't corner, couldn't figure out. I got out of there and went over to the park, thinking I could get myself settled down."

"And did you?"

He looked at me and said, "My life changed."

"You think any of that is just accident? Coincidence? Do you?"

He grinned happily. "No. Now that I look at it that way, I know it wasn't coincidence. I was chosen too. I was chosen!"

"Johanna knows the two of you are eternally linked. And I think by now that maybe the two of you are getting that too."

Noah turned to me with a grin, and I looked back, blushing.

"Wow," Noah said. "Well, we came here to talk about Jill, and we've just been babbling about ourselves."

"Oh, believe me," Tia said. "What we've been doing is exactly what we need for Jill; there hasn't been a wasted moment."

We fell silent, thinking on her words.

62

Noah leapt to his feet. "Dammit. Dammit! I should have seen this earlier."

"What?" I asked.

"Keegs, have you got your wallet with you?"

"Sure."

"Can you show me Jill's business card?"

"No."

"Why not?"

I shrugged. "Why would I have Jill's business card? I know her number and address."

"Exactly!"

"Oh, my God," I cried. "You're right! Jill wouldn't have my business card in her wallet."

"Someone put it there."

"The same person who cleaned out her wallet."

"And the same person who beat her nearly to death." Noah shook his head. "I should have seen this earlier. There's only one reason why someone would take her ID and leave that card."

"Why?" I asked.

Noah's eyes darkened. "To make damn sure you'd be contacted by the hospital."

"Me? What in hell does this have to do with me?"

Noah leaned forward and gripped my arm. "You know that someone's been after you, don't you?"

"So someone has done this to Jill—because of me."

63

I set up a time with Tia the next morning, and when I arrived, she greeted me with a pot of oolong. I draped my coat on a chairback and sat across from her.

"Little Bird, you're moving into a storm now with Jill and even more that's coming at you. I think you need a stronger support team. What do you think about you and Johanna coming together?"

I smiled. "I'm ready. I'm past my fears."

"Then close your eyes, and let's open ourselves to her."

She led me into a beautiful place, a stillness filled with light and peace.

"Breathe in total acceptance now. Johanna's here; just accept her. Let her be inside you. It doesn't matter if you see her. Simply feel her presence, feel her loving you."

As I swam through that timeless realm, a precious little girl came to me, as light and innocent as a melody. Her presence was palpable, and I welcomed her into my heart. I couldn't help it. She was pure joy. As she looked at me, her thoughts were speaking in my mind. "I have known you all your life, dear Keegan," she said in thought. "I knew you as a child and watched as you gathered the necessary wisdom for your mission. I came to love you as my own daughter. When you were ready, I called you to the bridge. When I spoke to you and heard your voice, it became one of the best days of my life. And now, here you are, ready to know the whole story.

"That day, I did not die. I expanded into a wider dimension. I drove to the bridge, knowing you would be right behind me. When we spoke on the phone, I poured myself into you before I slipped away. That body Noah saw was not me; it was already empty. I am still quite alive, Keegan, and I am always nearby, watching you. And watching Noah. You both have the wisdom of ages with you now. You two will do more than even I did."

From the recesses of my conscious mind, I wondered if I had become Johanna.

"No," she said, laughing. "You are not me. You are your own precious self who accepted the quest of the Three. I watched as you discovered acceptance and then being in the now. Soon you will find the third of the Three and be home. And as you awaken, your love dwelling in Noah awakens him too. My daughter, remember: I'm always here with you."

Then, though I continued to feel her presence, she was gone.

Tia was watching me when I opened my eyes, wiping away tears. "Oh, it's just my happiness," she said.

64

An hour later, Noah picked me up and dropped me off at the hospital, then went to the police station to check leads.

Jill was still unconscious and had been moved to a private room. I had just put my purse down when a doctor came in. He was a short middle-aged man with a pleasant, round face, thinning blond hair, and glasses. "I'm Dr. Johnson, Jill's doctor."

"Yes," I said. "Jill's told me about you. I'm Keegan Tate."

"And Jill told me about you. You're the attorney." He looked through the papers in his hand. "I see here that Jill's family has made you her advocate, which makes it a lot easier for both of us."

I looked at Jill. Her face was still swollen. "Dr. Johnson, what's Jill's prognosis?"

He tucked the papers under his arm and went to stand by her bed, raising his eyebrows and pursing his lips as he studied her. "There's a lot we still don't know yet," he said. He pointed his laser pen at points of Jill's face. "There's a small skull fracture here that I think will heal okay. There's also a bit of intracranial swelling, and we're keeping an eye on that. But we're not seeing a brain bleed, which is good news." He pointed to her bandaged face. "There is a left frontal orbital bone fracture, and the left eye was damaged. We don't know if she'll be able to see with it. We'll just have to wait."

"Doctor, is she going to wake up for sure?"

He turned to me. "Yes, I'm cautiously optimistic that she will. But things happen in trauma as deep as this. It could still go either way."

He turned back to the bed. "We're keeping a close watch on her brain activity." He moved around a step and pointed his laser pen at her chest. "She has three broken ribs, two on one side and one on the other, which means whatever took place was on both sides. The ribs are stationary, and it doesn't look like they damaged any organs. Again, good news."

"And what is your opinion? Do you think she will wake up and be . . . be herself?"

He regarded me briefly, then looked back at Jill, nodding. "Yes. Right now, I think so. She's a strong young woman, so I'm fairly confident."

I sighed with relief. "Can you guess what might have happened?"

He shook his head. "No, not easily. But I can tell you that I know only a few things that can cause injuries like these. The first is falling from a great height and bouncing off something like stairs or a mountainside."

"And the second?"

He crossed his arms and looked at me over his glasses. "Jill's not a rock climber, is she?"

"No."

"Then I can only assume she's been beaten in such a way that her attacker intended her to die."

I gasped.

He put a hand on my arm. "But we are doing our best for her, and we'll know a lot more when she regains consciousness."

65

Three days later, the hospital called to tell me Jill was waking up. I called Noah, then drove through cold wind and blinding rain to be at Jill's side.

Her face was still swollen and bruised. Even with fewer bandages, she was still barely recognizable.

"Jill, can you hear me? It's Keegs."

She peered through the slit in her right eye. "Keegs," she croaked.

I turned at the sound of the door opening. It was Noah with red roses. "How's the patient?"

"She's awake."

"Hello, Jill. I'm Noah."

Jill smiled weakly. "I know about you," she whispered.

"Oh, someone's been telling tales." He pulled up a chair and sat by her side, smiling warmly. "Jill, can you tell us what happened to you?"

Jill looked at him blankly, and for a minute, I didn't think she had heard him. Finally, she breathed. "No idea."

"Well, dear lady, you got pretty badly beaten up by someone."

She seemed to be coming more into focus when she said through a mouth that barely moved, "Oh, well. It's not the first time."

Then she drifted off to sleep, and Noah sat back in thought. After a bit, we slipped out the door. As we walked down the hallway, I vacillated between joy and worry, grateful that she was awake, yet afraid that she wouldn't remember what happened or even be completely Jill anymore.

I went home, tossed my keys on the coffee table, and made tea. I had just settled on the couch to catch up on two days' worth of newspapers when something on the floor caught my eye.

Once again, someone had slipped an envelope under the door while I was in the kitchen. I went to pick it up, filled with dread. My name was across the front in bold letters.

Donning a pair of gloves, I picked it up and took it to the kitchen counter, slit open the envelope, and shook out a folded note and bloody tissue. The tissue had red hair stuck to it.

Noah showed up minutes later, tossed his jacket on the couch, and came into the kitchen. He donned the gloves I handed him. He held the envelope up to the light, then opened it with tweezers. "I can't believe the guy's this stupid!"

The writing was small and neat but the words were badly misspelled, written by someone not familiar with the English language. We read it together.

> So you thot you would get away with being a
> bitch and you could just keep laughing I cuold take
> you out right now but I like watching you suffer
> It will be fun to see your face when your frends
> and your family get paid back for the shit you did
> Lock your doors bitch

Despite the misspellings and lack of punctuation, the message was chilling. I looked up at Noah.

He put an arm around me. "Hey, you okay, Keegs?"

"Am I okay?" I asked him, my voice a whisper. I leaned my head on his shoulder. Then I became angry and pushed away, whirling to face him. "Am I okay, Noah? This is the same sonofabitch who hurt Jill. He beat her up to get to me.

Ran that car off the road and almost killed that little girl and her dad, thinking it was me. Now he wants to hurt my friends and my family."

Then it hit me. "Oh, my God, Noah—my family!"

"Give me their address and phone number," he demanded, his voice forceful. "Now, Keegs!"

I scribbled down the information, and he called the FBI. "I'm a police lieutenant in San Francisco. I need to report a serious crime threat that is about to take place in Missouri."

He covered the phone and looked at me. "Call your parents right now and tell them to get out of the house. Tell them to go to the local police station and call you when they get there."

Then he uncovered the phone. "Yes, thank you. This is Lieutenant Noah Parker with the San Francisco Police Department. We have a situation that needs FBI attention right away. A woman here was beaten almost to death. Her friend, a deputy district attorney here in San Francisco, just received a note from an unknown person who admitted to the crime and says he plans to do the same to her family and friends. We're deeply concerned for her family in Missouri."

While Noah reported the threat, I called my folks. Dad answered on the third ring in his Missouri mellow. "Hey there, sweetheart. Hang on, let me get your mother. She's downstairs."

"No, Daddy, wait! Just stay on the phone and listen to me. You and Mom need to get out of the house right now. Don't ask questions because there's no time. Do it now, Dad. Hurry! Go to the police station and call me from there."

"Oh now, hang on a minute there, sweetheart! Just take a breath and settle yourself down and tell me what this is all about."

I gripped the phone and raised my voice. "Dad, you listen to me now! I don't have time to explain anything to you. You have to trust me. You and Mom are in real danger. Drop whatever you're doing and get out of there. Do it now!"

He paused, and when he spoke again, his voice was strong. "Okay, I got it. I'll call you from the police station."

Noah was still talking to the FBI, but when he saw my frustration, he excused himself, covered the phone with his hand, and said, "Keegs, they've already sent the information to Missouri. Things are moving. Now they need the full story. Don't worry. They're handling it."

I nodded, then went into the bathroom and threw up. Then I leaned my head on the sink and sobbed. A few minutes later, Noah knocked at the door. "Keegs? Can I come in?"

I opened the door and collapsed in his arms. He held me while I cried. Finally, I pulled away and blew my nose. Then I was back in his arms again, feeling his solid body against me, smelling his goodness, and not for the first time, realizing how deeply I loved him.

We went to the living room to wait. It wasn't long before my phone rang. It was Mom, calling to say they were at the police station. Noah took the phone and talked to both her and my dad as well as the police chief. Then Mom and Dad were back on the phone with me, and they agreed to check into a motel for the night.

I relaxed as soon as we hung up, but Noah snapped back into action. He picked up his phone again.

"What is it?"

"It's Jill, dammit! She's unprotected!"

He called the nurses' station. Within minutes, a hospital security officer was headed to Jill's room, and two squad cars were on their way.

66

We parked and ran through the hospital, took an agonizingly slow elevator, and were finally in Jill's room. She was safe, thank God!

I listened while an officer told Noah that, when they arrived, a man was standing by Jill's bed. He fled past them and out the door before they could react, and though the description was vague, one thing was certain: he was a middle-aged man with dark brown hair. His left arm was in a sling, and he wore a glove on his right hand.

Noah put an arm around me. "They found his sling and a syringe in the staircase. They're being sent to the lab for analysis. But if the guy wore gloves, we're out of luck on prints."

"Noah, you just saved her life. If you hadn't figured out that he was coming for her, she'd be dead right now."

He nodded. "Yeah, well, this is my job."

We both turned at the sound of Jill's quiet voice. Noah went to her side to ask if she had seen or heard anything. In a whisper, Jill said her eyes were closed when the man came into the room, and she was so used to technicians and nurses going in and out that she ignored him until he spoke. She opened her eyes just in time to see him dash past the officers. She remembered he wore a brown jacket and dark pants.

"He spoke? What did he say?" asked Noah.

"It was when the others came in." She paused to breathe. "I don't know what he said, something like 'sies' or 'shys.'"

"Do you speak any foreign languages?"

"No. Yes. Spanish . . . and a little French."

Noah stuck his head out into the hallway. "Jake, can you come in here and take some notes?"

The officer guarding the room stepped in and fished a notepad out of his pocket. Noah turned back to Jill. She had closed her eyes again.

"I know this is going to be tough, Jill, but I need you for one more minute. Can you hang with me that long?"

"Sure," she breathed, forcing her eyes open.

"Please help me figure out exactly where the guy was when you first saw him."

"Okay," she said. "I'll try."

"Where was he in the room when he said that word? Tell me where to stand."

"Move closer to that counter, between there and the door. More to your left. A little farther. He was right about there."

"And his back was to you?"

"Yes."

"How tall do you think he was. Taller than me?"

"Shorter."

"Okay, I'm going to bend my knees. Tell me when you think I'm about at the right height." He bent his knees, keeping his back to Jill.

"Stop about there," she whispered.

"Jake, can you measure this?"

"I got it, Lieutenant."

"Good, good!" Noah straightened up, facing away from Jill, and said, "Now I'm going to stand in this exact position. Were the lights on or off?"

"Only the nightlight was on," she said, her voice fading.

Jake turned off the lights, and Noah squatted back down. "Still about this tall?"

"Yes."

"Okay. Now I'm going to say the word you might have heard. Tell me if it sounds right."

Jill had closed her eyes again. "I'll try."

Noah spat out a word angrily. *"Scheisse!"*

"Oh yeah, that's exactly what he said."

Noah walked over to Jill and gently put his hand on her shoulder. "You've done great, Jill. Now rest. There will be an officer outside your door day and night to make sure no one bothers you again. I will do everything I can to keep you safe."

I kissed Jill's forehead as she closed her eyes. She fell asleep instantly, and I followed Noah into the hallway. "What does that word mean?"

"It's a German swear word. He said it when he realized he was caught."

"You speak German?"

He shrugged. "Enough to know the swear words anyway. Hopefully, it'll narrow the field a bit."

"So what happens now?"

"We check security cameras in the hospital, then we wait. Maybe we'll get lucky."

We did get lucky. Two hospital cameras caught the man's face. Interpol then identified him through their facial recognition software as a German contract killer, Otto Beck. They—and Noah—thought Beck might be the same person who ran the car off the road. Noah figured someone who didn't want to be identified found Jill near death and brought her to the hospital.

A doctor had told us that it was not unusual for people to not want to get involved, But Beck had made a mistake: our tough Jill had survived his monstrous beating. And yet it seemed he was still under orders to fulfill his contract.

We sat in Noah's car in the hospital parking lot. I looked at him and wanted to reach out and touch him, feel him against me, and soothe the angst churning inside me.

"I think he did want to kill her when he beat her," I said.

"His beating her was a message to me; he never intended for her to survive. He didn't know her strength."

"I agree," said Noah. "He was sure she wouldn't make it. And you're right: it was a message to you. This was personal."

I shuddered. "Then why doesn't that rat bastard just come after me? Why Jill? Why my family?"

"Hmm . . ." He closed his eyes and wrinkled his forehead. "Now, that's a question we should look at more closely. Maybe he wasn't trying to kill you by running your car off the road. Maybe he was just trying to terrify you and never intended the car to go over the cliff, just to crash against the guardrail."

He looked over at me. "I think this guy has screwed up his job. He's supposed to be making you suffer, not kill you. If I'm right, whoever's paying him doesn't want you to die yet. They want you to suffer."

"Well, that's sure as hell working." I shook my head in frustration. "I guess I must have done something really bad to someone!"

67

It was a cold afternoon with a storm blowing off the Pacific. Rain rattled against the windows. I leaned against Noah on the living room couch, wondering how I could have gotten through this without him.

"Noah," I said, "this Otto Beck. Will the police ever actually find him?"

He looked into space and was quiet. "Not right now, I don't think; Beck's gone to ground."

Just then my cell phone rang, and I looked at Noah. I knew it was Beck before I picked it up.

Noah nodded. I picked it up and hit the speaker button. "Hello?"

His voice was nasal and higher than I expected, almost whiny. "So you now search for me, yes?"

Noah was punching numbers into his phone, and I was praying he had some way to trace the call.

I stood up as if confronting an opponent in court. "Otto Beck?"

"Ah, so you have my name. Good, and now I have one more message for you."

"Just stop, Mr. Beck. Stop and tell me what you want from me. What have I ever done to you?"

"You shut up now!" he barked. "I am talking, and you are listening now!" He paused. "You are listening?"

"I'm listening."

"Your sweet life is over! Now you will pay for a life you smashed. You have loved taking people out of their families and watching them die. Now, you *schwein*, you will see how it is to lose the people you love."

"Mr. Beck, I don't know you. I never prosecuted you. I've never even met you."

"Not me, no, but good people, yes?"

"But not you! So you're working for someone, right? Someone hired you to hurt me?"

The line went dead. I looked at Noah, my heart hammering like a machine gun. My knees had turned to jelly. I dropped into a chair. "Did someone get the number?"

"Yeah, we got it. It's a payphone, and we know where, but he'll be long gone before anyone gets there. Still, we might get some prints."

"Prints? What good will fingerprints do? We already know who he is."

"We'll check them against prints in international databases and confirm it's Beck, then maybe get some background. It's not catching him, but it maybe gets us closer."

I looked at him. "Noah, he called me! He has my cell phone number, and I had him on the phone! I talked to the bastard who beat up Jill. And I froze! I should have played it cool. I should have gotten more information, but I was paralyzed. I couldn't think. I did nothing."

"Oh, not true," Noah said, shaking his head. "You did plenty."

"Oh yeah? Like what? What did I do?"

"Keegs, we now know that whoever's targeting you is someone you prosecuted. That narrows down the list. Now we go over cases you won and see who shakes out. And we also learned that the game's changed; he's not getting paid to kill you but to toy with you, to make you suffer. And much as I hate saying it, that's good news because it means we know what he's up to. Besides, if he's working alone, your parents are safe because he's here in San Francisco."

"And if he's not working alone? Then what?"

"The FBI is setting up a sting. They're putting an older couple in your folks' home as bait."

"Noah, my parents really are safe, aren't they?"

He looked out the window where the wind rattled rain against the glass, then looked back at me. "Listen, Keegs. I've got a good friend down in Sarasota, Florida, who just lost her husband. Her house is way too big for her, and she's been begging me to visit. I know she could use some company. Would your folks go to Sarasota to stay with my friend if they're invited?"

"Oh yeah, you bet they will," I said, nodding. "I'll make sure of it."

"Good. I'll call Beth and get that ball rolling."

Then something else occurred to me. "Noah, Beck's going to come after you too!"

He grinned. "Oh, if only he would come after me! But he's not going to do that. He's not stupid enough to come after an armed police officer."

"Yeah, but you're not always armed."

He looked at me strangely. "Of course I am."

I raised my eyebrows. "Noah, what about right now? You're not armed now, are you?"

"Well, no," he said. "My gun is not in my pocket; it's in my jacket. Listen, Keegs, my job right now is to keep you and the people you love safe, and you can bet that I'm damn well going to do it."

His cell phone rang. When he answered it, I went to make tea; when I returned, he had just hung up. "Beck was gone from the payphone, but they got prints. Now we'll make sure it was him."

"How would he not know to wipe down the phone?"

"He was in a hurry," he grinned. "You scared him."

"How? By saying he was working for someone?"

"Yep," he said, and nodded. And that tells us that he's afraid of whoever hired him. Our Mr. Beck is scared of screwing this up and getting himself killed."

I found that hard to believe. "A contract killer is afraid of someone killing him?"

"Oh yeah," Noah said. "There's always someone more dangerous than him. He knows that."

68

When we arrived at Jill's room the next morning, her bed was raised and she was partially sitting up, conscious, alert, and happy to see us.

The swelling in her face had gone down some, and the bruises were turning yellow. I fought back tears.

"Hey." Jill couldn't smile yet, but her eyes were brighter. "You brought chocolate, right?" Her voice was amazingly clear and strong.

"Well, I guess you're feeling better if you want chocolate," I teased.

"No, no," she said. "I don't want it; I need it. I need lots of chocolate to get me well."

How could she have come back so fast? This was unreal. This was a world of miracles, and I was just waking up. "I'll go down to the gift shop and get you some chocolate. But first, tell us what the doctor's saying."

"He came in this morning and did some tests. He said I'm getting some of my eyesight back."

"Are you actually seeing out of that eye?"

"It's pretty blurry, but the doc says that's normal for now."

"You are getting well so fast, Jill!"

"Maybe, but I'm really dull-headed. I might have lost some brain function, so my IQ will drop even lower."

"You nut!" I said. "If your IQ drops twenty points, you'll still be a genius."

Noah had stayed back, but now he came around me and handed her a bouquet of red roses.

"Ooh, how pretty!"

"For a pretty lady." Noah flashed his smile.

"Ha!"

"Let me go find something to put these in. Be right back."

"Ooo, he looks yummy. Where did you find him?"

"He's the policeman from the park I told you about. And yes, he is yummy."

"Then you take good care of him, you hear?"

"Yes, dear sister, I hear you. But right now, I want to know how you're doing. Are you in pain? And other than chocolate, what can I get you?"

"Patience. This damn bed makes my butt sweat. I feel like a wadded tissue in here." She sighed. "You have no idea what it's like to be stuck in a bed this long."

"I can imagine."

"But hey, I am getting well, and other than a little pain, it's all good."

"What an attitude, lady. Can I borrow it?"

Noah returned with the roses in a glass vase.

"They really are beautiful. Thank you, guys!"

"Don't thank me," I said. "That's Noah's deal."

"Thanks, handsome!"

"Don't you be flirting with my cop, you vamp!"

Noah asked, "Jill, you feel well enough to talk about what happened?"

"I'll try."

"First, I want you to know that, because of your help, we discovered who this guy is and what he's up to. And you'll be under constant protection until we get him."

Jill put a hand to her chest. "Why would anyone want to hurt me?"

"The guy's name is Otto Beck. He's a German hitman. He came after you because Keegs here loves you."

"Because Keegs loves me? Why hurt me because I'm close to Keegs?"

"We think she sent someone to prison who wants to hurt people she loves."

Jill looked at me, frowning. "Are there more, then? More people who are being attacked?"

I didn't want her to know about the car incident. "No, Jill. Not yet, anyway. My folks are safe. The other two people that I love are both in this room."

She looked at Noah and me in turn, then said, "You love this big galoot?"

I felt my face warming. "I do. Yes, I do."

Noah dropped his head, suddenly bashful. "Jill, we're going to keep you safe. We'll catch Herr Beck, and when we do, we'll find out who hired him. This will all end very soon. I promise you that."

She nodded confidently. "That's true, Noah. You'll catch him very soon and then plant a trap to find out who hired him."

Noah frowned. "What do you mean?"

Jill looked at me, then said softly. "I don't know how to tell you this, Keegs, but I'm now in your twilight zone. I'm seeing things . . . knowing things."

"Oh, my God, Jill. I am so sorry."

"Sorry? Hey, don't be sorry. I told you at the house that I wanted what you have!"

"But did you have to get nearly killed to get it?"

"Well, if that's what it takes. Maybe it's my initiation or my tuition."

I grasped her hand. "Then I have some excellent news for you. We have a dear woman who understands all this and is our coach."

She tried to smile, but it didn't come off. "Are you talking about the sweet old Mexican woman with the amazing eyes?"

I looked at her, incredulous. "You've met Tia Ana?"

"Well, I didn't know her name till now, but she came and

sat with me when I first came in here. She told me what was happening. She said: 'You are unfolding into the Light.' When she said that, I started glowing inside. And she said she was going to help me. After she left, I felt grounded in a new place. I love this place."

"She actually came here?" Noah asked. "She sat in this room?"

Jill cocked her head. "Is that so strange?"

"She told us she'd seen you but didn't come here in person; she came another way."

Jill shrugged. "Well, I'm just looking forward to spending time with her." She turned her head slowly, obviously in pain, to look out the window. "I've been looking for her all my life."

The door opened, and in came a police officer with a large bowl of ice cream covered in chocolate sauce. He set the bowl on Jill's tray without a word, swung the tray over her bed, nodded to Noah and me, then left.

Jill picked up the spoon and prepared to dig into the creamy mound. "Chocolate ice cream with chocolate sauce! Someone's been listening to my prayers."

"Stop!" I said. "Don't eat that!"

69

Jill froze. "Good lord, Keegs! It's only chocolate. What's your problem?"

I looked at Noah and whispered, "She said someone was listening to her prayers." I turned to Jill. "Did you ask someone to get you chocolate ice cream?"

"No, but I'm sure going to eat it!"

"No," Noah whispered, taking the bowl away. "No, you're not." He turned to me. "Keegs, jam that chair under the door handle when I leave. And don't let anyone in. I mean no one!"

He slipped out the door, and with my heart racing, I wedged a chair beneath the door handle.

Beyond the door, I heard him demand an ID. Then there was banging, grunting, and scuffling that seemed to go on forever. My heart was in my throat. I looked at Jill; she was watching me. I wanted so badly to open the door, terrified I would lose him.

Then there was silence. I looked over at Jill. "He's okay, Keegs. He's fine."

Someone knocked on the door. "Keegs, it's me!"

I pulled the chair away and opened the door. Noah's shirt was ripped and pulled out of his trousers. Blood flowed from a deep gash on the left side of his forehead. Out in the hallway, a man lay face down on the floor. His shoes were off, his hands were tied behind his back with shoelaces, and his pants were pulled down around his ankles.

"My God, Noah, what the hell's going on?"

He grinned and pointed his chin toward the man on the floor. "Allow me to introduce you to Herr Otto Beck."

My mouth dropped open. "That's him? That's Otto Beck?"

"Yes, my dear, that's him. Now, let me get this little cut handled before I bloody up everything."

"I've already called for a nurse," Jill said. She held up her cell phone. "I also called the cops. Your buddies are on their way up."

"Damn, lady!" Noah exclaimed. "You are definitely on this team."

We soon learned that Beck had lured the guard officer away, knifed him, and stuffed his body in a janitor's closet. He knew the nursing shift was about to change, and he'd heard Jill ask for chocolate, so figuring the shift change was his best opportunity, he got a dish of chocolate ice cream from the cafeteria and dosed it with a deadly toxin.

As I listened to Jill and Noah talk, their voices began to fade, and I felt myself being pulled up and out of the room into that vast, quiet peace where Tia often took me. It no longer felt foreign; I traveled farther each time, and I'd grown to love it.

I excused myself, stepped into the hall, leaned against the wall, closed my eyes, and fell deep into that endless dimension. I focused on knowing each step necessary to keep my loved ones safe.

I returned to Jill's room in time to hear her ask Noah, "So he's off to jail, and we're all safe?"

Noah shook his head. "No, not safe yet." He put his finger to his lips and motioned around the room that it still might be bugged. Jill nodded.

"Jill," he said, "we've decided to move you someplace safe later this afternoon. Right now, we're putting two guards outside your door."

"And," I said, "I'm staying with you today."

"Oh good, a slumber party!" Jill tried smiling through broken lips.

I turned to Noah. "Where is this somewhere safe?"

"I'm going right now to find a place," he said. Brushing a kiss on my lips, he was gone.

I took a book out of my bag and sat by the window to read. I had chosen *The Wind in the Willows* because I needed that simple and honest melody again in my heart. Before I could open the book, Jill was fast asleep. I had read for nearly an hour when Noah slipped quietly into the room and sat beside me.

"It's handled," he whispered, putting an arm around my shoulders.

Almost as if she felt us, Jill woke up. "So what's happening?" she asked sleepily.

"I've got great news," Noah said. "We found a studio apartment for you, Jill. It's out on Masonic, just off Geary. We'll take you there tonight by ambulance and get you in without anyone seeing you."

In an innocent voice, Jill asked, "But what about my doctor and my meds?"

"Not to worry," Noah said. "We've figured that out; we'll disguise your doctor as a UPS driver. He'll go over every day with a package."

"But won't I need police protection?" Her mischievous grin told me she was enjoying the game.

"No, no. Any officers in the area will look suspicious. You'll be alone there, but you'll be perfectly safe."

"Okay, then," Jill said. "I trust you."

70

At one o'clock the next morning, a female police officer with a bandaged head and makeup bruises was wheeled out of Jill's room, put into an ambulance, and taken to an apartment. Two plainclothes officers, already inside, would hide with her there for a week. The apartment was stocked with enough food and supplies to last. Jill was moved to a private room on a different floor an hour later.

The first night in the apartment was quiet, and the three officers got a full night's sleep. The next day, Noah and I visited, bringing a bouquet of flowers.

The second night at three in the morning, a shadowy figure jimmied open a window to the bedroom. He had only taken a few steps toward the bed when the lights went on, and he was facing three guns.

Noah and I recapped the events over breakfast at my place the following morning.

"He's just like Herr Beck," Noah said. "Even after over an hour of questioning, he won't tell us who hired him. Whoever that guy is, he must be powerful enough to have both this guy and Beck afraid to talk."

As soon as Noah said that, a thought erupted. "Noah, I think I know who it is. Damn! Why couldn't I have seen this earlier?"

"You do? You think you know who it is?"

"I prosecuted an eighteen-year-old kid who stabbed a woman nine times during a store robbery. He was sent away for life."

"A teenager? This isn't the work of a teenager, Keegs."

"You'll see—let me get the files."

I called Frank and asked him to pull the files. Noah sent an officer to pick them up. Two hours later, we looked at a photo of David Ricci, a sweet-looking young man with thick black hair and big brown eyes. I remembered him well because, despite his sweet nature, he showed no remorse for having butchered the mother of three young children. At the time, his gangster father, Benedetto Ricci, was serving a sentence for armed bank robbery.

Noah leaped into action. "Let me call and find out what we know about these two Ricci gentlemen."

I went to the kitchen and put some cookies on a plate, and when I came back, Noah was staring at the ceiling, his hands behind his head. He saw the cookies. "What is this? Every time we hit a snag or get a win, here come cookies and tea?"

"My cookies are brain food, so just shut up and eat!"

"I think you found him," he said. "Benedetto Ricci got out of prison two months ago. According to the warden, a few weeks earlier, he had a run-in with a couple of guys who wanted him dead, but he was mobbed up, so he was protected. A week after his release, his son David was stabbed to death in the shower; it was payback for whatever Benedetto did."

"So Benedetto Ricci is blaming me for his son's death?"

"Looks like it, because you put David in prison. We're chasing down Ricci's parole officer now. Let's hope he knows where he is."

The parole officer had not seen Ricci since his last home visit fifteen days earlier. But a bulletin went out, and a week later, Ricci was picked up by police in San Diego. Noah flew down to see him.

Ricci wasn't hiding his hatred of me in the least. He vowed to butcher every one of my relatives and friends, even from prison. When I heard it, my gut knotted. But Noah said they were idle threats Ricci couldn't carry out. When he went to trial, my old boss, Frank, prosecuted him.

He was found guilty of attempted murder and accessory to murder. He was sentenced to life without the possibility of parole.

71

Jill got better and Noah wanted to ask Jill questions about something she said earlier. We came to her hospital room bearing an extra thick hot chocolate.

Jill's face lit up. "Ooh! Just what I needed today," she told Noah. "You're an angel."

"Now, can I ask you a personal question? Not about what happened here but about something else."

Jill took a sip of her cocoa and closed her eyes. "You bring me extra rich hot chocolate, you can ask anything. And yes, I'll marry you!"

"Okay, so that's out of the way. But seriously now, what did you mean the other day when you said that being beaten was not new for you?"

Jill set her drink down and gazed into the distance thoughtfully. "Well, I'll tell you guys this one time. But it's not a pretty story."

"It's all right," I said. "We need to hear it."

She looked at Noah for a long moment. "I had two childhoods. One was playing with my friends and going to school. I carried myself so that it looked to my friends like my life was normal. But underneath it, I was a festering sore."

She wiped away a sudden tear. "Now, don't feel bad; I'm not crying for me but for that little girl. We're not the same person anymore."

Noah frowned. "What in hell was going on, Jill?"

"Well, I had a brother, Bart, Bartholomew. Bart was four years older than me and hated me from the day I was born. When I was an infant still in my crib, my mom caught him trying to strangle me with a lamp cord. The family laughed and told the story for years; they thought it was funny. That was only the beginning. Bart seethed with his hatred of me. He was never my brother. He was a monster."

She stared out the window as if seeing it all again. After a few minutes, she sighed and went on. "I had my mom's red hair and blue eyes, and I shared her love for music. Bart hated me for that. He was dark-complected like my dad, but unlike Dad, Bart had an inner rage, one I eventually learned was pathological sadism. As a psychologist, I came to understand him. He tortured animals, and when he couldn't find animals, he tortured me. He'd grab my skin in sharp, twisting pinches, stomp on my toes, and punch me where the bruises wouldn't be seen. He'd hold and twist my breasts and laugh when I cried. I hated him with all my heart, and I wished he would die. I know he would have killed me if he could have gotten away with it.

"When I showed my mother the bruises and told her what he was doing, she scolded him. 'Bart,' she said, 'women are softer than men. You have to be more gentle.' He hung his head and said, 'Gosh, Mom, I'm sorry. I was only teasing her.'

"Then Mom would look at me and say, 'And, Jill, you stop being such a big baby. Your brother loves you. Can't you be just a little nicer to him?'

"Well, after that, I stopped telling on him because it always came back on me. That's how clever he was. Mom and Dad loved me but refused to see our family as less than perfect. Their denials gave Bart the freedom to raise all the hell he wanted. He spit in my food, he stole my dolls and dismembered them, and he wiped his butt with his finger and smeared it on my face. That and more, constantly. But in front of our parents, he was a polite, almost humble boy, asking how my day was, pretending, always pretending, and getting away with it. My parents bought his act, hook, line, and sinker.

"Then when I was about twelve, his cruelty became sexual. I told Mom again, and she just shook her head and told me to be more careful around him. At first, he just felt me up, then he started forcing me to touch his penis. He grabbed me by the throat many times. He threatened to kill me and both our parents if I told a soul. I totally believed him because he had gotten away with doing whatever he wanted all those years.

"Every night, I prayed he would die. I begged God to let a rattlesnake bite him or a truck crush him. But it never happened. He just went gleefully on, destroying me.

"During those years, Mom and Dad always worked late, giving Bart all the hours he wanted with me. So I just stopped going home after school. I found a little spot to hide along a river bank a few blocks from our house. I sat there in the afternoons, day after day, doing my homework, reading, and daydreaming until it got dark. I went home only when I knew my parents would be there.

"Then one day, he followed me. He jumped into my little sanctuary, laughing. He slammed his fist into the side of my head and called me his little whore. My hearing in that ear never came totally back. He knocked me on my back and jumped on me with his full body. I actually felt my ribs break."

She paused and closed her eyes, and we were quiet. Finally, she continued, her voice barely more than a whisper. "He choked me until I saw only blackness, then he tried to rape me. But he couldn't penetrate me, so he jammed a stick up inside me instead. It felt like I was being torn apart. "He kept saying, 'Like this, don't you, little whore? Feels real good, doesn't it, little whore?'"

She looked back at us, her face drawn. "To this day, I remember the look on his face: it was pure evil.

"When he was finished, he leaned over me and waved his finger in my face and said, 'Now you listen, you little bitch. You tell anyone, even one person, and I'll find out. And when I do, I'll kill you, and I'll kill Mom, and I'll kill Dad.' He straightened up and grinned down at me. 'And you know I'll do it.' He was smiling when he said it.

"I could barely breathe, much less speak, but I nodded. He got up, stomped on my stomach, and then strutted away, whistling, like he'd just won a battle.

"I lay there for the longest time. I've never felt such pain and so degraded. Oh, God . . . I wanted to die! But I finally pulled my clothes on and sat on that riverbank, crying. I cried for the longest time. My life was over. I wanted so much that day to jump in that roiling water and go to the bottom. But why bother? I felt like I was already dead, so what was the point?"

My heart broke for my friend, and I wept freely. Jill and I had been like sisters, yet she had somehow kept this hidden from me. I wiped my tears, but they just kept coming.

"When finally I did stagger out of the woods, a neighbor woman saw me and saw the blood on my jeans. She scooped me up and took me to the hospital. I was in there about a week while they dealt with internal injuries and infection. I had a concussion and some broken ribs."

She forced a smile. "So, my dears, me and my ribs have danced this dance before. And you know, being in the hospital is awful for most people, but back then, it was the first time I'd ever felt safe."

"What happened to Bart?"

"The hospital called the police, and they arrested him. And of course, he had his story ready. He said when I didn't come home, he went looking for me and found me by the river having sex with a big black guy. He said I was blaming him to cover up for my lover."

"Sounds like he hated blacks?"

"Oh yeah. Bart hated everybody. But yeah, he hated blacks. He talked about them like they were subhuman. I now realize the truth: he was scared to death of them."

"Did the police find out what happened?"

"I heard later that they kept grilling him until all his lies fell flat. That's when my parents finally realized that their son was a sociopath, a monster. Of course, they were steeped in shame when they realized how they'd let him torture me all those years."

"Did you forgive them?" I asked.

"Yeah, I did. It took me a lot of years, but eventually, I did. They are good and loving people; they were just asleep. My anger at them was hurting all three of us. I also had to wake up."

She shrugged one shoulder. "It's hard to believe, but sometimes intelligent people just can't see what is outside their comfort zones."

"And," I said through my tears, "that's just how monsters like him, and even like Hitler, get their power: by people unwilling to see."

"So what happened to Bart?" asked Noah.

"He never came home. He went to a juvenile facility. After three years, he got out, but he never came home, and we never saw him again. I heard he joined a gang in Chicago, and then there was nothing. Then two years ago, my folks told me Bart had been killed in a shootout with the police.

"I cried for hours when I heard. But I wasn't crying for Bart; I was crying for my lost girlhood and whoever else he'd hurt. Those tears purged me. That's when I finally forgave my parents."

"Damn," said Noah, shaking his head. "Jill, I'm sorry you've now had to go through this again."

Then as best she could with her swollen mouth, she smiled. "Hey, don't be sorry. Something really cool happened in this."

I raised my eyebrows. "Something cool happened in this? Jill, you're kidding."

"No," she said, and shook her head slightly, wincing from the pain. "I'm not. Look, all those years of that dark place in me, subconsciously feeling like I was trash, thinking that being tortured and raped must have had something to do with who I was as a person not worthy of being loved and protected? Until now, that black hole in me had never completely dissolved. For my whole life, I would wake up sometimes in the night filled with self-loathing and hatred for Bart. I felt that a good part of me, an innocent part of me, had been permanently destroyed.

"But you know what? Now it happened again—but this time I'm not a naïve little girl. Now I'm seeing through a new viewpoint: both Bart and Beck are monsters, and who they are and what they did has nothing at all to do with me, nothing to do with who I am. That old pain, that dark, ugly Bart pain? That's gone now. I'm clean and free, and life is good."

She smiled. "And I'm with you two goofballs, reinforcing how much I'm loved. And I got to know Tia Ana, the woman I've spent my whole life waiting for."

Three weeks after she was attacked, all the bandages were gone and she could see a bit with her injured eye. The eye doctor was optimistic that her full vision might return. She would have permanent scars along her hairline, but that didn't seem to bother her. "Makes me look tough," she said. "Now I can walk on the dark side, and no one'll screw with me."

72

My folks were still in Florida and enjoying it more than they thought they would. My dad had insisted he go home to work on the farm until I finally convinced him I had the funds to pay for laborers and that the work would get done without him there. So he went fishing.

I was winding my way home from the hospital on another cold, windy day when my phone rang. It was Johanna's son, Clement. I pulled over to speak to him.

"Keegs, my good sister! I hope you are well."

"I am well, Clement, and it's nice to hear your voice. How are you, and how are Angela and Bernadette?"

"We're all well, thanks. They send their affections."

"How can I help you, Clement?" I almost didn't want to ask in case there was a problem with the will.

"Well, this is a bit awkward, Keegs, and I hope you'll take it the right way. Mom wasn't the only one in our family with *the gift*. Her brother, my uncle Benjamin, is even more . . . well . . . spiritually advanced."

"God, Clement, how wild must it have been to grow up in your family!"

He laughed. "Wild is right. It seemed either Mom or Uncle Benjamin were always making some magic happen."

"Oh, this stuff was even happening while you were growing up?"

"Oh yeah, for sure. Mom and Uncle Benjamin were always talking about stuff before it happened. You know, Keegs, we each have a little of their gift, but none of us has opened ourselves to it entirely. Not like them, and surely not like you."

"I can understand your reluctance to swim in this river, Clement. It took me long enough to get the hang of it."

"But you know, Keegs, once that door opens, you've got to step through. If you don't, you eventually have to look at how much you goofed by ignoring it."

"Clement, are you talking about you?"

"Yes, I sure am. I could have been expanding my consciousness for years. I'm only now beginning. And I have you to thank for that. Did you know that?"

"How is that?"

"Because you took a bigger risk than any of us. You were a successful practicing attorney with a settled life, and you were willing to toss it all away for this."

"That's because I finally came to see what 'this' is. It's a damn sight more rewarding and maybe even more valuable than what I was doing."

Then thinking how pretentious that might sound, I added, "Of course, that's me. Your mom selected me. I tried my best to go back to my old life, but it just didn't work. Your mom was dead right." *Dead right?* "Oh God, Clement, what a terrible thing to say. I'm sorry!"

But he was laughing. "Oh man," he said with a laugh. "Dead right. I can't wait to tell the girls. That's hilarious."

"Thanks for taking it that way."

"No problem. Now, back to business and why I called: Uncle Benjamin wants to meet you."

"He wants to meet me?" I asked in surprise. "What in the world for?"

"Keegs, Uncle Benjamin knows who you are. He's known for years because he and Mom talked about you. Now he feels he can help you move forward. What do you say? Will you meet with him?"

"Well, of course I will. I'd be honored to meet him."

"Good, good. Then he'll be in touch. Incidentally, Uncle

Benjamin is one of the kindest men you'll ever know. I'm sure you'll come to love him as much as we do. And be prepared for a pleasant surprise. I won't tell you what it is."

I got home, kicked off my shoes, and called Tia. We'd only talked once since Otto Beck was arrested. Noah was out of town, testifying on a case, which meant I had Tia to myself. I arranged to meet with her the next afternoon.

73

As if on schedule, the rain stopped the next day, and mare's tail clouds drifted on a high blue ceiling as I drove through Haight-Ashbury, enjoying candy-colored homes flushed with afternoon sunshine.

Tia greeted me with a hug and led me to our usual table. "I'm glad you're here," she said, "because I have a surprise for you."

A surprise from Tia could mean anything. Then I saw the table was set for three, and I thought Noah must have returned. It was the kind of surprise that would make my day.

But then a man appeared from the kitchen, and I couldn't stop staring at his dark ebony complexion, his snow-white hair and beard, and his endless, truly endless blue eyes. He wore a light blue shirt and tan slacks, and his visual and spiritual presence filled the place. I had never experienced such an immediate personal impact.

And there it was again: I knew him. I had no idea how, but I had known him my whole life.

I was to learn that this man was the soul of kindness and humility. I was to realize that it was simple humility that made him so enchanting and delightful.

He reached out and took my hand, smiling. "Keegan Tate. Thank you for agreeing to meet me."

"Oh my! You're Benjamin Gooding!"

He laughed. "Yes, I am. And I'll bet Clement told you I'd be a surprise."

"Yes," I admitted, "he did, and he also told me it would be a pleasant surprise. And again, he was right."

Then I saw Tia drying her hands on her apron and smiling at us.

I looked from one to the other in disbelief. "You two know each other?"

They exchanged glances. "Yes," Tia said. "We know each other."

"But how . . . I mean . . . for how long?" I was lost.

"Oh," Tia said, placing her hand on Benjamin's arm, "I've known this sweet man for more years than I can count. But we only met in person yesterday."

Benjamin sat across from me as we ate lunch.

"You must be wondering," he said, "how a black man could be part of the Gooding family."

"Something like that."

"I was eight years old and living in an orphanage in Nigeria when the Goodings heard about . . . my gift. They flew over to meet me, and then they adopted me. Not a very dramatic story, I'm afraid, but that's it."

"It's a good story," I said. "Thank you."

"And my blue eyes? Well, that's a mystery, like yours of blue and brown. It's fun, isn't it?"

I nodded, smiling. "With your skin and those blue eyes, you've been blessed."

Benjamin sipped his coffee, his eyes closed. Then he looked at Tia, nodded, and turned to me.

"As you know, Keegan, many of us are born with this ability, and if we let it guide us, it grows as we mature. It's actually pretty unusual, yet not unheard of, for it to awaken at your age and at the ages of your two friends. But of course," he said with a shrug, "it was always there in you. It was just being covered up by a mind that thought other avenues were more important."

"So this awakening: it can happen to anyone?"

"Oh, sure it can, because some level of this gift is in every one of us. Still, it usually lies dormant because of religious teachings and intellectual demands and such. People don't even allow themselves to see it, much less accept it."

"Yep," I said, and nodded. "That was sure me!"

"I know," he said. "Some in our community were concerned it might be too big a shock at your age. And yet you and your two friends are moving along quite well. I now see that we needn't have been concerned."

"Well, that's because of Tia. She's been nursing us along with her ruthless yardstick and her great cooking."

Tia laughed. "You haven't seen the yardstick yet. That's at your next level."

Benjamin said, "Yes, you three are coming awake nicely now. Our whole community is watching."

"Community?"

He smiled. "I call it the community because it's an affiliation of those in this dimension of love."

"Wait a minute—of *love*?"

"Okay," he said. "I know that sounds a little strange. Love must be the most overused and least understood word in any language. I'm saying that those living in this consciousness, in this awareness, are in an expanded reality. They experience more color, texture, and wonder. That can only be love."

"Well, love's an emotion, right? Love's an expanded emotion."

He looked down at the table for a moment and then at me through those snowy eyebrows, "Not an emotion, Keegan. No, love is life—is energy—the only energy in this universe. When we are one with that energy, we are nature, nature as God. We are love."

He paused to drink his tea, then looked away into the empty restaurant. "When you're in this place, you and all others in this place are connected. We're family; we're a community."

"Does that .. does this community get together ever? To meet each other and to talk?"

He glanced at Tia, who watched him intently. "No," he answered. "The vast majority of us never see each other. And yet we're connected. I can't tell you how we come to know each other. But let me ask you this: when you met Ana here, and when you met Noah, did you feel like you'd always known them?"

I nodded. "Yes . . . I sure did. I also knew you."

"So when we're awake, that's what happens. We meet ourselves in others. It's like coming home to family, isn't it?" Because we're connected in that wonderous and mysterious way. We know each other."

"So," I said with a smile, "what's my next step?"

He looked at me, his blue eyes boring into my psyche. "I think you know that. Right? My sis asked you to find the Three."

"She did, yes. And I'm well on my way to it. Let me ask you this: when I've found the Three, will I have made it? Will this constant need to change and grow level out and get easier?"

Benjamin nodded to Tia, who said, "Yes, it will get easier. A lot easier. Because you'll be in the flow of nature, in the flow of this universal energy. But the challenges will grow with you; they'll always be greater."

I sighed. "That doesn't sound like much fun."

"Oh, but it will be because you'll be empowered. As Benjamin says, you'll be love, not simply loving. That's all power and wisdom, as you. It won't ever level out because, by its very nature, it is *constant expansion into wisdom and joy*."

"This path's forever, Keegan!" Benjamin chimed in. "It never ends. And it's always exciting and more surprising."

I glanced at Tia. She was watching us closely.

"Well, I guess that makes sense," I said, "because that's sure true for me. Right now every day is filled with wonders."

"Like your clouds?" Benjamin asked.

"Do I have no secrets?"

"Ana and I see you expanding. We see new portals opening in your life. Not so long ago, you told Ana that you felt like you were free-falling. What a wonderful expression! Now you're changing the falling into flying."

Tia went to the kitchen and returned with steaming bowls of vegetable stew and a plate of sliced apples with chunks of cheese.

Benjamin bowed his head and blessed the food in a soft voice, and we ate in silence, savoring the rich vegetables and the light-as-air dumplings.

When we finished eating, Tia said, "My niece, one day you will realize that your life before now was lived deep in a cave where you were convinced that the shadows on the back walls were reality. Then along came Johanna, and you turned around and stepped outside into this vast foreverness. Now you're becoming one with it."

"Foreverness sounds a little scary," I said."

"Yes," said Benjamin. "Scary and exciting."

Then while Tia and Benjamin talked, I listened to their stories of miracles and miracle workers from long ago in faraway places. And as I listened, I realized how vast this new consciousness was: a vast society of sacred warriors moving throughout the world, healing and creating harmony. It was neither cult nor clan but rather members of the human family waking up together in different parts of the world.

I was thrilled, realizing I was now one of them.

74

I called Noah. "I ordered a pizza."

He chuckled. "I'm on my way."

He walked through the door and into my arms. It was like being folded into a clean blanket that smelled of warm cinnamon.

We ate pizza as he told me the trial had not gone well. "The judge disallowed the critical evidence because someone in the cop shop did a sloppy job putting it together."

"Didn't the prosecutor know that that evidence would be disallowed?"

He snorted. "We needed a Keegan Tate."

I smiled. "Keegan Tate's prosecution days are over."

"Really? You've decided that?"

"Well, it's pretty much been decided for me, hasn't it? It's not my job anymore. I'm going in another direction."

"And that would be?"

"Cooking breakfast for you," I teased.

"Now, that I can handle!"

I put the pizza box in the trash and washed our plates while Noah dried.

"You talked to Tia today?" I asked.

"No. Why?"

"There's a new man on the scene named Benjamin. He's Johanna's brother. He says his job is to keep us—you, Jill, and me—moving forward."

"Hey, I'm liking him already."

The phone rang. "That's him now," I said, knowing it was.

"Good evening, Benjamin. We were just talking about you. What? Oh, sure he's here. Just a minute."

I put the phone on speaker and set it on the table.

"Hello, Noah." Benjamin's voice was smooth and deep. "I'm looking forward to meeting you."

"Yes, me too. Keegs has been telling me about you."

"Now, something important has come up, and we three must deal with it immediately."

"We three?"

"Here I am, signing you up for something, and we've not even met. I apologize, but the timing is critical, and we must move quickly. When can we meet?"

Noah looked at me, and I nodded. Then he said, "How about right now?"

He gave Benjamin my address.

"What the heck?" I asked after he hung up.

Noah shrugged. "Got me. Sounds pretty important, though."

"Here we go again," I said. "I think our lives are about to turn another cartwheel. I guess this is what we signed up for."

"Signed up?" He raised his eyebrows. "Who the hell signed up? We got drafted!"

I took his hand, grinning. "Then let's run away. Let's go to a tropical island and live on mangoes and fish."

75

A knock at the door interrupted the fantasy, and I invited Benjamin in. I made tea while the two men got acquainted and brought it to them in the living room. While the tea was steeping, I asked, "So, Benjamin, what's our urgency?"

He leaned forward, gazing at the floor, seemingly lost in thought. Then he sat up and looked at each of us in turn. "I apologize for barging into your home like this, but I need your help. A good person is about to do something dangerous that might destroy her. We must help her see the danger of her plans. I've not been able to budge her on my own."

"Do we know this person?" Noah asked.

"Yes. It's your own Tia Ana."

Noah and I stared at each other in disbelief.

"Yes," Benjamin said, and nodded. "Ana is right now heading into certain danger."

"Well, that makes no sense," said Noah. "How can that possibly be?"

"Yes," I agreed. "How could Tia ever be in danger? Is that even possible?"

Benjamin clasped his hands and held them to his chest. "I do know it's hard to believe. Hard to believe this wise woman would walk into a situation that might be fatal, yet she is determined to do so."

"Will you have a cup of tea?" I asked.

"Yes, that's what we need now: a cup of tea and a bit of bliss to get us on the right track so our decisions are correct."

We drank our tea silently for a few minutes before Benjamin set his cup down and said, "Let me tell you a bit about

Ana, something you may not know. Ana grew up in a simple, happy family in the mountains of New Mexico. A mom, a dad, an older brother, and a younger sister. Her father was a farmer, and her mother was a schoolteacher. Her brother Daniel was two years older, and her sister Elisa was ten years younger. Our spiritual gift was in Ana when she was born, and at a very young age, she could already see and know things that adults could not. And even though she was a child, adults often sought her advice."

He sipped his tea. "Her life was good. But through the gift, she sensed a coming tragedy and tried to put it out of her mind. Then on her fifteenth birthday, her parents both died in a car accident. Later that same year, her brother died in Vietnam. Elisa was five years old. From that day on, Ana was Elisa's support and her parent. At fifteen years old, she was raising her little sister alone."

"How in the world did she do that?" asked Noah. "Where did the money come from?"

"That I don't know," said Benjamin. "I just know that she was and is the foundation of security in Elisa's world."

"I never knew any of this," I said.

Benjamin continued. "There's good news about early trauma for some people; sometimes it opens them to spiritual awareness. Tia was ahead of the game already, but those years of service to Elisa were precious."

"Then why doesn't that happen to everyone going through early trauma?"

"Because some of us see ourselves as our trauma; we see ourselves as our pain. Then our pain becomes suffering. Others can objectify their pain and their trauma. They become open to deeper realizations."

Noah leaned forward. "I knew Tia's story because I grew up in her home," he said. "Elisa was my little sister. Tia never talked about her sacrifice for Elisa and me. Never. I never realized how that could have expanded her and made her wiser. I think now that I took it all for granted."

"You've shown your gratitude. I've seen you do it," I said.

"Yeah, I have. But I just didn't get what else was going on. She shielded me from it."

"And yet she always knew you would eventually be right here," Benjamin said.

Noah laughed. "I guess she did."

"You had a wonderful example, growing up in Ana's home under her wing. Now you see how every experience, no matter how small, is a step for us toward spiritual awakening. They are seeds to be accepted and cherished."

I couldn't help but laugh. "And the experiences I've resisted became weeds in my garden. Thank you. That's clear now."

"Right," said Benjamin. "Then we're forever on our knees, pulling what we think are weeds from the gardens of our minds and never knowing their fruits."

The room fell silent.

"Benjamin," Noah asked, "this danger has to do with Elisa?"

"It does," Benjamin said, and nodded. "Elisa became a different kind of angel than her sister. She dedicated her life to helping people in need, which brings us to the present. Elisa went to Mindanao in The Philippines last week to take supplies to an orphanage. On her third day there, she was abducted by a gang called Ang Malalakas. They're demanding $500,000 for her release."

"That's half a million dollars!" Noah exclaimed.

"Yes, half a million dollars. So Ana is determined to go there and plead for her sister's freedom."

"Oh, wait just a minute," I said. "I've got the money. I'll happily pay the ransom."

"Of course," Benjamin said. "Of course you will. But you see, I have the money too, and I'd also be happy to pay. But money isn't the only issue here; the gang is the problem. No amount of money might be enough. They often demand more and more and then behead their hostages anyway."

"Oh, my God!" I cried.

76

"Yes," he said. "The person who pays the ransom keeps delivering more money until the hostage is released or, in some cases, found dead. If the person paying is there and available, they can easily be the next victim."

Noah studied the older man. "You've had time to think this through, Benjamin. What do you suggest?"

Benjamin stood up, placed his hands in his pockets, and silently paced the room. Then he said, "I think we better all see Ana now."

While the two men discussed plans, I called Jill to fill her in. She was a part of us now and needed to know what was happening.

She took it in with surprising calm. "Oh, another challenge. How fun!"

"Fun? Don't you think it's damn scary?"

"Well," she answered, "maybe fun isn't the right word. But my life is changing so fast, and I'm learning that when the big changes hit us, they open new realities, and then we expand."

"We're expanding pretty fast, my sis!"

"True. Life is exciting. Now, keep me up to date on this, will you?"

"I will."

When the three of us were in the car, we brainstormed about saving Elisa while protecting Tia, wrestling with options all the way to the café. When we arrived, it didn't take long to see that we'd been swimming against the tide because Tia had already committed to leaving immediately for The Philippines.

Nothing we said deterred her. "I'm going," she said. "Any one of you would do the same thing."

We all knew it was true, yet her plan seemed weak, and I continued to plead with her. "Tia, if you go, then they'll have two hostages. How is that going to help?"

She smiled at me, then at each of the others. "You've all three done your best, and I love you for it. Now I'm going."

No one spoke as we looked at each other, hoping to find another solution.

At last, Tia Ana broke the silence. "They only keep prisoners a short time. If no one responds, they'll execute Elisa. I'm not going to let that happen."

Noah tried again. "Tia, can't we use positive thinking and spiritual power to change the guys who have your little sister?"

"Perhaps, but I have to go and be in the field where the action is happening. Do you understand? I have to be in that energy to change it."

Noah frowned. "And you can't do that from here?"

"Just stop now, all of you," she said firmly, then got up and went into the kitchen while we sat in uneasy silence.

After a moment, she reappeared with cups and a pot of tea.

"Do you remember the story of Gandhi?" she asked, sitting down. "That dear man proved, absolutely proved that love is the most powerful energy in this universe. He did that, didn't he? He could not have done it from South Africa or China. He had to be immersed in the problem before finding a way out. You can't ride a horse while watching from the fence. If you're going to be effective, you have to saddle up and mount up."

I sighed and looked at the others. "This is our biggest test so far, letting our Tia walk into a lion's mouth and trusting that love will save her."

"Let's remember the lessons of Gandhi and Dr. King," she said.

"They were both assassinated," I observed.

"My dear," Tia said, "if you get on the horse, you might get bucked off, or you might find him to be a friend who will carry you. But there are times when sitting on the fence just won't do, and this is one of them. I have to go to The Philippines to save my little sister. Now, that's all there is to it."

"Tia," Noah said softly, "this scares the hell out of me. I can't help it. How can you hope to overcome terrorists in a foreign country?"

"Listen. Please listen." She looked at each of us. "We've come to a crossroads now; we all have, including our Jill. The choices we make here will set a course for our futures. Is it perilous? Yes, of course, it is. But does life ever change without risk? So let's remember who we are and what we're doing here."

She paused, and the room fell silent.

"Do you remember how Great Britain once controlled every part of India? It was their colony, and they owned it with thousands of soldiers. And they demanded the Indians buy products only from them—products that the people of India could make for pennies on the dollar. They couldn't even collect their own salt; they had to buy it from their British rulers. So Gandhi led his people on a salt walk. He started out with a few dozen people, and they walked for over 240 miles. Sixty thousand of his followers were arrested. Gandhi himself was beaten and arrested. Still, he persisted until he succeeded. And even though the British had the strongest military force, it made no difference. Gandhi led his followers through peaceful protests until Great Britain was defeated and sent back home, not by military might but by the power of love. And that same love and energy is what we have going for us right now. I'm taking that love to The Philippines, and I'm bringing my sister home."

She looked at Noah. "And yes, my son, it is going to work."

Benjamin had been quiet for some time. Now he addressed

the rest of us. "Ana is right. We can't win them over with physical force because they have guns, knives, and Elisa. We really have to rely on something more powerful."

I felt the attorney rising in me. "Listen, please, Tia. I've spent years dealing with people like this. This is what I know how to do. We're talking about people who have no conscience, and they won't develop one just because we play nice with them. The only thing that will save Elisa is stronger energy."

Tia patted my hand and smiled. "Exactly!" She stood up. "A stronger energy. That's what I've been talking about here. So now, excuse me, I'm going to make my airline reservation."

"Well, then, make it for two," I said, "because I'm going with you."

"Oh, no—"

I cut her off. "So what are you going to say now? That it's too dangerous?" A smile spread across my face. "Hey, we're a team, right? I am coming with you!"

"Keegan," she said, "this is something I have to do myself. Elisa is my sister, my family."

"You're also my family," I told her, "and I am going with you. Let's not argue about this. I'm going."

Tia Ana studied me for a long time. No one else spoke.

Finally, Benjamin broke the silence. "Ana, is there nothing I can say to change your mind?"

"No, Benjamin. I must do this."

"Then make that reservation for three."

Later, when Noah and I lay together in the darkness, he asked, "You're not afraid?"

"Yes, sure, I am. But I'm breathing through it."

"That Ang Malalakas gang sounds like a dangerous bunch, and thinking of you confronting them scares me. I'll take time off and go too. You're going to need protection."

"Thank you, Noah, but no. Tia said we must go with just our open hearts. She says that's our strength."

He sighed, then was quiet. "Okay," he said finally. "Then we'll do it Tia's way."

I snuggled against him, feeling his slow heartbeat. "To be really honest," I said, "I do think we're going to need a miracle."

"Okay, then, let's make one."

77

Our plane landed in heavy heat and drenching rain. My blouse was plastered to me before we even found a cab. The cab ride was itself an adventure. We were soon at a hotel that would rival any in San Francisco for its elegance. Tia and I checked into a luxurious suite with a living room, a kitchenette, two bedrooms, and two bathrooms. At another time, the accommodations might have made for a fun vacation. This trip was, for me, loaded with concern.

As I unpacked my suitcase on the king-sized bed, I was surprised by my aching for Noah; surprised because I had lived almost my entire life without a man, and now after being with Noah for less than six months, he had become part of my heart.

I had insisted on paying the ransom, and Benjamin and Tia eventually agreed. My money was transferred to his bank in Manila before we left the States. Soon after we got to the hotel, he disappeared for several hours and came back with a canvas duffel. "All the money is in there," he said. "Cash bundles. You must keep it safely hidden."

"How about the downstairs safe?"

He scratched his head. "This much money? No, I don't think so. Think you can keep it safe here?"

"Yes, I'm sure I can."

"Then do it."

He left, and I dumped the money on my bed and stood there dumbfounded by the sight of it. I'd never seen that much money. And to think I owned it! I called Tia in, and when she saw it, we both laughed. Then we stuffed it back into the duffel, and I put it on the back of the overhead in my closet and covered it with clothes.

We ate an early supper downstairs with Benjamin. No one spoke; we were all exhausted. We went to our rooms, and from mine, I called Noah to let him know we were safe. We talked for a while, then I bade him good night and fell into a deep sleep.

78

The next morning, we met for breakfast in the atrium, a lovely room with sunlight splashing around us and tropical flowers growing under tall windows. How, I wondered, could I be bathing in such beauty while Elisa was nearby in the hands of killers? As I held Elisa in my heart, feeling the pain of it, I realized that nothing is one thing. So even with the pain, I allowed myself to drink in the flowers, the sunshine, and the beauty of the room, and savored every bite of my breakfast. I knew that joy was to be my strength now.

Benjamin went to the restroom, and as the waitress cleared our dishes, a strange man approached our table.

"Can I help you?" I asked, standing to meet him at his level.

The man smiled. "It's okay, Miss Tate. I'm here to help. Please, let's sit. We need to talk."

I frowned at him. "How do you know my name?"

He smiled. "It will soon be clear. Let's just relax,"

He sat at our table and ordered coffee from a passing waitress. Then he turned back to me. "You will soon know that I am your friend."

Just then Benjamin reappeared. The stranger stood, and the two men embraced. Benjamin broke away with a broad smile. "Ana and Keegan, please meet Danilo Torres. We have known each other since childhood, and we're like brothers. Danilo has been in the top echelons of law enforcement and government for years. Please accept Danilo as you have me."

The man acknowledged the introduction with a bow of his head. "I'm here to help you."

"I apologize for being rude." I smiled. "I guess I'm a little suspicious right now."

"This is a difficult time, Keegan. I don't blame you for being suspicious."

Tia touched his arm gently. "So, Mr. Torres," she said, "you know why we're here?"

"Yes, I do, and please call me Danilo."

We waited to speak further while a waitress poured fresh coffee. When she was gone, Danilo spoke. "Ana, please tell me exactly how you heard about your sister's abduction."

"I got a telegram, and then I got a phone call."

"Do you have the telegram with you?"

She dug it out of her bag and handed it to him.

"And how was this delivered to you?"

"By a Western Union courier. He came to my café, my home."

"Do you know how the kidnappers knew your address?"

Tia blinked. The question seemed to startle her. "Well, now that I think about it, they couldn't know unless they got the address from my sister."

Danilo turned to Benjamin with a sigh. "So that raises some questions before we start anything. To my knowledge, Ang Malalakas has never used telegrams before. Never. Perhaps we're dealing with another gang pretending to be Ang Malalakas."

"Why would they do that?" asked Benjamin with a frown.

"Well, because it makes them look more powerful, more dangerous."

"But," I asked, "if it's a lesser gang, that could be good news, right?"

Danilo shook his head. "No, not necessarily. Sometimes a renegade gang is more dangerous because they're less predictable. They often have no single leader, no one in command."

"But masquerading as Ang Malalakas would be dangerous for them, I should think."

"Oh yes!" Danilo nodded. "Very dangerous. Which proves my point: if it's a splinter group, they're living on the edge. They're taking more risks and caring less about who gets hurt. In fact, some of the horrors ascribed to Ang Malalakas are actually done by some of these smaller gangs."

"So what do we do, then? Do we call the number Tia has?"

"No, not yet. First, we'll talk to your Noah and see if he can find out who delivered this telegram."

I didn't question how Danilo knew about Noah being a policeman, but I was in acceptance. Surprises that were once disorienting were becoming commonplace.

Danilo talked to Noah for several minutes, asking him about SFPD's procedures for finding the source of a telegram. Then he returned my phone and turned to Benjamin. "Benjamin, we need to find out who we're dealing with here. What say you? Let's call that number."

Benjamin nodded. "Yeah, let's do it."

Tia dialed the number and put her phone on speaker. A man's voice answered on the first ring. "Who is this?"

"I'm calling about my sister," Tia answered.

"You came alone?"

"No, I brought a friend. A young woman."

There was a pause. "We told you to come alone. Why did you bring her?"

"You said no such thing about coming alone. She's here to help me."

"You brought the money?"

"Yes."

"Five hundred thousand dollars?"

"Yes. I just want my sister back safe."

"You'll get your sister when we get the money."

"You can have the money, all of it. But only when my sister is returned safely."

The man spoke angrily. "Now you've done it! Now your sister is dead."

Tia Ana looked at Danilo, who immediately reached out and took the phone from her. "This is Danilo Torres. You don't know me, but you're going to be dealing with me from now on. Now, you listen closely, dumb shit. You want the money or not? Because if you do, then you'd damn well better stop playing games and do as I say. Number one, you take very good care of that young lady. Do you hear me? She gets even slightly hurt, you don't get a cent. Do you understand me?"

The man on the other end of the phone grunted.

"I need an answer, damn you! Hurt one hair on her head, and you get no money. I need to hear your agreement."

There appeared to be a small scuffle, and then someone else spoke. It was a man's voice but higher pitched and almost whiny. "So you think you're a big man, huh? You ever see a woman get her head cut off? I'm going to send you a video. It will be ugly, but you know something? I love doing it. And I'm going to love cutting off this lady's head."

"Look," Danilo said softly, "I hear one more word like that, just one word, and I hang up. Then you go ahead and kill the lady. You're probably planning to do it anyway. Then you also kill $500,000. It's all here right now, all in cash, and we intend for you to have it. You have one and only one thing going for you: that's the well-being of that young lady."

"You talk big, Mr. Danilo."

"Listen to me, tough guy. You can cut the crap, cut the macho talk! Do you want this $500,000? We want your hostage back safe and in one piece. Mess with her, hurt her in any way, and you get nothing. You think you're smart enough to do that?"

"You still talk like you think you're a big man," said the voice. "I'm the man in charge here!"

"Oh, you think so?" Danilo was still speaking softly. "I've got half a million dollars in a duffel bag right here, and that makes me a very big man. You have nothing but a hostage. Can you spend that? Now, do you want this money or not? Then show us Elisa so we can see she's safe."

"No! You get her when we get the money. Don't call back until you are ready to pay."

The line went dead. We looked at each other around the table. Tia touched Danilo's arm again. "Thank you," she said. "I could not have done what you just did."

He patted her hand. "Don't be put off by what that guy said. His reaction tells me that he's way out of his league. Now, Benjamin and I are going to leave for a while. I've got a cousin who's somehow connected to Ang Malalakas. I'm hoping he can put us in contact with them."

"Danilo," Tia asked quietly, "how much time do you think we have?" We all knew what she meant.

Danilo sighed and held her eyes. After a moment of thought, he said, "Ana, we've got at least a couple of days. Maybe more. Way more time than they want us to believe. But we do need to move as quickly as possible. The longer this takes, the greater the danger."

I looked at Tia and then at the men. "And what are we to do in the meantime?"

"You both know what to do," said Benjamin. "But you must stay inside this hotel. Another kidnapping would totally destroy us, destroy our leverage."

"We have leverage?"

Benjamin nodded. "Oh yes, we do, and now we're going to get more. If you two will just be patient and do your part, we'll win this. We'll bring Elisa home."

79

The men left, and Tia and I went up to our room. In the elevator, I stared at the door. The entire situation was unreal. I was in a foreign country in a luxury hotel with the possibility of Tia's sister being savagely murdered if we made a mistake. We were in the grip of terrorists while living in luxury.

I was wealthy and should not have been as surprised as I was to learn that wealth did not protect anyone from these tragedies. Somehow I had assumed rich people didn't deal with such things.

While unpacking, I sank into despair, unable to stop envisioning what that man had threatened. I drifted into the living room, where I found Tia sitting at the window. When she turned, she saw my state, reached out a hand, and brought me beside her.

"Do you think maybe we should meditate?" she asked.

It was not a question; she was guiding me.

We sank into comfortable armchairs, and I followed her voice. "Breathe in through your nose, and allow that soft breath to go into every cell of your body, awakening each of those cells so that your entire physical self—from the tips of your toes to the tips of your fingers to the top of your head— is filled with relaxation and with peace. If your thoughts try to intrude, simply come back to your breathing. Take all the time you need."

After a short while, I floated in a river of what could only be called grace. I have no idea how long I swam in that sweet river before her voice guided me again.

When I opened my eyes, she was watching me. "Little Bird, this mission is going to take us into a dimension you've never known, and getting there and staying there will be the greatest test of your life. Our thoughts are real things. They alter reality. Elisa's life depends on our thoughts. So beginning now, you and I will coordinate our thinking. We will see the truth of Elisa, safe and happy. Despite any contrary evidence that comes to us, you and I must keep our courage strong and hold the vision of Elisa safe and happy."

She nodded to me, watched for a minute in silence, then went to the kitchen, probably to make tea. I remained in my chair, staring across the room and out the window at a deep blue sky. I knew then that, if I were to be effective, I had to view Elisa's kidnapping differently. I could no longer be one of its victims; I had to see it through the eyes of a healer. I was again reminded that I was powerless without accepting what is.

Tia brought in the tea, and we sat sipping it in silence, each lost in our thoughts. It occurred to me that, although I had come to The Philippines to support Tia, she was doing the supporting. I needed to step up for her and Elisa and bring my best self to this game. I needed to show up and step up.

80

That long morning walked slowly into an even longer after-noon as we waited for the phone to ring. Restless, I rum-maged through the kitchen, found complimentary food and drinks, and made us each a hot chocolate. "Are you surprised they haven't called us yet?" I asked, handing her a steaming mug.

"Well, they don't see the need to call. They're trusting that we aren't just sitting idle, but we're working right alongside them."

Her voice and her mannerisms were calm and relaxed. I was surprised. "Tia, this is your sister. She's being held as a prisoner by terrorists. And yet here you are. You're more relaxed and trusting than I am. It's all I can do to not bite my fingernails."

She nodded. "I see that. And it's true; I'm not feeling anxiety like you are. Now, why do you think that is?"

"I don't know. Probably because you're on a much higher level of consciousness."

"There are no levels of consciousness, only levels of waking up."

I laughed. "Okay, got me! But hey, I am waking up. Slowly, I know, but I'm reaching for it."

"Stop reaching, will you? Stop looking outside yourself and know you're already there: whole, perfect, and com-plete."

"I'd feel less useless if I were confronting those terrorists. We're here right now, reliving the old story of how the man is the leader who goes out and does the important things while the woman, as the meek follower, stays home, wrings her hands, and hopes for the best. Like in this case, the men went off to do real, dangerous work, and here we sit, you and I, just staying out of the way. That's one reason I became an attorney; I didn't want to spend my life being an observer. It never felt right, passively waiting on some man to save me."

"So you're feeling a little resentment, are you?"

"Well, yeah, I guess I am."

"Then I have some excellent news for you, if you're ready."

"Oh, I am so ready!"

She leaned forward. "So you think we're just bench-warmers here?"

"Yeah, that's sure what it feels like to me."

She studied my eyes for a moment. "Listen carefully, Little Bird: we did not come across the ocean to be passive observers. And we are not. The work we will do right here in this room will be every bit as effective and as necessary as the men's work. Without us, their efforts might even fail. I haven't stopped working since we left home.

"Now, my niece, can you join me? So we can work alongside the men? All of us focused on the vision of Elisa's safety."

Her answer exasperated me. "How in the hell are we going to be even the least bit effective while we're parked here in this hotel room, waiting for them to call?"

Tia tilted her head in the way she did when something was about to change my life. "Thank you for asking that question. Now, let me tell you how women make things happen while staying out of the fury. We use the greatest power ever known."

She must have seen the skepticism on my face because she laughed. "You'd better get ready for a shift in your conscious-ness now, young lady!"

I spread my arms and dipped my head twice. "I'm very ready!"

She sat back in her chair and watched me for a long time. I waited while clouds moved across the sky, sinking the room in deep shadow, then moved to bathe us in a sea of colors.

Finally, she said, "The power of women, Keegan, is love."

I stared at her, waiting for elaboration, but it seemed she had nothing to add. Finally, I said, "For months now, I've been waiting for you to tell me the final big revelation, and now here it is? Love? The power of women is love? That's something new?"

"And yet," she said, "after all our time together, you still think love is a feeling, don't you?"

"Well, of course, love's a feeling. What more could it be?"

As the shadows shifted through the room, I saw her face become as ancient as her New Mexico ancestors. "If we see love as just a feeling, then that's what it becomes. And then we'd better stop calling what we're doing here love. Because what we're doing is not a feeling, my niece. Not at all. Love is pure energy. And so we can both be on the same wavelength, I'll call it grace; it's the same thing. Now, I'm pretty sure you won't say grace is a feeling, will you?"

"Grace?" I asked. "Grace is power?"

"Grace is like water, isn't it? Soft, gentle, and cleansing, and yet it carves canyons in the earth."

I closed my eyes and looked at this. Was that grace in me? If so, why wasn't I feeling it?

81

"Grace and love: one and same thing. The energy and power of all universes in all time."

"So we're back to love, then, aren't we? Only now it's grace." I paused, looking into space. "Yeah, I can see that. And if I'm getting it right, it changes how I see love. In fact, it changes the way I see everything."

She watched me, saying nothing. The clouds passed across the sun again, changing the light in the room, and her face changed with it. She was very old, then very young. In her face, I saw the faces of men, of children, and of ancient wisdom, and with each change, I loved her more.

I found my voice. "Grace as love, love as grace. And it's not just a feeling in me. It's all energy and power in all time and space. Grace, the source and the result. Okay, why does this sound like one of Johanna's Three?"

She laughed aloud. "Because it is. It's not one of her Three—it's all of them, all three within one. Grace is acceptance of the now. And grace is also the next step, the one that ties the three together."

"And of course you won't tell me."

"So you can get it intellectually? No, I think not. But there is something I will introduce to you, if you're ready."

I leaned forward. "Oh, I'm ready."

"Then look at this: grace, as you said is all energy in all space and time. And it's also all intelligence, all wisdom, all information in space and time. Grace: all of everything everywhere. Now, you chew on that while I go make fresh tea."

When she came back, I said to her, "I really do want this, Tia, but I feel like I'm being a little slow."

"You're not slow; you're blocked. You're stopped by your illusions of reality."

I shook my head in disbelief. "So now I'm lost in illusions? What have we been doing all these months if I'm still lost in illusions?"

"This is the next big step for you. If you get it intellectually and not consciously, I'll have done you a disservice."

"Please, Tia. I'm ready."

"Your mind is creating this reality here, right now. It doesn't even exist but in your mind. You are creating it by thinking, coupling together what makes sense to your subconscious, your amassed memories."

"Are you saying that you are an illusion? That you're not seeing this same room, this same reality I am?"

"No, I'm not. I'm seeing my reality, the reality I'm creating."

I stared at her. We did not see the same reality?

"Did you see the room darken when the clouds passed over?" I asked.

"Yes, I did."

"There, then," I said. "Same reality."

"No, not the same reality. Because my experience of that was different than yours. We are two different people, Keegan. Two different minds, two different lenses into reality. We're two different instruments in the orchestra of life, each hearing and playing our own part."

"And illusions?"

"There is a truth underlying all our experiences and interpretations of them. It is grace. It is infinite wisdom and love. It is right now creating this universe, including your body and mine."

"How can I get there?" I whispered. I was awed by what she had said.

"Surrender."

"Surrender to what?"

"To not believing anything. To let yourself see the magical pattern unfolding in this room and in me."

"I saw you change. I saw you young and old and even as a man."

She smiled. "See how near you are to truth?"

82

She folded her hands on her lap. "Every solid thing in this universe is made of energy, right? It's all vibrating energy. Every solid thing is made of energy."

"Right."

"Most people think of grace as some spiritual fantasy thing, a beautiful idea, a concept. But it's reality, the only reality there is. It takes the form of solid objects, but it remains flowing energy. The only energy in this universe or any universe is grace. The energy that makes the planets orbit, the energy that makes wind and tides—all of it is grace."

"Then how is grace love?"

"Love, my dear, is our expression of grace."

"'Our expression of grace' sounds like a philosophy."

"Oh, you're so right about that. It is philosophy when we're discussing it. But when we stop talking about it and *be it*, things happen. Miracles occur."

"Gandhi!"

"Exactly."

"So we're here creating a reality that keeps Benjamin, Danilo, and Elisa safe. And that's grace? That's love? How do we do that?"

She leaned in closer to me. "Here between us, we'll expand that energy of grace, of love until it reaches out to them and gives them the clarity, the courage, and the confidence to work miracles. Our men are facing dragons. It's our job to defang those dragons. We'll recruit them to our team. We'll fill them with love. We'll move beyond any doubts and visualize our wish as already done. We'll do it with total acceptance of what is, then we'll set a vision of what we want to be. With acceptance as our anchor, we'll do this, Little Bird. With love, with grace."

She looked out the window at the changing light, then turned back to me, "Tell me, Little Bird, if we are in acceptance, being in the present, and feeling love and grace surrounding us, what will we be feeling?"

I didn't have to think long. "Joy. We'd be feeling joy."

"Okay, good. Let's focus on that for a minute. Is that joy the same as happiness?"

"Yes, it is ... No, wait. It's more than that, more than happiness. It's ... it's a feeling that's deeper than happiness. It's, well ..." I laughed. "Tia, you've been teaching this all along, and now finally, I'm seeing it. I feel so foolish. Why didn't I see this before? Joy is my state of being. It's my foundation, the foundation you've been trying to get me to see."

She was beaming. "Welcome to my world."

I sat quietly while that new truth opened windows inside me. My whole thinking process was being rearranged by joy. A state of being, not an emotion, not the result of something. Happiness was a reaction to something. But joy? Joy was me as a tiny child before I learned to have concerns and doubts about myself and the world, before I learned to worry. Just in this minute, this blessed minute, my life was shifting, and I was feeling a freedom I'd never realized existed. The filters had been taken off my eyes, and I saw the world not as "out there" but as inside me to hold in whichever way I decided.

She had been watching me. "That's our power, you see. That's what women of the ages have done while the men are on their battle lines. Joy, as you're experiencing it right now, is love. It's as old as life itself, and it's the greatest power in the universe."

"Tia, I get it. I'm totally on board and convinced. But I

honestly have no idea how to harness this joy, this grace, and send it to those guys."

"Oh, but you do know. You know because you're now living those first two steps: *acceptance of all that is in this instant.*"

She leaned forward. "Did you know that you and Noah were the most effective parts of Jill's healing?"

"No, I didn't know that."

"Well, know it now. And know all the things you've been doing with your good heart."

I laughed. "Like I'm going to keep score of all the good I might do."

She tilted her head like she did when she was about to zap me. "If you don't recognize the miracles you work, how will you ever build confidence as a miracle worker?"

"Well, I've never been too big on self-praise."

"Oh, but I'm not talking about self-praise here. I'm talking about honesty. I'm talking about being one with what is."

I closed my eyes. "I wish I could make this journey easier."

"And you can. I taught you how, didn't I? Meditation is how you come to know yourself beyond body and mind. That's how you build your confidence as a miracle worker."

She waited while I considered her words. Then she said, "Shall we?"

"Okay, sure. Let's do it."

83

I steadied my breathing and sank deep into the armchair. Within moments I was in space, complete, not needing or wanting anything. I was totally content. In Tia's presence, reaching this state was so easy.

She spoke, her words soft but penetrating. "Let's now focus our breathing as an intention on our men being well and on Elisa being safe. It's true for them as we see it and create it with our hearts. Let them be filled with our streaming love right now."

Silence.

"We see it not as something we want to happen but as something already happening."

Silence.

"We don't ask for it. We know it, and we give thanks for it being so."

Silence.

"Whatever we want to see regarding Elisa and our two men, we accept that it already is, and we are giving thanks."

Silence.

"Let us repeat our intention so we get clear, so we erase any doubts. Let's say, *It is already done, and we are giving thanks.* Let's say it twenty times while seeing Danilo, Benjamin, and Elisa as safe and happy."

Twenty times, we said with one voice: "It is already done, and we are giving thanks."

"Now then, let's open our eyes and stay in this space of joy, deep peace, and acceptance of what is true. We will both live our afternoon with grace flowing through us into those in the field."

I opened my eyes and looked around the room, still in my quiet mind.

"Ready for the next step now?" Tia asked.

I nodded.

"Then let's harmonize our hearts in joy so we feel the vibration of grace, of love between us. And then let us watch Elisa walk into this room, whole and well."

I closed my eyes and saw Elisa in the room.

"Is this a kind of praying?" I asked, my eyes still closed.

"Yes, it is. It's the only kind of praying. It's what Jesus did when he was working miracles. He told us to pray, knowing our prayers are being answered."

"Tia, I'm all in on this, but I must admit that a few doubts keep popping up. Am I sabotaging our efforts with my doubts?"

Tia got up and went into the bedroom. She returned a moment later with a small plastic bag that contained a piece of folded white paper with tape attached. "I thought we'd come to this point, so I brought this from home for you. Here, take it. What do you see?"

"Well," I said, "it's a piece of paper with some tape on it."

"Look more closely. Look at the tape."

I held the paper up to the light. Sure enough, there was a tiny dark speck under the tape. "Okay, I'm seeing a fleck of something. So what am I looking at?"

She smiled. "It's a mustard seed," she said. "A mustard seed. Now turn the paper around and read what's on the other side."

The words were small, written in purple ink in beautiful calligraphy. "If you will have faith the size of a mustard seed, you will say to this mountain, 'Move from here to there,' and it will move, and nothing will be impossible for you."

I put the paper down and stared at her, sensing that I was flying, like I could leave my chair and soar around the room. This amazing day! Everything washed away my old certainties and immersed me in wonder.

"Everyone has doubts, including me. They'll always be there. We accept them and move them aside. We want a miracle to happen, so we look into that darkness and find one tiny light, one tiny bit of assurance, even as tiny as that mustard seed. Then through that tiny light, we create a miracle."

With those words, she stood and left the room, and I sat alone, holding the tiny seed. As I pondered her words, I saw my doubt for the first time as paint, a thin coating that had nothing to do with the truth underneath. My doubt then drained away like an outgoing tide. When Tia returned later with a towel wrapped around her head, I was at peace.

She sat across from me, removed the towel, and finger-combed her hair. "Now, Little Bird, which do you think is harder: to move a mountain or to free Elisa?"

I smiled at her, saying nothing.

"Let's focus only on that part of us that knows—even if it's the size of a mustard seed. Are you ready?"

"Ready."

At that moment, the phone rang. We looked at each other, and it rang again.

I answered. It was Benjamin. I put it on speaker so we both could hear.

"We need you with us here," he said, "and we're both feeling your presence. I'm calling to tell you it was definitely not Ang Malalakas that took Elisa. We don't yet know who it was, but we're getting real close. We're now going to try and get Ang Malalakas on our team, which may take a miracle, but hey, that's what we do, right? Please stay with us now. Together we'll win this."

"We're here with you, my brother," said Tia. "Stay open to us and our love, and know that it's constant. Feel our presence; we're right there with you."

"Okay, then, now we go forward, the four of us. We'll bring Elisa home. We see it and know it right now."

"A mustard seed," Tia said.

"A mustard seed," he replied.

Then he was gone.

84

There was clarity, almost a brilliance in me I'd never experienced before. I felt like I must be glowing. My whole self
was filled with certainty and goodness. I closed my eyes and
breathed in the sweetness of it all. I kept my eyes closed and
let the peace float me like a leaf on a quiet woodland pond.

I heard Tia's voice, soft and distant. "We see the existence
of all possibilities now. We accept everything exactly as it is
right here in this instant. We see creation ongoing, all in
harmony. We travel with the winds singing through the trees
of the high country. We swim with the dolphins and the great
blue whales. We live in grace, in love, and in truth. We are
here now in the realm of unlimited possibilities, where the
new and beautiful are easily available. We see Elisa safe and
Benjamin and Danilo celebrating with us."

"I see your sister as whole and well and free," I said softly.
"I know it."

"We are swimming in sacred and forever goodness."

I sank deeper into the void, surrounded by a beautiful,
gentle presence.

"Now we are pure joy. We are eternal. We are nature."

Her voice was a sweet song, caressing me, a gentle breeze
of grace.

"We are joy and love now, and our joy and love join with
Benjamin's and Danilo's. Divine Presence is breathing
through each of us."

I heard faint chanting, echoing as in a great hallway.

"What you are feeling now, my niece, is your truth. This is
who you are."

I became as light as a child dancing in a summer meadow. I felt tears rolling down my face.

"Are we ready to bring into reality what we wish now?"

"I am."

"You must be sure."

"I'm sure. I see white clouds drifting on the blue sky and your sister cuddled in your arms. She's crying, but she's safe. I hear children laughing."

"Hold that vision while you come back. Take your time. Bring with you all that you have discovered."

I had no idea how much time passed before my eyes opened. I was surprised to see that the colors of the room had changed. Tia had changed; she looked younger and more beautiful.

When I could finally speak, I said only "Thank you!"

"So now you see that those who go into combat as conflict warriors must fight against one another. Those who go as brothers and sisters find no enemy, only family. They are warriors of Light."

"I see that," I said, "and I know it's real."

She smiled at me for a moment. "Can you see now that the invisible is more real than the visible?"

I nodded. "Oh yes, and the invisible is malleable. It's not fixed."

"Less than one ten-thousandths of one percent of the material world is matter. Did you know that? Less than ten-thousandths of one percent! The rest is grace, the spirit of life that moves in all things. And when you saw Elisa? That was every bit as real as this table."

Her joy radiated around her, and I was bathed in it. Her goodness felt like a choir singing inside me.

"You are now one of us, Little Bird, a traveler through time and space, where all is miracles."

"Will I always be able to do that?"

"Work miracles? Sure." She laughed. "Well, you probably can't turn a camel into a tree. But little things like saving my sister? Oh sure, you can do that."

"Tia, you create miracles almost every day, but you don't always go into meditation to do it. How is that possible?"

She laughed again. "Keegan, I'm never out of meditation. Meditation is my life."

"Wow, that sounds lovely. I hope I'll get there."

"You already are getting there. It's becoming your nature too."

And with those words, we again fell silent. I drifted into the wonderful feeling of peace and assurance, holding Benjamin, Danillo, and Elisa in my love and knowing that all was well. I had changed, and I felt the change. Only a few hours ago, I was uncertain and worried about what we were trying to do. Now I felt completely confident that we would have Elisa back with us, whole and well.

85

When the phone rang again, Tia was not in the room.

It was Benjamin. He said he and Danilo were on their way to an outer island to meet a leader of Ang Malalakas. "We're docking now," he said. "We're going to be out of touch for a few hours but still in this same river of energy. We both feel your presence. Thanks for that. Please keep the grace flowing. We're winning this."

He hung up, and I called out to Tia. "Benjamin thanked us for the grace. He used the word grace. Tia, Benjamin and Danilo know exactly what we're doing here."

"Of course they do," she called back. "We've been doing this since the beginning of human civilization."

She came back into the room and stood looking out the window. "Women stay behind in the camps and hold the men in their hearts," she said, still looking out. "Since ancient times, tribes have depended on men's bravery and women's spiritual flow of energy into them and their challenges. Have you seen the tribal beadwork, blankets, and pottery made by native women? Those are not just objects of utility; they are prayers of affirmation made of the grace from women's hearts."

"Right now I'm feeling pretty honored to be a woman."

"As well you should be, especially because you are one of the chosen."

As she returned to sit with me, the room darkened unexpectedly, as if a cloud had passed between the sun and the earth. Tia closed her eyes, and I followed her lead. In my mind, I saw Benjamin and Danilo surrounded by men with guns pointed at them. I gasped, recognized what I was doing, and began smiling. I smiled until that old pattern melted, and I saw them both doing well.

When I opened my eyes, the room was again flooded with sunlight, and Tia was watching me. "You do see how it works, don't you, Little Bird?"

"Yes," I breathed. "I do."

I stood up and went to look out the window. "Tia, I'm shifting inside. I'm not seeing anything the way I used to. I've never felt this way before. I'm so filled with energy . . . I don't know. It makes me almost giddy."

Less than an hour later, the phone rang again. it was Benjamin. I handed the phone to Tia and sat beside her. She listened for a long time, then hung up and returned to the window.

"Bad news?"

"Ang Malalakas," she said.

I went to her side. "So what does it mean? What are they doing?"

"Benjamin said the Ang Malalakas leaders are furious, and he thinks right now that they might help get Elisa back. He'll know more later tonight or maybe not until tomorrow morning."

"Such a long time to wait."

She turned to me. "Can we talk about Johanna's Three?"

"Sure," I said, and shrugged. "But I have no idea what the Three has to do with what's happening right now."

"It probably has everything to do with what's happening now."

"Okay, then, let's talk about it."

"Where are you in that process?"

"Well . . . I am one with acceptance, and I am in the now. I just need the third."

"Why do you think you don't have it yet?"

That question hung in the air between us. Finally, I said, "Because I'm not ready?"

"Do you remember how acceptance was not so easy until you got to be in the now? And then acceptance got easier."

"Yeah, I remember. They came together and became one: I am acceptance, and I am right here, right now."

"So tell me what acceptance means to you."

I caught my breath. "Tia, I'm in such joy from our work today, I feel like I'm not even me anymore."

She laughed. "Or maybe you're becoming you. Tell me what acceptance is."

I didn't hesitate: "It's gratitude and forgiveness. It's gratitude and forgiveness for everything past and present. I don't just accept certain things; acceptance is total."

She was watching me.

"And then the second is being present, and acceptance is complete. I can't imagine how the third could make it better. Do you think it will?"

She smiled. "What do you say we order dinner?"

"Hey, what about my question?"

"What question?"

I laughed. "You're a big help!"

We ordered dinner, and when it arrived, we ate slowly and savored every morsel.

And we waited.

And waited.

86

The moon was high in the sky when I snatched up the phone on its first ring.

"You got the money?"

"Who is this?"

"Don't play games with me, lady. You got the money or not?"

"I'm not answering your question until you tell me who you are."

I looked up to see Tia staring at me from across the room.

"Bring the money down to the lobby in fifteen minutes."

I stalled, hoping we'd hear from Benjamin before I gave the money away. It was not the money I was concerned about; I'd already released that. It was simply that as soon as they got the money, our leverage to get Elisa was gone.

"I can't get the money in fifteen minutes. It will take me at least an hour."

"You don't get an hour; you bring the money in fifteen minutes, or I bring you this lady's head."

I surprised myself by saying, "Okay, you cut off her head, and you cut yourself off from half a million dollars. So go for it!"

I heard nothing but his breathing on the other end of the line. I prayed I had said the right thing. Finally, he said, "Why do you need a half hour?"

"I didn't say a half hour. I said an hour."

"Okay. One hour. Bring the money to the lobby." I heard muffled voices in the background, then he spoke again. "Don't go to the lobby. We'll come to your room. One hour!"

"Wait!" I cried. "What about Elisa?"

But the phone had gone dead.

"Now it's getting dangerous," I told Tia.

The phone rang again. It was Benjamin. I told him about the call.

"An hour should give us enough time. You two sit tight and don't answer the phone again or the door." Then he hung up.

"Men seem to like hanging up on me today."

Tia laughed at that, and it broke the tension.

I followed her into the kitchen, where she made tea and put out a plate of cookies.

"You know something," I said, "Benjamin seemed almost happy about the guy asking for the money."

"It's all working out exactly how we see it, Little Bird. Now let's enjoy our tea." She picked up the two cups, and I carried the cookies into the living room. I looked around the space we had occupied for what seemed like days. It had been shrouded in darkness when we first arrived. Now it felt like the arena of a contest between light and dark forces. Rather than intimidated, I now felt fully engaged.

"Tell me, my dear auntie, my teacher, is the kitchen your temple? Do you connect with spirit through serving food?"

"Sure I do. Sharing food is communion, you know. It's sacred. We're having communion right now. As we are one in spirit, we eat the same cookies and drink the same tea, and in that way, we also become one in our bodies."

I picked up a steaming cup. "We are one in cookies and tea?" The image made me laugh.

"Precisely." She picked up a cookie but didn't eat it right away. "Listen, Little Bird. Over the next hour, we will be put to the test. All we've talked about over the past months will be tested. Are you ready? Can you maintain your harmony? Your joy? Your love?"

I could hear the rattle of sabers as I breathed—once,

twice—and repeated my mantras. "Tia, my dear, whatever happens, I am accepting it right here and right now. I've never been more ready."

We talked lightly and smiled. We were like soldiers before the big battle, keyed up but seeing the energy as love and not dread. Then as if on cue, Tia looked at the door just as someone rapped loudly.

"Who is it?" I asked.

"You know who it is. Open the door."

"I need another half hour."

"You don't have another half hour. Open this goddamn door now or I'll break it down."

I hesitated, but he didn't wait. With a crash, the door broke opened and was left hanging by one hinge. Two short burly men walked in holding pistols. One was dressed in dirty jeans and a tight black T-shirt. He had long black greasy-looking hair. The other, older and bald, wore jeans and a faded orange T-shirt. He went to search the bedrooms while the first man held us at gunpoint.

"No one here," the older man said when he came back.

I studied them as I would defendants in court: both well-muscled. The one holding the gun was in charge. "Now! The money!" he said.

I recognized his voice as the one on the phone at the breakfast table with Benjamin and Danilo.

He waved the gun at us. "You got two choices: the money right now—or you both gonna die—right now."

I stood up and calmly walked over to him. I looked into his eyes and saw fear. My voice was level. "Where is she?"

87

I blinked, and the next thing I knew, I was on my back, looking at the ceiling. I had not seen his fist coming. Pain stabbed my jaw; it must be broken. I tasted blood. Yet I realized as I lay there that, inside me, nothing had changed. I was acceptance, gratitude, forgiveness, and in the moment of now, completely at peace. I got to my feet and moved closer to the one who had hit me.

He had an ugly snarl on his face, and I smiled at him. "My friend, let's make this easy," I said. "Just tell us where she is."

I was stalling, hoping our men would arrive before I had to surrender the money.

The man's face went blank, and he lifted the gun to my face. The hole in the barrel was inches from my left eye. "Now, in two minutes," he said, and with his other hand, he held up two fingers, "I'm going to make a call. Then"—he shrugged—"if we don't got the money, I make the call, and that lady's head comes off. And also I just shoot the two of you. I have nothing to lose; you do."

From the corner of my eye, I saw Tia nod, so I went to the closet and pulled down the duffel bag. The man who had punched me grabbed it and dumped the bundles of money on the carpet. He quickly rifled through the stacks, then stuffed them back into the bag. Then he reached into his pocket, whipped out a switchblade, walked over to the phone, and sliced the cord.

"Now," he said, stepping so close to me that I saw the blackheads on his nose and smelled his fish breath. I didn't step back from him; instead, I stepped closer until our noses were almost touching.

He stared into my eyes with malevolence and also with confusion. He was wondering why I wasn't afraid of him.

"You two want to say alive?" he asked us. "You stay right here in this room for two hours. You got that?"

"Where is she? Where's your hostage?" I asked again.

He backed toward the door with a wicked grin. He looked at Tia, "Old lady, you made one big goddamn mistake. We told you to come alone, right? And you brought this one," he said, jutting his chin at me. "That girl we had?" He scoffed and shrugged. "Hey, she's dead already."

He patted his chest, still grinning. "I did it myself. I whacked her head off. And man, what a mess she made! You wouldn't believe it."

A chill washed over me. Then I breathed it away. This wasn't my reality.

"And those two guys you sent after us?" He chuckled. "They were babies. Ha! They're dead too. And that's on you, lady; that's all on you." He moved to the doorway. "You two want to stay alive? Then don't leave this goddamn room for two hours. You do, you're both dead."

The other man pulled the duffel to his chest, and the two disappeared through the shattered doorway.

"Tia?" I turned to her.

"Hush, now, Little Bird. This is not the time to doubt. Nothing's changed.

"But he said . . ."

"Oh, I heard him," she said, and waved a hand dismissively. "But I don't think I'll have that guy creating my reality, will you? Those two are creating darkness around them. They're relying on force; we're relying on grace. Which do you think will win?"

"Gandhi, right?"

"My niece, this is your time. Right now. Time to step fully into the Light. Do it right now. Do not buy into that man's reality. Bless him and chase him out of your mind. This is *our* moment, Little Bird, yours and mine and Benjamin's and Danilo's and my sister's. Today is when you come into the powers Johanna gave you. You saw my little sister being well and happy? Well, hold that vision."

My jaw throbbed. The pain was all the way down to my collarbone.

"Okay, I still see Elisa and our guys being well. I accept that reality. I do, and I know it's true." As painful as it was, I smiled.

"And the man who hit you?"

"Oh, he's all right. He's just living out his reality, not mine. I don't want revenge. But I would like this pain to ease up."

Tia came over and gently felt along the edge of my jawbone. "Well, it's not broken. Any loose teeth?"

I searched my mouth with my tongue. "Nope, they seem to be in place." Then I felt the split in my lip, which seemed to be the source of the blood dripping on my blouse.

"No real damage done," Tia said. "Just a split lip and some cracking pain. Probably could use a couple of stitches in that lip. But if you trust me, I'll butterfly it so it won't scar."

"I trust you. And if it does scar, hey, I'll match Jill."

"Well, she'll be very impressed with that bruise. It's going to be a beauty."

She closed her eyes and put the palms of her hands on either side of my face, and within seconds, my pain was nearly gone. Was there nothing this lady could not do? She found Band-Aids in her travel kit and cut out butterflies, which she gently tapped on my lip. She made a cold compress from a dish towel and ice cubes and had me lie on the couch.

88

"What do we do now?"

"Now we relax our minds and hearts, we stay focused on our vision, and we radiate love. Oh, and also we drink oolong tea to keep our spirits strong and to heal our jaws."

"*My* jaw," I muttered.

"No, dear, *our* jaws. Neither of us goes through this alone, and I'm feeling your pain and grateful to be sharing it with you."

I studied her, seeing who she was, and I realized something new: she was teaching me by her example—she always had been. She taught me that love was more powerful than any other energy in the universe. She had taught me that by herself being love.

She had just been told that her sister was dead, that Benjamin and Danilo had been killed. Instead of succumbing to worry or despair, she doctored my jaw and made my favorite tea. Would I ever grow to that level of serenity? Especially in the face of such darkness?

And yet even now, I felt a warmth expanding in my chest that was love. I recalled one of my favorite lines from *Alice in Wonderland*: "It's no use going back to yesterday because I was a different person then."

I lay on the couch with my jaw covered by an ice-filled dish towel, realizing I had become different. Instead of thinking and worrying about outcomes, I knew things would go our way. All outward evidence showed the worst was happening, yet that was not where my mind was. Something had shifted within me, changing my consciousness of truth, of what is. I saw that this day had been predicted months ago by Tia. She told me then that I would one day see I had been living in a cave, convinced that shadows were the only reality. She said one day I would find an opening and step outside, that I would step into *foreverness*, and she was right. Here I was.

I had come home. For my entire life, without knowing it, I had been struggling for this wholeness, struggling to feel complete. I saw on that awful afternoon that all I ever needed was to dare changing. Once I could shake off my beliefs and opinions of truth, truth emerged. I felt such gratitude for Tia's guidance and the love of Noah and Jill.

I came back from my thoughts and saw I was holding a half-empty teacup. I put it down, closed my eyes, and drifted inside myself, then into a beautiful meadow where an ancient, silver-haired woman greeted me with a smile. She knew me—she had always known me. I smiled back at her, and we became one. Above her was a soft sphere of golden light. She reached up and cupped the sphere in both her hands, then watching me, she held it to her heart and sighed. The sphere became a pitcher. She reached out and poured golden light over me, into me, and it flowed through my head and body. With her soft eyes, she watched me as the light's grace flowed through my system, rinsing away self-doubt and filling me with quiet assurance. In that moment, I came home to foreverness. I would never leave there.

Tia sat across from me when I came back, waiting and watching. The two of us held eye contact, and after a time of silence between us, I nodded.

"Tia, I see it now. You brought me here to show me this way. You planned all of this."

"Me?" she asked, raising her eyebrows innocently. "Why, my niece, as I remember, you insisted on coming."

"Yes, and of course you knew I would. How can I ever thank you?"

"One day you will pass it on. That will be my thanks."

I looked around the room. The surroundings had become familiar, and yet nothing looked the same. "My whole world has changed."

"And isn't it exciting?"

It was almost midnight, but neither of us could sleep. We ordered a late-night meal from room service and ate together in silence.

89

I finished the last bite of soup and looked up to see Benjamin standing in the mangled doorway. He was watching Tia. She had already seen him and was holding his gaze. She shook her head slightly.

He turned back into the hallway and spoke to someone, looked back at us and smiled, and then Elisa was standing beside him.

She flew into her sister's arms. They wept together, and as I watched, I was weeping with them. Benjamin came to me and cradled me in his arms.

After a bit, he and I went into my bedroom. He sat in a chair, and I sat on the edge of the bed, still trying to stop my tears of joy.

"My God, Benjamin, what a whirlwind this has been for me. I finally grew up. I did. And you and Danilo. Where is he, and are you both okay?"

"I'm fine. We're both fine. Danilo said he'll see us in the morning." He nodded at me. "It looks like you ran into a flying fist."

"Hey, nothing serious," I assured him. "A minor battle wound."

"Well," he said, and smiled, taking my hand, "we won."

I leaned forward. "Benjamin, I'm so deeply grateful for you and Danilo."

He put up a hand. "And we're equally grateful to you and Ana. Without your help, I'm not sure how we could have accomplished this."

"How in the world did you get Elisa back?"

"Danilo's strategy and connections. Because of how he handled it, Ang Malalakas eventually came around to our side and went after the guys who took her."

I touched my jaw. "They came, you know. They came and took the money."

"All of it?"

"Yep."

He glanced at my jaw. "And you tried to resist."

"Well," I said, laughing, "I think that was part of my awakening."

"Doesn't look too good. How bad does it hurt?"

"Not much. It hurt like hell at first, then Tia touched it, and the pain was almost gone."

"Of course it was."

We heard men's voices in the hallway, some of them sharp and angry. Benjamin went out to investigate. When he returned, he said, "Nasty business, lawlessness, and death."

"The money?"

He shrugged. "It's gone."

He stepped out again, and when he came back, he said, "The hotel's sending a crew up to hang a new door. Should only take a few minutes."

Tia joined us in my room. She had helped Elisa bathe, dressed her in a nightgown, and tucked her into bed. "She'll sleep now, then she'll eat something, then she'll sleep again. She'll come back to this reality gradually. It'll take time for her heart to heal and to realize she's safe."

"I'll get another room," I said. "You take this bedroom."

"No, I'm going to sleep with her tonight so I can hold her. That's what she needs."

She went over to Benjamin and kissed his cheek. "More than anything, I'm grateful to you, my brother. You got Ang Malalakas to work with us. You risked your life for us."

He smiled and shook his head. "No different than you'd do for me, Ana." Then he yawned and stood. "Now, if the two of you will excuse me, I need a hot shower and a good night's sleep."

"Go with God," said Tia.

90

The next morning, Elisa came out of Tia's bedroom, smiling shyly at me. "Thank you!" she whispered.

Tia followed her and took her hand. "Come now, Sissy, let's get ourselves down to breakfast. There's a nice surprise—the dining room's a beautiful atrium."

We rode down together in the elevator, and I wondered aloud if Benjamin would be joining us. When we entered, the atrium was even more splendid. The last time we'd been here was on a mission of darkness. This time we were celebrating life.

Danilo was at the table, waiting for us with a big grin. We all three hugged him and thanked him, then we settled into our chairs, wondering where Benjamin was. No sooner had we settled in and begun enjoying the ambiance of greenery, flowers, and guitar music than he appeared, carrying my duffel.

"Can anyone join this party?" he asked, dropping the duffel beside my chair.

I gasped. "My gosh! Is this possible? How in the world could you have possibly gotten this back?"

"Long story," he said with a shrug. "Danilo mostly. I just hope it's all there. Shall we order?"

We had just begun scanning our menus when Danilo joined us. We ordered, and when we had steaming cups of coffee or tea before us, the men told us their story. They had followed lead after lead until they found an old associate of Danilo's, a first cousin to an Ang Malalakas leader. Through him, they connected with that man and the other leaders.

At some point, Benjamin himself might have been taken for ransom, except for the fact that the gang wanted even more to find those masquerading as them. They stormed the camp where Elisa was being held and killed two of her kidnappers. Then they tracked down the rest, and when they found them, they also found the duffel. They returned it to Benjamin early this morning in gratitude for Danilo's and his help in tracking down the pretenders. Neither Benjamin nor Danilo had thought to ever see the money again.

My money was back, and even if they'd kept some of it, which I imagined they probably had, it was still a gift because I'd already released the whole amount.

"I'm surprised Ang Malalakas didn't want to keep the money," I said.

"Well," Benjamin said, smiling across the table at his friend, "Danilo's a pretty convincing guy."

We ate our breakfast, laughed, and shared our stories. I was surprised and felt rewarded by the men saying how our participation at each step was as relevant as theirs. It reinforced all I had learned.

After breakfast, Benjamin left to take the money to the bank, and we continued talking.

I was watching Elisa. At first, she was shy and didn't join the talk, but as we continued, she opened up and finally told us her story. The men had taken her to an island, locked her in a tiny dark room, and refused to talk to her. She was sure they intended to kill her and didn't want to have feelings for her. At first, she was terrified. Then realizing that her life was over, she sank into depression. She said the days she spent in that dark room felt like months. Eventually, she began to see her sister's face in that darkness and realized she was not alone. From that moment on, she waited, knowing she was safe.

We thanked her for her story and especially for her courage.

Danilo stood. "Well, my dear friends, I am going. But I must say this one thing: we are now family. It is a bond that will never be broken. You keep thanking me, and I appreciate it, but it is just what family does for each other. You'll return the favor very soon, sooner than you can guess. That's the way it will be between us from now on."

He reached to shake each of our hands, then he was gone. His saying we'd return the favor baffled and yet touched me.

We went to our rooms, packed, checked out, and headed for the airport.

91

Tia and Elisa were ahead of me in the line for boarding passes. A man two persons beyond them caught my attention. He was a middle-aged man with straight black hair, combed back. He was wearing brown corduroy trousers and a black pullover. His shoes were black and needed polish. He turned to look back, and I saw wire rim glasses on a face set with grim determination. I didn't know why he stood out to me at the time, but it was impossible not to notice him. It was as if something burned inside him.

We boarded the airplane, and as I arranged my belongings, I was delighted to find Benjamin in the seat next to me.

I buckled my seatbelt, and the plane took off. As I looked around the cabin, I saw the man from the ticket counter sitting across the aisle three rows ahead of me. To take my mind off him, I turned to Benjamin to strike up a conversation, but it was useless. The man's presence vibrated in me. Looking in his direction, I felt his energy—dark, tragic, and powerful.

Since I couldn't forget him, I started studying him. He sat stiffly upright, neither eating nor drinking nor reading. He did nothing to pass the time.

Why was I so concerned about him? And then I realized again: I was not the same person who had flown across this vast ocean only three days earlier. I was new, and my life was new.

I opened my journal to write about the recent events but couldn't focus. That strange man kept tugging at my heart.

After a time, I stopped writing and resumed studying him.

He continued staring straight ahead. Finally, when I couldn't stand it any longer, I went to the woman sitting on the aisle seat next to him and asked if she would mind trading seats for a few minutes. She agreed, took her book, and went to my seat. I sat down in her place.

The man seemed unaware of what had happened next to him.

After sitting for several minutes without either of us speaking, I asked casually, "You want to talk about it?"

He turned and frowned at me. "What?"

"I asked if you wanted to talk about it."

"Talk about what?"

"I think you know."

"I think you should mind your own business."

"This is my business. I'm a friend, and I want to know how you're doing."

He turned to face forward again. "Please go away and leave me alone."

"Well, that's the last thing I'm going to do."

A man across the aisle had a book open on his lap but wasn't reading. He was listening.

I spoke again. "You see, if you don't talk to someone about this, you're going to destroy yourself and lots of other people too."

He turned to look at me again, daggers shooting from his eyes. "Who in hell are you, lady. And what do you want from me?"

"Well, I'm your friend. And right now, you need a friend."

He turned to face forward again, ignoring me.

"I can see a dangerous darkness in you."

He turned to me. Now he was visibly angry. "What in hell are you even talking about?"

"I'm talking about you, my friend. I'm talking about the pain I see around you. I see that you've been hurt more than anyone can understand. I can feel your pain. And it's breaking my heart!"

He turned away from me again, but this time he answered. "My son," he said softly. "He was just a boy. He went to America to become a doctor."

He turned back to me, his face melting in sorrow. "Now my boy's dead. He's dead because of one stupid, evil woman." He hissed through his teeth. "She was driving drunk. She ran over him in a crosswalk."

His agony was inside me, but I could step aside and use its energy now. "And so you have to punish her, don't you?"

"Yes," he said, nodding vigorously. "Yes, I do. Someone has to!"

"Well, that's what the law's for, isn't it? She'll pay. How is that your job?"

He bristled at me. "So you think she'll pay, huh? Well, you're pretty naïve because that's just not the way American justice works. This woman is rich, so she'll get off scot-free. They'll slap her hand and say, 'Don't do it again,' and that will be all. Then she'll go right out and do it again."

"And that's why you're justified in killing her."

His jaw tightened. Then he nodded.

I had to reach him. "Okay, so you're going to kill her. That makes sense. After all, she might be a bad person, maybe even an evil person, because she didn't care enough to stay out of a car when she was drunk. And she ran down your son. She took the life of a gentle, sweet boy. Think of all the lives he might have saved if he had become a doctor. Now he's gone forever."

"That's right," he said, tears streaming down his cheeks. "That's right."

"And now that boy's father, a good, kind, respectable man with a heart full of love, will become a killer himself. And he is not doing it because he is a mad or evil man. He is doing it because he's drunk, drunk on rage and pain. Rage and pain go into the blood just like alcohol, and they're intoxicating just like alcohol. And just like that woman, he's refusing to deal with it. Tell me: is one more evil than the other?"

His jaw quivered, then he dropped his head into his hands and began to sob.

"Feel the goodness inside you, Adrian. In your life, you have only ever loved. Can you do this terrible thing and live with it? Can your family live with it?"

His sobs continued, his back heaving. When his breathing slowed, he wiped his swollen eyes and looked at me again. "How do you know my name?"

I shrugged. "Hey, I know some things I can't explain. But that's not important. What's important, Adrian, is that you cannot do this thing you were planning to do."

He wiped his tears with the back of his hand and sighed. "Okay, you're right. Oh God, I know you're right."

"How about I help you get on the next plane back to The Philippines when we land? Will that be good?"

"Yes, please. I'm done with this. I just want to go home."

92

THE THREE

When I returned to my seat, Tia had taken Benjamin's place in the seat next to me.

"And that, my dear," she said as I sat down, "was your Three."

My eyes opened wide, and I stared at her. "What? That was the third?"

She elbowed me playfully. "Come on, get with the program here. What happened to you just now?"

I looked ahead to where Adrian was sitting. "I didn't know who I was or even who it was that was talking to him. It was like someone else was me, loving and helping him." I turned to her. "How can that be the third? I don't even understand it."

"Oh," she said in a teasing voice, "then we're back to needing to understand? My oh my!"

"Okay," I said, and grinned. "I don't need to understand. I don't even want to understand."

"Then consider what just happened with Adrian." *Of course she knew his name!* "What do you know? Not understand, but know?"

I hesitated, looking down at my lap. "I know I was filled with beautiful energy, with a deep love for that man. I felt it flowing through me, and I was in a river of . . . of grace, I guess. I don't have a name for it other than sweet energy or love. Wait! That's it. It was love—I loved him. I was filled with so much love that I went to him and didn't care if he rejected me."

Tia sat quietly, looking at me with a gentleness that caressed my heart.

Finally, she said, "Then let's look at the Three, starting at the beginning."

"Okay." I folded my arms and looked up. "Acceptance was first. It was so powerful. It changed my life."

"How?"

I looked at her and saw the face of a child. How did she do that?

"In the beginning, it was revolutionary in my mind, in my life. But that was before I knew that acceptance was made up of gratitude and forgiveness. It took awhile to get on top of those two, but when I did, acceptance set me free. Then it got super easy because I felt like the weight of the world had fallen off me. I was light and happy. Your mantra became mine: *It is the way it is; it is the way!*"

"And number two?"

"Ah, talk about changing my life! When I truly understood that there is no past and no future, that they're both fantasies, then all the garbage I'd been toting around my whole life just slipped away." I paused. "Wait, now. When I said 'slipped away,' it didn't just happen. I had to train my thinking, and it took weeks and months of keeping my mind in the now. It still slips into old habits sometimes."

"Those two," Tia asked. "How did they work together?"

I didn't hesitate. "I thought I really got acceptance until I started living in the now. I realize that there is no past and no future but that everything in all time and space are right here on the tip of this needle called now. Then acceptance stopped being a concept and became who I am. I am acceptance of all that is here right now. Everything else is an illusion and not mine to deal with."

Tia rested her chin on her closed hand and looked deeply into me. "And number three?"

Then I saw it. "Tia, when I went up to Adrian, I was just loving him, feeling his pain and needing to serve him however I could. Nothing mattered except him. I knew I could guide him out of that darkness; I didn't doubt it for an instant. I felt free, free to be me and to flow my love into him without fear. And yes, the Three are all One. I'm acceptance, right now, and love is in me, as me, guiding my every step."

I turned to face forward, and she put her hand on my arm. "And that mysterious figure on the beach?"

I laughed. "That was me."

Her cheeks were wet with tears as she hugged me. "Welcome home, my Little Bird."

93

The plane circled San Francisco Bay, and below I saw the Oakland Bay Bridge and smiled. "Thank you, Johanna."

The Customs line was long, and I longed to see my love. When I finally passed through Customs and was waiting at the carousel for my bag, I realized that it was only three days ago that I'd come through this airport. In that short time, my life had changed. The Three had become One, and that One was now my consciousness, my way of life. I collected my bag and pushed through the door into the lobby, and there was Noah, grinning like an eight-year-old boy. I ran to him and fell into his arms.

He held me close, and I felt his heart beating with mine. Then he pushed me away to arm's length. "Oh, nice jaw."

"Well, I am a spiritual warrior, you know."

Yeah," he said, "I see that. Did your spiritual jaw get it too?"

"Oh no," I said with a laugh. "That jaw got stronger."

A voice called out from behind him. "Okay, okay, make some room here. Make some room!"

And there she was: beautiful, tall Jill, all smiles. She wrapped her arms around us both, and as I snuggled into the two of them, I knew we'd become one.

When we finally separated, I said, "Jill, your scars are almost invisible! You look twenty years younger."

She laughed. "Well, I am younger. That's because of you and your gang of weirdos. And, Keegs, look at your poor face. Did my truck hit you too?"

I shrugged. "Well, of course it did. We're sisters, aren't we? You're not having all the fun."

As soon as Tia, Elisa, and Benjamin emerged from Customs, we walked together to a small alcove where we could sit facing one another. Benjamin reached for my hand and smiled. "Keegan, I'm proud of you."

I squeezed his hand. "Thank you, Benjamin."

"Keegan's life changed, and my life changed too," said Elisa, who had been quiet. "I'll tell you this: it's pretty great being Ana's little sister."

Then she looked at Benjamin and me. "I'll never stop thanking you two. And yes, I've got a few wounds, but nothing that won't heal. I grew up a lot sitting in that dark room. I've become my own woman. For the first time, I know who I am. For that alone, it was worth it."

"Well, Danilo made this mission a success," Benjamin said. "Let's not forget about him,"

"Thanks for remembering my dad," said an unfamiliar voice, and a stranger stepped into the area where we sat.

We all stared at him.

"Excuse my intrusion. I'm John Michael Torres. Danilo's my father."

"John Michael!" cried Benjamin, jumping to his feet. "I haven't seen you since you were a boy."

"I know," John Michael said, and smiled. "I've been watching you, Benjamin, marveling at the man you are. My dad has always been full of praises of you."

Benjamin introduced John Michael to each of us. When he got to me, I suddenly recognized the young man. "You were sitting across from a man I was talking to on the plane."

"Yes, that was me. I was on the flight because of Adrian, who's an old friend of my dad's. Dad knew about the death of his son and suspected what Adrian was up to. He sent me to keep him safe."

He looked at me with raised eyebrows. "I watched you, Keegan Tate. I watched you work with Adrian, and I was amazed. I was truly amazed. Thank you, good woman. You may have saved several lives."

He glanced at his watch and stepped back. "Hey, I've got to run. My plane back to The Philippines leaves in an hour." He hugged Benjamin again, waved to the rest of us, and disappeared into the terminal.

We sat in silence for a few minutes. Tia Ana looked carefully at each of us, finally resting her eyes on Benjamin, who also was studying us.

"Well, Ana," he said, "I guess we've finally made it. We now have the team, and I think we can begin."

Jill, Noah, and I looked at each other. We were the team!

If only we could have imagined the adventures coming our way.

Acknowledgments

Since my childhood, being an author was my dream. Thanking all those who encouraged that aspiration would take volumes. Here is a short list of those who changed my life:

Mary Trask, my pal, who reminds me daily of the power and the beauty of love.

My daughter, Chauncey Trask, who reminds me that we are winning all the time.

Tyson Gorsuch, my son, whose gentle heart is my blessing.

My editor and friend, Julie Klein, whose patient guidance determined the wholeness of this book.

Katherine Loh, my Malaysian publisher and friend.

Peter Morgan, who always has my back.

Oscar Dystel, who assured me that I am truly a writer of stories.

Joe Lamanno, Amie Santerelli, and Richard Robertson, who are my life tutors.

And my deepest gratitude to these who stand always by me as I navigate the tides of life: Chuck and Suzie Beringer, Erik Bjornsen, Marie Bjornsen, Gordon Bradford, Josh Bradford, Jim Chiarottino, Mike Chiarottino, Eleanor Clift, Marilyn Cooper, Claire Daly, Anne Devolin, Lorie Dwinell, Paula Forget, Paul Frehe, Vicki Harnden, Chris Hooykaas, Ellen Kastler, Penny Madden, John Mason, Helena Morrison, Kenny Roos, Marilyn Sheer, Bill and Patti Shiels, Tan Shiow Shyan, Jimmy Spackman and Kaayla Tomlin.

Printed in the USA
CPSIA information can be obtained
at www.ICGtesting.com
LVHW051510140324
774484LV00001B/27